THE ANGEL TASTED TEMPTATION

THE ANGEL TASTED TEMPTATION

SHIRLEY JUMP

This is a work of fiction. All of the characters, organizations, and events portrayed in this novel are either products of the author's imagination or are used fictitiously.

eISBN: 978-1-937776-32-9
ISBN 13: 978-1-937776-83-1

CHAPTER ONE

One of the first things to greet Meredith Shordon to Boston was a man in a pair of Fruit of the Looms, playing a set of bongos.

She'd come here looking for a man—but not one like that.

Meredith stood in the middle of the bustling airport subway stop and stared. Exactly like every other tourist beside her. If there was one thing she hadn't wanted to do, it was look like a gaping Midwesterner who'd never seen a big city in her life.

Well, there went *that* plan.

Heck, she'd been gaping since she left Indiana. First, there'd been the quartet of Patriots fans who'd been on the second leg of her flight, returning from an out-of-town game. They'd brought the ongoing celebration with them, from the red and blue stripes painted on their faces to the way they yelled "Go Pats!" at odd times, like they had a rare, two-word form of Tourette's syndrome.

Then, the clouds had parted and revealed the massive skyline through the oval window of the jet.

She'd forgotten the NFL fools behind her and stared at the massive stone behemoths of Boston's skyline. It looked more like Neptune than Heavendale, Indiana, where she'd been a few short hours ago. There were none of the wide expanses of green land and patchwork quilts of farms she was used to.

She'd stopped staring long enough to get off the plane and through the overwhelming crush of people to meet her cousin's friend, Maria Pagliano, and to claim her baggage without looking too much like a bewildered farm girl.

Until now.

The man tum-tummed on the two drums hanging from a leather strap around his neck, his long, dark, curly hair swinging in concert. He danced to the rhythm, a contented smile on his face, as if bongoing hit a high sex never could.

He caught Meredith's stare, hit his bongos harder and thrust his slim hips to the left, toward a big white bucket with a handwritten sign that read TIPS FOR THE HIPS.

Meredith drew her caramel leather trench coat closer around her, resisting the urge to button up. She hadn't seen a man this naked since she'd walked in on Bobby Reynolds getting his football physical at the end of senior year.

Unfortunately, she'd opened the locker room door right in the middle of his hernia screening.

For two years after that, she'd been unable to look Bobby in the face. Or eat pork products ever again.

"Don't give a dime to Bongo Boy," Maria said, grabbing Meredith's arm and hauling her away. "He makes more than most investment bankers."

"He does?" Meredith craned her head over Maria's, casting one last look at Bongo Boy's swiveling anatomy.

"He heard about that naked cowboy who plays guitar in New York—"

"There's a naked man playing guitar in New York?" Geez. She needed to travel more. Scratch that. Travel, period, considering this was only the second time in her life she'd left Indiana, if she even counted that trip to the Ohio State Fair.

And this time she hadn't *left*. Exactly. More like *run away*. She'd abandoned a whole lot of people's expectations, leaping at the chance for something new, exciting, different.

She just hadn't expected the first exciting thing she saw to be a man in his tightie whities pounding out *Yankee Doodle Dandy*.

"The Naked Cowboy isn't *really* naked. I saw him once in Times Square." Maria shook her head, clearly disappointed. "I tell you, there's no truth in advertising anymore."

The instant she'd met her, Meredith decided she liked Maria. Maria was one of the trio of business partners at Gift Baskets to Die For, along with Meredith's cousin, Rebecca Hamilton, and another woman named Candace Woodrow.

A buxom Italian brunette, Maria wore a bright red dress and medium heels that set off her fabulous legs and made virtually every man in a thirty-foot radius stop and stare. The complete opposite to Meredith's long, straight and uninspired blond hair and dark blue eyes, all about as exciting as a Honda in a lot full of Ferraris.

Brash, outspoken and unafraid of color in her clothes, Maria was everything Meredith was not. Most of all, Maria was a perfect friend for what Meredith wanted to accomplish while she was staying in the city: a major overhaul of her life and her self.

"I think it's great that you're doing this for us," Maria said, shouting a little to be heard as they made their way through the crowds. "Dropping everything to come and help Rebecca while she's on bed rest. We were desperate for the extra help."

Desperate was something Meredith understood. When Rebecca had called yesterday morning to ask if Meredith could help out while Rebecca was home working on a healthy pregnancy, Meredith couldn't say yes fast enough. Undoubtedly, her blue-ribbon past at the Indiana State Fair and familial loyalty made her the first choice for helping them out of a jam.

Meredith circumvented a businessman with a lethal briefcase that kept swinging into her knees. "When Rebecca called, it took me about a half second to give my notice at Petey's Pizza Parlor, hang up my uniform for good, pack my bags and hop on the first plane out of Indiana."

Maria laughed. "A little eager to leave?"

"Oh *yeah*. I'd have *crawled* to Boston from Indiana to finally find a life that involved more than cows and corn." She glanced back over her shoulder at Bongo Boy. "I just didn't expect to have it thrust in my face, percussion complement included."

"Hey, get used to the unusual. That's part of what this city is all about."

Bongo Boy's native pounding was silenced when she and Maria stepped onto the subway car and the doors swooshed shut behind them.

Crowds shoved their way through the jam-packed Blue Line conveyance. Meredith thought of the hundreds—maybe thousands—of hands that had touched those silver poles today. She wasn't so sure she wanted to hold one, not without some gloves and antibacterial gel.

"Come on, let's grab a seat," Maria said.

"But they're all full." Besides, who knew what had sat in those seats? She was glad she was wearing long pants. Didn't want anything ... foreign crawling up her legs.

"Not for long." Maria turned and flashed a flirty smile at two men with bright yellow construction hats, sitting side by side on the long plastic benches. A second later, the two men rose and gave up their seats.

"I thought men didn't do that kind of thing anymore. Chivalry is dead and all that," Meredith said after they sat down.

"You just have to know how to work with men, Meredith, and they'll treat you right." Maria crossed one leg over the other. Above them, the two men watched her bare legs move with undisguised appreciation. "And remember to use the top view to your advantage."

"It helps that you *have* a top. I'm a little barren up there." Meredith glanced down at her 34Bs, looking flat beneath her jacket and white turtleneck, and sighed.

"Different strokes for different folks." Maria winked. "I hope Bongo Boy didn't give you a bad impression of Boston."

"Not at all. Calvin Klein should snatch him up, though."

Maria laughed. "Now that's an ad I'd like to see when I open up my *Cosmo.*"

Meredith clutched her purse in her lap, holding it tight to her chest. For the third time since she'd landed in Boston—and the tenth time since she'd left her apartment that morning—her cell phone vibrated against the inside of her bag. She peeked inside, glanced at the missed call list and let out a sigh.

She doubted even the witness protection program could hide her from her mother.

The subway car rushed around a curve, sending the bench of people against each other like a human wave. The lights flickered. Across the aisle, a burly man in a winter cap and a holey gray sweater gave Meredith a toothless smile. The scent of humans—sweat, perfume and desperation—swept through the enclosed car.

The closest she'd come to such a confined space was Elmer Tyne's annual Halloween hay ride. Most of the smells on that one came from Elmer's plodding and gassy mare, Heloise.

"Boston is just a little different from what I'm used to." Meredith shut her purse without answering the call. "But I'm still going to do what it takes to experience it all while I'm here."

"I can show you the Prudential and the Aquarium—"

"I didn't mean that kind of experience." Meredith started to lean back against the seat, remembered the germ quotient, and straightened. "I come from a town of three thousand people," she explained. "I haven't exactly lived yet. Heck, I've barely seen the "real world.""

Maria laughed. "If you want the real world, you've come to the right place. It doesn't get any realer than this."

The train continued its rushing path along the tracks, the riders journeying along, looking as passive and unanimated as the ads for safe sex and language schools that decorated the metal walls. No one here looked real. Heck, they didn't even look alive.

"Good," Meredith said. "Because I want..." She glanced around, then lowered her voice to a whisper. "A man."

Maria blinked. "A... a man?"

"Yeah. I want to ... well, fill in the gaps in my education." She raised a brow to complete the meaning of her sentence. "Hopefully more than once."

Maria leaned back in her seat, a smile of appreciation on her lips. She thrust a hand out to Meredith.

"Welcome to Boston, Meredith Shordon. I'm *definitely* going to like working with you."

Meredith's phone vibrated again, as if her mother was sending a protest all the way from Indiana: *Don't think about sex. Doing it, watching it or even spelling it in a crossword.*

Ignoring the call was cowardly, but it bought her some time. Time to figure out who she was, what she wanted and how the city of Boston could change Meredith Shordon.

For the better.

But...

That little word grumbled inside her brain and sent an arrow of doubt through her hastily arranged plans.

If she'd found men playing bongos in their underwear here, what else did the city of Boston hold that Meredith hadn't expected ...

And wasn't prepared to handle?

Travis's Regrets-Can-Be-Drowned Hangover Remedy

1-1/2 ounces vodka
3 ounces tomato juice
1 dash lemon juice
1/2 teaspoon Worcestershire sauce
2 to 3 drops Tabasco sauce
Salt and pepper
1 celery stalk

It's been a hell of a night and an even worse morning. The best thing to do is forget both. Start by mixing the vodka, juices, Worcestershire and Tabasco. If you're a glutton for punishment, use a blender. Or if your head feels like it's been the bass drum in a rock concert, then use a spoon. Doesn't matter how you do it, long as you get the damned thing mixed and poured over ice.

Season with salt and pepper, that is, assuming your tongue doesn't feel like a leftover scrap of Berber and will even notice the taste.

Shove the celery stalk in there and call it breakfast.

While drinking, promise yourself you will never, ever end up in this situation again. At least not before Happy Hour starts tonight.

CHAPTER TWO

Travis Campbell reached for the Tylenol, shook out a couple, swallowed them dry and swore never again.

Never, *ever* again.

He was too old for this. Too old to be chasing skirts and drinking past dawn. It was time to start being responsible, time to act like the grown-up he really was.

His pounding head stammered out an agreement between pulses of pain.

'There's a girl at the front door, asking for you," Kenny, his roommate, said, stumbling into the bathroom and swiping at his face. "She might have been at the party last night. Might not have. I dunno. After a case of Bud, they all look the same to me."

"Tell her I died." Travis turned the bottle of Tylenol around, read the precautions about overdosing and shook out a couple more anyway.

"There's a party at Lou's beach house in Hull tonight. If we sleep all day, we'll be ready to go by nine." Kenny belched, splashed a little cold water on his stubble-ridden face, didn't see a towel and opted for his T-shirt instead.

Kenny Gerard was a whiz at work, a man who could make it through a twelve-hour day without looking or acting like he'd spent the previous twelve hours making his way through the alcohol in a bar like a starving man at the Ponderosa buffet.

In his job as the Assistant to the Director of New Product Development at Belly-Licious Beverages, Kenny was Travis's right hand man. And at a party, Kenny was the man who made sure Travis—and any-one within a five-foot radius—made good use of that right hand by always keeping it full of intoxicating drinks.

A friend, drinking buddy and conspirator to a life of depravity. Kenny was just the type of guy Travis had always liked having with him on a Saturday night.

Until now. Until the consequences of all those Saturday nights came swinging at him with what felt like a hell of a right hook.

"I'm not going to Lou's beach house." Travis slipped the Tylenol into the pocket of his shorts for later, leaving the bottle on the counter.

"Man, you're going to miss a killer party. I hear he's getting strippers." Kenny sauntered over to the toilet and sat down on the closed lid. He picked up last month's issue of *Playboy* and began flipping through the pages, pausing to drool over women he'd never have.

"I'm done, Kenny."

"Yeah, I'm pretty toasted myself, man. I am done. D-O"— *belch*— "N."

"E."

"E?" Kenny blinked at him, his brown eyes bleary. Spindly red lines crackled across the surface, like a map of the interstate highway system.

Travis shook his head. "Never mind. I'm done with parties. And women. And acting like I'm seventeen."

Kenny scratched his head, his sleep-styled dark brown hair flopping with the movement. "Why?"

"Because—"

"Travis Campbell, I am going to kill you!" The bathroom door burst open and in strode a redhead in high heels, a clingy white pantsuit with matching trench, and an oversized bright plum-colored purse.

He'd met her last night. Or was it last week? Damn. All those parties had started to run together, like a river of tequila and vodka.

Her name started with a T, that much he remembered. Tiffany. Maybe Tammy.

"I'm in the *bathroom*," Travis said to her, indicating the sink and Kenny on the toilet with his magazine. She stood on his linoleum, clearly not caring that she'd walked in on his morning ablutions. The bright blue shower curtain behind her looked like one of those TV blue screens, making Travis feel like the whole thing was surreal, unnatural.

Or maybe that was the leftover rum in his system talking.

"Listen," he said, rubbing his head, "can we talk about this later?"

She parked a fist on her hip, the purse swinging to the front. "You don't remember me, do you?"

"Of course I do." *Tawny. Terry.*

"Then what's my name?"

He swallowed. Beside him, he could see Kenny smirking. Damn. Why couldn't she have shown up *after* the Tylenol had had a chance to start working?

Tara. Tess. Tilda.

Shit. He'd about run out of T names and not one had felt mentally right. He'd take his last resort then— turn the tables on *Thomasina-Thelma-Tasha.* "Listen, you clearly don't like me anymore. Wouldn't it be best if we forget about each other? Move on. Get a little closure?"

If he spouted enough Dr. Phil maybe she'd leave.

"Oh, I won't forget you," she said. "Or what you did to me."

"What I did to you?" Oh shit. What the hell did she mean by that? He'd been drunk, but not *that* drunk.

Had he?

"I-I-I—" She sniffled, shook her head, then directed her gaze at him again. "I thought you loved me."

Travis swallowed. Had he used *that* word? That alone was a sign he was drinking too much. That was it. The rest of the case of beer was going down the drain.

Wait. That might be too rash. Better just to put it in the bottom bin of the refrigerator. Outta sight, outta mind, outta mouth and outta trouble.

"How could you think that?" Travis asked. "I barely—" He caught himself before he said *remember you*, and reworded. "We barely dated."

"I felt a connection." She swiped at her eyes. "Right in the first few minutes, when we started talking on Brian's sofa."

Brian's sofa. Okay, he remembered a conversation with a redhead—*Tori, Trista, Trixie*—at Bri's party last night, but nothing that would have caused him to hear wedding bells ringing. "Uh, I'm sure we had a great conversation ..."

Toni. Tracy. Tricia.

"... but I think you got the wrong idea," he said.

"Oh, you do, do you?" She pursed her lips. "I only got the idea you gave me, Travis."

He put up his hands. "Hey, I'm not a commitment kind of guy. It was a pleasure meeting you last night, but—"

She cocked her head to the right and zeroed in on his gaze. "You don't remember me at all. Do you?"

"Well, I—" He finished on a self-deprecating half laugh that he hoped begged forgiveness and turned on whatever charm he had left after a night of drinking and making a fool out of himself. "I'm sorry—"

"Olivia Tate, you jerk!" And then she swung the massive purse right at his head.

He wasn't prepared for a pocketbook blow. He felt a slam—what'd she have in there? A watermelon?— then felt himself fall to the floor in a crumpled, hungover heap.

From his vantage point, he watched a pair of black heels pivot and stomp out of his bathroom. Behind him, Kenny laughed so hard, Travis could hear the pages of *Playboy* fluttering like applause.

Her *last* name started with a T. *His* first name was the one that began with T. No wonder the Budweiser company was so wealthy. They'd sucked all his brain cells out and into the brown bottles he used to worship.

No more beer. No more parties. And no matter what, no more women.

Travis moaned and reached up, feeling along the counter for the Tylenol. He drew the bottle down to his level and flipped up the top with his thumb.

Empty.

Now that was poetic justice.

Momma's All-You-Need-Is-This Tuna Casserole

12 ounces flat egg noodles, cooked and drained
2 7-ounce cans tuna, drained
1 cup mayonnaise
1 large onion, chopped
1 green pepper, chopped
1 celery rib, chopped
1 teaspoon salt
Dash pepper
2 10-ounce cans cream of celery soup
1 cup milk
2 cups Velveeta cheese
1/2 cup Parmesan cheese
1/2 cup French-fried onions

Nothing's wrong with you that a good home-cooked meal can't fix, that's for sure. You don't need that fancy city food. The basics will do you fine and get you right back to where you belong—at home, in the loving arms of your family, living out your destiny.

Start by preheating the oven to 375 degrees. Then mix the tuna, mayonnaise, onion, pepper, celery, salt and pepper in a bowl. No need to get pretty, just stir it all together.

Meanwhile, heat the soup, milk and Velveeta in a saucepan over low heat. Don't scorch it now, who knows what kind of cancer comes from burned food? Once it's all melted, mix it with the ingredients in the bowl, stir in the Parmesan, then dump the whole thing into a 3-quart casserole dish (now you know your Momma gave you a Pyrex set for your hope chest. She's still hoping, so you better get it out of the chest). Sprinkle with the onions, then bake it for 30 minutes.

That's plenty of time to think about a certain bad decision you made. And if you don't start doing some thinking quick, Momma's going to have to send out the cavalry to help you.

CHAPTER THREE

An hour later, the Motorola won. Meredith finally answered the twentieth—or maybe it was the twenty-first—call, before her phone could explode like a bottle of nitroglycerine that had been aggravated one too many times.

She'd barely had half a second to greet her cousin before her cell phone had started again. Meredith waved a quick apology to Rebecca, then slumped into an armchair and faced the consequences.

"I hope you at least brought protection, dear," her mother said, not even waiting for a hello.

Oh yeah, she'd brought protection. Not her mother's idea of it, though. In her purse was a thirty-six-pack box of Ultra Thin Lubricated Trojans. She doubted Walgreens would let her return them.

Nor did she intend to.

When she'd run away from Heavendale, Indiana, she'd done it without looking back. She had no intentions of returning home until she was different— very different.

She might be here to help her cousin. But most of all, she was here to shed the small-town Meredith

Shordon, who was as common as rain in the spring and weeds in the garden. The first place to start was with a man.

"Meredith? Are you all right? I worry about you, dear."

"Momma, I'm alive. I'm breathing. Stop worrying."

"A girl can't be too careful, you know." In the background, Meredith could hear her father echoing agreement with a grunt. An Engelbert Humperdinck song played on the radio in her mother's sunflower wallpaper kitchen. "Especially in a city like that. You need all the help you can get."

Meredith raised her eyes heavenward and prayed she wouldn't be struck down in the La-Z-Boy for lying. "I packed it."

"*Both* economy-size containers of Purell I gave you?"

The instant hand sanitizer lotion was sitting in the back of her apartment closet in Indiana, but Meredith didn't say that. Her mother and Sam's Club were a dangerous combination. "Yep."

"*And* the Lysol?"

"Of course."

"Have you been ..." At this, her mother paused. From a thousand miles away, Meredith could picture Martha Shordon looking around for any listening ears. Little teapots, she called them, though neither Meredith nor her two older brothers had ever resembled beverage containers. Nor were any of them, now in their mid-to-late twenties, too young for whatever words her conservative, God-fearing mother might say. ".. . putting those paper covers on the toilet seats before you . .. well, you know. Number one, number two and all that."

Now that was one thing Meredith *had* done. Who knew what kind of diseases lurked in public restrooms? "Yes, every time."

Her mother let out a long breath of relief. "Good. I'm just concerned about you, dear. That's all. This isn't like you."

For a moment, Meredith felt a twinge of regret for leaving like she had. For letting everyone down. She heard the concern in her mother's voice and knew that even though Momma was a germophobe to rival Mr. Clean, she handed out those Clorox Wipes with love.

"I'm fine, Momma," Meredith repeated.

"Have you stopped by to say hello to your Aunt Gloria yet?" Momma asked, referring to her sister, Rebecca's mother. "Maybe she can talk some sense into you. I just can't understand why you took off like a bat out of you-know-where."

"I don't want to talk about that right now."

Momma sighed. "Meredith, you can't just up and leave your responsibilities like that."

"I just got to Rebecca's. I want to say hello and unpack and—"

"Dear," her mother said, her voice lowering again, out of teapot range, "is her house clean?"

Her mother's perennial question. To her, some-one with a dirty house or untidy kitchen ranked in the same category as a potbellied pig with diarrhea. She didn't want either in her house, spreading what she called an air of disorder in her pristine environment

Cleanliness was, of course, the best way to equate oneself with godliness. To her mother, those who couldn't find the time or energy to de-germ their homes weren't worth a broken cookie at the church bake sale.

Meredith glanced around her. In her mother's eyes, Rebecca's disarray would be an offense against humanity, though Meredith didn't see anything potentially lethal in the room. Piles of preschooler toys grouped into colorful mini-mountains of lefto-ver play around the room. A blanket lay haphaz-ardly across the sofa, trailing onto the floor. And at her feet, a big, fat snoring beagle who smelled like mothballs.

"Yep, clean as a whistle."

"You make sure and watch how often she washes her hands and—"

"I know, Momma. I have to go. I love you."

Her mother let out a sound of discontent at hav-ing her hygiene lecture interrupted, then she soft-ened. "I love you too, dear. Be safe. And remember, Indiana girls are good girls."

Meredith ignored the flickers of doubt in her gut, said good-bye to her mother, then flipped the phone shut and stuffed it back into her purse. She was half tempted to turn it off, lest her mother call again, but had a sudden image of the cops surrounding Rebecca's house on good Shordon authority that only a hostage situation would prevent Meredith from answering.

Meredith turned to Rebecca, who had ensconced herself in the opposite armchair. Rebecca's second pregnancy, now nearing the end at thirty-six weeks, was well pronounced, like the baby was determined to introduce himself or herself into every conversation. Rebecca wore her shoulder-length, straight brown hair back in a clip that she said kept it out of her eyes— and out of reach of the hairstylist-to-be fingers of her four-year-old daughter, Emily. Rebecca was a beautiful woman, one of the few in the family who hadn't been cursed with the Shordon mini-chest or the mega-nose.

"Sorry," Meredith said. "When my mother calls—"

"I know," Rebecca said, laughing. "It's like a primal urge to let our mothers keep having input in our lives, even when we're long past the legal drinking age."

"It's masochistic."

Rebecca laughed. "At least your mother is a thousand miles away. Mine lives next door. One of these days, I swear Jeremy and I are going to have enough money to afford a house of our own."

Rebecca lived in a small Cape-style house owned by her parents, Aunt Gloria and Uncle Mike, bought years before as rental property after Uncle Mike had transferred up to Massachusetts with a promotion from American Airlines. The houses sat a few streets down from the Charles River, close enough to catch the scent of the fresh water and a glimpse of the boaters.

Their investment had paid for itself quickly in the desirable Cambridge area, so when Rebecca got married—and pregnant in quick succession—they'd rented the second house out to their only child.

"I'm sure it won't be much longer before you've got a mortgage of your own to complain about," Meredith said with a smile.

"If Jeremy ever decides he's got enough education it won't. Now he's signing up for his doctorate. At MIT, which will cost us a fortune." Rebecca reached for a basket of clean laundry and began folding the little pastel T-shirts and pants inside. "I swear, I'm going to go crazy living here."

"It makes finding a babysitter easier, though."

"I'd prefer a sitter who kept her opinions about my housekeeping to herself."

Meredith laughed. "Sounds like those tendencies run in the family, at least between those two sisters." She thought of Aunt Gloria, whose house was as chaotic as Martha's was pristine. Despite being on opposing cleanliness spectrums, the two sisters shared one common trait—they were both darn good Buttinskis.

Rebecca chuckled. "Want some wine? I'll live vicariously through you. I haven't had a glass in so long, I wonder if *I'm* fermenting. Being pregnant has put a serious kink in my social life."

"At least you have one. My idea of Friday night fun is getting off early from Petey's Pizza Parlor and waiting for Hester to lay a new egg in Grandpa's chicken coop."

"I remember how bad it was in Indiana when I was a kid. God, I don't miss that place at all."

Rebecca started to get to her feet, but Meredith waved her back down. "You sit. I'll get it. You're on bedrest, remember?"

"Ah, it is nice to be spoiled." A smile spread across her cousin's face. "Sure I can't talk you into moving in permanently?"

"Hey, I'm easily bribed." Meredith crossed to the kitchen to get the wine. While her cousin rested on the couch and gave directions, Meredith opened a bottle of zinfandel for herself and poured Rebecca a glass of ice water. It was after ten and the house was silent, with Emily asleep and Jeremy off with his study group, boning up on engineering principles.

"Labor pains okay?" Meredith asked from the kitchen.

"Much better now that I can't do anything but sit around the house. I'll be glad when this baby comes and I can move again.

"Speaking of painful stuff... How's Caleb?" Rebecca asked, when Meredith returned to the living room with the drinks. Her cousin patted an empty spot on the sofa beside her.

Guilt pricked at her. There was another thing she'd abandoned—her former fiancé. Caleb hadn't taken the ending of their relationship well at all.

Good thing he'd had that paper bag in the glove compartment of the hearse. That, and a trip to DQ for a soft-serve chocolate cone, had taken the edge off the words "It's over."

"He's okay," Meredith said, taking the proffered seat. "Still thinking we'll get back together, though. But we won't. Besides, I think I'm allergic to the smell of formaldehyde. Every time I was with him, I felt ill."

Rebecca laughed. "I'm sure you'll meet someone different from Caleb, especially here. Not too many embalmers hang out in the local bars."

"I want more than different. I want a guy who ... well, who knows what he's doing." Meredith arched a brow of hint. "With *everything.*"

Rebecca looked at Meredith. She blinked twice. "That is totally not you. At least not the Meredith I remember from the summers at Grandpa's lake cottage."

"I know. It's the most insane thing I've ever wanted to do in my life."

Rebecca gestured at her with the water glass, the ice cubes clinking like quiet music. "Why didn't you do all this wild oat sowing back in Indiana?"

"You lived there when you were a kid. You remember what it was like. Everyone knows everyone in Heavendale. If I bought two percent instead of whole milk, the neighbors would tell my mother before I could get home." She shook her head. "Can you imagine what doing something like this would generate?"

Rebecca laughed. "A gossip tornado."

"Exactly." That was something Meredith couldn't afford, not back home. Everything that happened in Boston had to stay in Boston. If word leaked back to the Heavendale papers, she'd ruin much more than just her own reputation.

And that was a price she couldn't afford to pay.

A smile crossed Rebecca's lips. She moved forward and drew her cousin into a hug. "I hope you know what you're doing."

"I do," Meredith said. "Sort of."

"You're playing with lit matches."

"That's what I'm hoping."

Rebecca drew back and gave a simple shrug that said she was going to support her cousin, no matter what. "Well, if you're sure you want to toy with fire, I can tell you *exactly* where to go to find some really cute kindling."

Kenny's Everything's-Better-With-a-Beer Fish

1 pound fish (haddock, cod, whatever you want)
1/2 cup flour
1/2 teaspoon salt
Pepper
1 bottle beer (definitely stale—don't waste a perfectly good beer on this!)
Vegetable oil

One warning: don't try to mix *drinking* beer with *frying* beer at the same time. I once had a hell of an accident doing that and ... Well, let's just say my performance was a little subpar for a while. So stay sober for now, then chug-a-lug when you're done.

Heat 1-2 inches of oil in a heavy saucepan until it reaches 350 degrees. Or if you're like me and wouldn't know a freakin' candy thermometer if your doctor brought it out at the annual physical, just improvise. The oil's ready when it sizzles like hell if you drop some batter in there. Easy, right?

In a pie plate (see Ma, I did pay attention to something other than the girls in home ec) mix the flour, salt and pepper. Add in the beer—from half the bottle to all of it, depending on how thick you want your batter to be. Dip the fish into the batter, then put the filets into the oil.

Yeah, that was hard, wasn't it? Feeling worn out? Grab a cold brewski. Don't worry, you got time. The fish will take five minutes on each side to get golden brown. You could down at least two in that time. Maybe three, if you work fast.

Drain the fish on some paper towels if you want to pretend you care what you're doing to your arteries, then eat.

Beer in your bottle and beer in your food. It doesn't get much better than that, my friend.

CHAPTER FOUR

"I told you, Kenny, I'm not going in there."

"Yeah, yeah. But you were hungover when you said it."

"I'm serious. I'm done drinking. I'm done with women for at least a month."

Kenny drew in a sharp breath. "Be careful what you say out loud, buddy. It's bachelor blasphemy."

Travis paused on the bottom step and gripped the wrought iron railing. It was Sunday night and they'd just left the gym after a particularly humiliating game of racquetball, made worse by the purse-sized bump on Travis's head that kept aching, like a reminder of past sins. To be standing here, outside Slim Pickin's bar, was the height of stupidity, considering his resolve that morning. But like an addict seeking that regular high, Travis had followed Kenny here.

Every Sunday, they came to Slim Pickin's. Monday was Mortie's Place. Tuesday, another bar, Wednesday sometimes another visit to Slim Pickin's, then a fourth on Thursday, until the weekend came and Brian or Lou or someone else would chip in for a case and fire up his grill. As regular as clockwork, as if he were standing on the assembly line for early liver disease.

Travis turned to Kenny. "Don't you think it's time we grew up?"

Kenny blinked. "Uh ... why?"

"Because we're in our late twenties; thirty is just around the corner, and we're still acting like we scored a fake ID and a case of Coors."

"And your problem with that is ... what?"

"I have a job. I can't be doing this every night."

Kenny climbed back down the two steps and laid a hand on Travis's arm. "Travis, you and I convince people to buy *beverages* for a living. That's not a job. It's like being Gopher on *Love Boat*."

"Exactly. And why do you think I haven't been promoted? Or tried really hard to get a new job? You know how I hate working for Larry."

Kenny shrugged. "Because you figured out a cake-walk job with a decent salary is the smartest thing you ever fell into?"

"No. Because I come in bleary-eyed and with a headache more often than not. This isn't the life I planned on, Kenny."

His friend turned his head right, then left, peering down the empty sidewalk. "Well, I don't know whose life you think you've got, pal, because you're the only Travis Campbell I see in front of me."

"That I don't know." Travis let out a sigh and ran a hand through his hair. "But I intend to find out."

"Dude, you're not making any sense. First you want to quit drinking. Then you start talking crazy about giving up women. Now you don't even know who you are? Have you been hit on the head recently by falling debris? We can sue for that you know."

"No, I haven't. I was, however, hit by a hell of a purse."

"Oh yeah. I forgot about that. Maybe it knocked a few brain cells loose." Kenny draped an arm over Travis's shoulder and tugged him up the last step and into the entrance. "And I have the perfect solution for lost brain cells."

"What?"

"Why lose some more, of course. It's what beer does best."

Meredith sat on a corner stool at Slim Pickin's, an untouched margarita on the rocks before her, and drew in a breath. This was a crazy plan. The kind they put on women-in-jeopardy movies. "She should have known better," the announcer would say as the opening credits rolled, "than to go looking for trouble."

That was precisely what Meredith wanted, though. Trouble—and lots of it—before she had to return to Indiana. She knew it wouldn't be long before someone came looking for her. She had to hurry up and make this change happen.

If anyone tried anything, she had the box of Trojans in one pocket of her purse—best case scenario—and a small bottle of pepper spray in another pocket—Lifetime movie special scenario.

The pepper spray had worked on Mrs. Beedleman's obnoxious, overfed and too-pampered chocolate Labrador. She figured it should work on anything male lunging at her, whether it was looking for kibble or not.

She settled herself onto a stool and looked around the dimly lit sports bar. It wasn't a bad place and, being on Mass. Ave., it was close to Rebecca's. Like most bars, the wall decor was ESPN, Fox Sports and HBO Boxing. A half dozen pool tables peppered one side of the room, while a square of booths formed the perimeter of a small dance floor headquartered by a brightly lit jukebox.

It was early yet, just after seven on Sunday night, and only a few people, mostly couples, sat at the tables. Avril Lavigne's latest song began drifting from the jukebox speakers, causing a few men to groan, a couple of women to dance in their seats and one guy to plunk down a pile of quarters beside the juke and start thumbing through it for better future selections.

So far, there wasn't an eligible male in sight. Not that Meredith intended to drag the first single man she saw off to the nearest Holiday Inn, but she didn't want to wait too long. She needed a man.

And she needed him quick. Before her resolve left her as quickly as a bull escaping his spring castration.

Two men came into the bar, one short and dark-haired, with end-of-day stubble on his chin, the other tall and tanned, his hair the color of the chocolate on a KitKat bar. As the taller of the two approached the bar, she could see that his eyes were a deep, dark green, like the shadowed corners of a lush forest. Something hot quickened in her gut.

The man moved easily about the bar, as if he'd been here a hundred times before. He had a strong, taut body, not too muscular, not too thin. Clad in jeans and a fitted dark blue Henley, he looked—

Perfect.

At the other end of the smooth oak surface, a heavyset man in his early sixties lifted his glass toward the bartender. "How about another round, Bud?" The words came out slurred and slow, as if he were concentrating on getting them right.

The bartender, who didn't look a day over twenty-one, scowled at the older man. "My name isn't Bud and you're done here. The last thing I need is a drunk snoring on my bar."

The tall man left his friend's side and sauntered over to the other end, laying an elbow on the bar beside the bigger—and drunker—man. "Hey, Jim, what kind of customer service is that?" he said to the bartender.

"The kind that keeps my ass from getting sued because this guy plows into someone's living room after I serve him one too many."

"You could at least be nice about it."

The bartender shrugged and started drying glasses. "He's drunk. He won't even remember me tomorrow."

"He's still a human being."

Meredith watched the entire encounter, fascinated by the tall stranger who'd defended a drunk. How many men had she known who would do that? She'd known far more whose idea of being nice meant letting their girlfriends take the first sip off the head of a fresh draft of Bud. She hadn't met many who'd go out of their way to defend a guy who'd gone way past 0.08 percent.

The tall man slid onto the stool beside the older man, who was now rooting in the nut dish for an elusive cashew. "Hey, Mike," he said. "Whatcha doing here on a Sunday night?"

Mike looked up at him with bleary eyes. "Wife left me, Travis. Took the damned dog, too."

"She took Chester?"

Mike nodded, reached for his glass, saw it was still empty and put it back on the bar with a sigh. "I screwed up again."

"Ah, you don't need her."

He sniffled. "But I need the damned dog."

"Sitting here drinking yourself into a coma isn't going to bring Chester back."

The man heaved a sigh and clutched his beer mug like it was going to save him from drowning. "You're right."

Travis reached forward, removed the empty glass from the man's hand and pushed it away. It was an easy, gentle touch. Friendly, yet firm. "Let me call you a cab."

"You mean, go home?"

"Yeah, go home. Sleep it off and—"

"But Chester isn't there." A sob caught in Mike's throat.

"I know. I know." He put a hand on Mike's shoulder. "Listen. Get over to the animal shelter in the morning. There are a lot of animals there looking for someone who needs them. Hell, you already have the fenced-in yard." He gave Mike a grin.

Travis had a heart *and* a soul. Meredith hadn't expected to like the man she chose, but it was a nice bonus. Kind of like getting the free matching purse when she bought new shoes, only better.

Mike considered Travis's words for a long moment, then he nodded, his face brightening. "And if I get joint custody of Chester, he'll have a friend to play with when he comes for visitation."

Travis grinned. "Exactly." He signaled to the bartender for some coffee for Mike, then unclipped his cell phone from his belt and punched in some numbers. After a minute, he closed the phone and turned to Mike, sliding a freshly stocked bowl of nuts toward the man. "Cab's on its way. You gonna be all right tonight?"

"Yeah. Thanks, Travis. You're a great guy."

Travis chuckled and patted Mike on the shoulder. "You're drunk right now. When you're sober, you'll change your mind."

Mike opened his mouth to protest, saw Travis already had an argument ready on his lips, and reached for the mug of coffee instead.

After saying good-bye, Travis crossed back to his friend and started watching the Patriots on one of the thirty-inch screens circling the bar area.

Meredith squeezed the slice of lime into her margarita and considered Travis. Until he'd walked in, the bar had lived up to its name—*Slim Pickin's.* Travis, however, wasn't just gorgeous, he was nice. He seemed trustworthy, even chivalrous. Meredith didn't know a lot about cities but she did know not to choose a man based solely on looks. Ted Bundy had been kind of cute, too.

Meredith watched Travis, who kept his eye on Mike until the cab arrived a few minutes later, then screwed up her nerve. She took a long sip of the margarita. Damn. Why couldn't the tequila hit her fast, before her self-consciousness had a chance to awaken and put her whole plan at risk?

"You two guys gonna order something? Or are you just here to decorate my bar?" the bartender said to Travis and his friend.

"Two rum and cokes," the short one said, pivoting toward the bartender.

"Except leave out the rum in mine," Travis said. His friend shook his head at him, then paid Jim for the two drinks. The men turned, putting their back to the bar again. The short one's gaze roved over the room, alighting on anything female. Travis, though,

37

kept his gaze on the pigpile of men in blue and red uniforms.

Meredith checked his left hand. No ring or evidence of one being there before. Maybe he was dating someone, which would explain his lack of interest in the women in the room.

Or maybe he was just waiting for the right woman to come along.

Meredith swallowed, then took another gulp of her margarita. Nope, no courage in the lime twist either. Just a slight buzz that made her skin feel flushed.

If she didn't move now, she'd never get past the label printed on the white sash draped across the mirror of her bedroom back home.

There was *no way* she was going to her grave with her greatest life achievement being "Miss Holstein."

She slid off her stool and headed over to the duo, her hand on her purse. Beneath the leather exterior, she could feel the box of Trojans. She took in a deep breath, forced a smile to her face and crossed to the one named Travis.

Travis stood there, like an oak tree, staring at the football game as if she didn't exist. He was a foot taller than her, maybe more. A whiff of his cologne teased at her nostrils. A bit of musk, a hint of pine.

And a lot of man. More man than she was used to. "Excuse me," she said.

The short guy's gaze swiveled toward her. "You looking for me?"

"Uh, no. I'd like to talk to you." She directed her words at Travis.

"I'm watching the game," he said, without looking down.

The short guy punched him in the arm. "Don't be rude, Travis. A pretty lady wants to talk to you."

"You know what I vowed five minutes ago," he muttered.

"And you know I think you're nuts," his friend muttered back. "So say hello and don't be a jackass."

Travis looked down at her. "Hello." Then his gaze went back to the television.

Cousin Henrietta, who'd been in Boston once for a wedding, had warned her that Bostonians were as rude as a litter of kittens in an ice bath. Maria, however, had proved to be the exact opposite. So had Rebecca, who, contrary to Momma's predictions, had stayed true to her sweet nature after moving to Boston when she was eleven.

Maybe it was just this guy. Maybe she'd chosen the wrong one.

"You know, it's too bad you're busy with the game," Meredith said, keeping her tone flip, unconcerned. "Because I was about to make you a very nice offer."

His gaze stayed riveted on the Patriots/Bears matchup as if the fate of the world hung in a piece of pigskin. "What's the offer?" the shorter one said. "If it's a drink, I'm all yours."

"Let her go, Kenny. I'm not—"

"Crazy, even if you act it," Kenny interrupted. "Don't mind him, he's grumpy."

"Maybe he's just obnoxious." Meredith started to walk toward her seat, then stopped midstep.

A man wouldn't walk away from something he wanted. He wouldn't let a little aloofness get in his way. He'd try a little harder.

And so would a city girl, Meredith decided. Small town Indiana girls gave up easily when confronted with big-city attitude. City girls told the man off.

She returned to stand in front of Travis. "Do you have something against women?"

He dropped his gaze to hers. "Not at all."

"Something against me in particular?"

This time, his gaze swept over her, slow and easy, inching down the details of her body. Meredith felt a slow burn of embarrassment creep into her cheeks.

And a slow burn of a whole other kind stirring in her gut.

"Not at all," he said.

"Then why are you being so rude?"

He blinked. "Rude? I... Well, I guess I was being rude."

"He has his reasons," his friend piped in, a grin on his face. "Stupid ones, but reasons all the same."

"Kenny, I'm having a conversation here," Travis muttered.

"But I thought you swore off—"

"*Kenny*," Travis said again, with more growl in his voice.

"I see a blonde I like over there anyway," Kenny said. "I'll leave you two alone. Provided I can trust you to go easy on my friend here." He gave Meredith a wink and hooked a thumb in Travis's direction.

"Go easy on him?"

Kenny's grin widened. "Don't tempt him. He's a weak man."

"Kenny, I swear I'll—"

"Leaving, leaving." Kenny waved a hand of defeat and walked away.

Travis Campbell was a man who didn't want to be tempted. Now *that* was exactly the kind of challenge Meredith had come to this city to find. It was even better than her original plan to find a man who was ready, willing and able.

A man who wasn't willing, wasn't ready but still able would force her to really act like a woman. Try out this new sexy siren persona she wanted to affect.

And help her shed the image of a girl steeped in cow manure and homespun roots once and for all.

"Can I buy you a drink?" she asked, forcing her voice not to shake as she spoke. Never before had she made a pass at a man.

Hopefully she didn't fumble it and end up overshooting the goal line. Like the guy in the blue-and-red uniform on the TV above them just had, eliciting a few frustrated groans and several curses from the male audience in the bar.

Travis turned to face her and rested his elbow on the bar. "I don't drink. Anymore."

Anymore. There was a word that invited questions. Meredith opened her mouth to ask one, then shut it again. Her objective wasn't to form a relationship here, just to... complete her education. For that, she didn't need to know what "anymore" meant.

"Meredith Shordon," she said, thrusting out her hand.

He paused, then took her hand in his and shook. He had a firm grip. Long, strong fingers.

Perfect.

"Travis Campbell."

"Nice to meet you, Travis."

"Where do you come from, Meredith Shordon?" He cocked his head and studied her. "Your alphabet contains the letter "r," so I know you aren't from here."

"Indiana."

"There are people who live in Indiana? I thought they all left after the finale of *Little House on the Prairie.*"

She laughed. "A few of us hung on in Walnut Grove."

He released her hand. "Well, it was a pleasure meeting you, Miss Indiana."

The beauty queen reference, coupled with the word pleasure, sent another round of heat roaring through her.

Now or never. She only had so much time before she'd have to go back.

Back to Indiana. Back to being Meredith Shordon. The woman everybody knew like the back of their hands. If there was anything Meredith hated about herself, it was her conventionality. All her life, she'd fit into the little square created by Midwestern values. No lying. No cheating on her tax returns.

And most of all, no sex.

She'd been a good girl. And what the hell had it gotten her?

A mortician as an ex-fiancé. A job as a waitress in Petey's Pizza Parlor, despite two years of college. An associate's degree instead of a bachelor's because somewhere along the way she'd convinced herself that was good enough.

And most of all, a fear of anything that took her outside that insular environment because that was where the big, bad wolves existed. Too much sin, she'd heard over and over again from Pastor Wendall at the First Presbyterian Church, and she'd be headed on a nonstop highway to hell.

Hell, Meredith had decided, didn't seem such a bad alternative to slogging pepperoni pizzas around and being kissed by a man who smelled of formaldehyde.

Meredith took a step forward and tossed all the rules she'd lived her life by out the window. "I'd like to make you an offer, Mr. Campbell."

He gave her an inquiring look. "You hardly know me."

"Exactly."

His mouth lifted up on one side. "Only because I'm a curious man, I'll ask what this offer is."

She swallowed. "As I mentioned, I come from a small town in Indiana."

He nodded.

"And, well, this is my first time in a city."

"A good city to pick for your first time." He grinned.

She met his dark green gaze. "Exactly."

The air hung between them, punctuated by a Sheryl Crow song. In the distance, a couple danced in the center of the room, another flirted in a corner booth.

Travis slid onto his stool, propping one heel against the steel circle on the base. "Are you saying what I'm thinking you're saying? Or am I just an idiot guy who's thinking with his lesser brain?"

"You heard me right." Meredith drew in a breath. "I want my first time to be in the city."

"First time?" he echoed again.

She saw him swallow. Who knew two words could have such an impact on a six-foot-two man? "That's what I said."

"Uh, I'm not what you think I am."

"You're not a man?"

He chuckled. "Oh, I'm a man all right I'm not a... well, a gigolo."

She smiled. "Good. I wouldn't want a professional. I suspect that would be about as fun as a breast exam from a gynecologist."

Travis leaned forward, resting a hand on her arm. "I know you're new in town and all, Miss Shordon, but that isn't the kind of thing you go up to a stranger and offer."

"I may be from Indiana, but that doesn't mean I'm an idiot, Mr. Campbell. I know what I'm doing." She took a step forward, placing her own hand on top of his. "Are you interested in the position?"

A hundred emotions flickered on his face. He swallowed, then cleared his throat and considered her again. "I'm really not the right man for what you want."

She frowned. "You can't perform?"

That got his attention. "Of course I can."

"No old football injuries or surgeries that prevent you from doing the job?"

"Of course not." He cocked his head and studied her. "But you don't know anything about me."

"I know enough." She'd seen him with Mike. Her gut told her Travis Campbell was a decent man, the kind who wouldn't turn her life story into a TNT special. Meredith collected her courage and drifted her hand down his chest. "I've seen the merchandise and I want to buy it."

He let out a long breath, as if her touch had taken away his resolve. "I'm not for sale."

"Then you can work for free."

"Don't you, ah," he watched her hand make its way back up his chest, "have a boyfriend back on the farm, or wherever it is you lived in Indiana, that can do this for you?"

She shook her head. "Not anymore."

A fleeting thought of Caleb ran through her mind. She could just imagine his reaction to her propositioning a complete stranger like this. He'd be horrified, unable to understand how she could do something so personal with someone she hadn't known all her life. What Caleb didn't understand was that was *exactly* why she wanted a stranger for this job. So no one would know but her and the whole town of Heavendale could keep their noses out of her sex life.

She sighed and took her hand off his chest. "Listen, I don't want this to get personal. Are you interested in the job or not?"

His gaze skimmed over her again. For the first time, Meredith was sure she had made a mistake. This was a crazy idea. It had seemed so sane when she'd left the farm and boarded a plane.

"Yes," he said after a moment. "I'll take the job."

She gulped. "Good."

"But first, I think you should know what you're getting yourself into."

Then he swooped forward and kissed her.

Travis had only intended to give Meredith Shordon a taste of her own medicine. But when his mouth met hers, an explosion of want burst in his brain.

She kissed him back, tentative at first, as delicate as a hummingbird. The innocence of her lips, so tender, so soft, told him to tread lightly. The quiet fragrance of spring flowers drifted off her skin, a sweet contrast to the salty taste of margarita on her lips.

He cupped her chin with his hand, tracing her jaw with his thumb. She opened her mouth to his and in one hesitant, gentle move, tasted him with her tongue.

Holy shit. What had he done?

He'd only meant to teach her a lesson. Instead, he found himself quickly drowning in desire.

As if she felt the same, Meredith pressed forward, her breasts brushing against his chest. She tangled a hand in his hair and again brought her tongue into his mouth.

Travis jerked back, ending the kiss before he jumped off the cliff and into bed with her. This was so not the plan.

"Still want to honor that deal?" he asked, hoping she'd say no. Praying she'd say yes.

Eyes closed, she nodded her head. "Uh-huh."

Oh damn. He didn't need to be getting involved with this woman. She was too sweet, too naive, too much of a—holy crap—a virgin.

Was he nuts? Any man with more than one functioning brain cell would leap at this kind of opportunity.

The little voice in the back of his head reminded him that he'd made a vow to stay away from all the things that got him into trouble. Namely, alcohol and women. Especially women who had "hurt potential" written all over them. The last thing he needed was a brokenhearted woman armed with a bigger pocketbook than Olivia's.

Travis glanced at Meredith and her wide, open, trusting blue eyes. When he did, he knew one thing: he needed to protect her from herself. She had no idea what she was asking for—or how another man with fewer morals would take it.

Who was he kidding? He didn't have any morals. Or he hadn't had any before Olivia had purse-slapped him across the temples.

Now he had morals. Well, at least he had good intentions.

"You're perfect," Meredith said. "Exactly what I wanted."

She said it like she was ordering a dress off a shopping channel. Didn't exactly do a lot for his already battered male ego. "I aim to please."

"And you did." She smiled, then stepped closer to him. A vibration started against his stomach. Holy Mother of God. She had toys with her, too?

His resolve *definitely* wasn't that strong.

The vibration turned into a ring. Meredith rolled her eyes and stepped back. "Excuse me. I have a call."

It was a cell phone, not something out of the *Adam & Eve* catalog.

Then why didn't he feel relief?

Meredith withdrew the phone, answered it and frowned. She smiled an apology at Travis, then moved back to where her margarita waited, condensation frosting the outside of the wide-rimmed glass.

Kenny honed in on the opportunity and was at Travis's side in a second. "I thought you swore off women a few minutes ago. Or was that the other Travis?"

"I did."

"Unless my watch is really wrong, I don't think your self-imposed thirty-day waiting period has passed."

"It hasn't."

"So what are you doing?"

"Saving that woman from herself."

Kenny laughed. "Now that's one I haven't heard before."

"I don't mean it that way."

"What does she want with you?"

"Let's just say she wants me to show her the best views in Boston."

"She can take one of the duck tours for that. I hear they even give out free quackers." Kenny chuckled at his pun.

"I meant the view from my bedroom."

"Your bed—" Kenny took a second to digest that. Then his eyes and his grin widened. "Oh."

"Yeah."

"Well, too bad you've sworn off women, my friend." Kenny puffed out his chest and ran a hand through his hair. "Seems I'll have to do your dirty work."

"Don't you go within five feet of her. I know how you are."

"Only because you're the same way."

"Not anymore."

"Yeah, right. I'll believe that bullshit when they make Coors the national drink."

"I'm serious."

"So you're not going to sleep with her?"

"Nope."

Kenny laughed long and hard. "Right. You're just going to show her the sights?"

"Yep. Be her own personal tour guide."

"I'll make sure the cleaning lady changes your sheets. Just in case."

"You're a pig, Kenny."

"And proud to live among the dregs of society." He grinned. "So tell me. Where'd this miracle come from? I didn't think there were any innocent women left in Boston."

Travis glanced over at Meredith, her back to him as she continued her cell conversation. As he did, he remembered what she had told him about where she came from and who she was. An idea began to brew in his head. A bad idea, one he shouldn't even be considering. But he did anyway. "She's from Indiana."

"Yeah, so? Corn-fed and all that?"

"Exactly." Travis's gaze hit Kenny's. It took a second, but he could see the wheels begin turning in Kenny's head, the same wheels that had been churning in his own a second earlier. "What did Larry say at the meeting Friday morning?"

"If we can make it fly in Topeka—"

"We can make it work anywhere." Travis took a sip of his soda and tipped the glass in Meredith's direction. "She's our key to making it fly in Indiana."

Kenny shook his head and reached for his drink. The lime twist had fallen into the glass and bobbed among the ice, like a Martian drowning in rum. "Is that what makes her so special?"

"Well, she does have amazing legs." Travis smiled.

"I thought you swore off women."

"I didn't *die* overnight, Kenny."

Kenny clapped him on the shoulder and grinned. "Glad to hear it, bud." He glanced over at Meredith, admired her legs—and more—for a moment, then turned back. "Promise me one thing, though."

"What?"

"That while you're, ah, capturing the thoughts of your newest focus group over there, you won't do anything stupid."

"Like what?"

"Like fall in love. We have a good thing going here with the bachelor life and I don't want you screwing it up. You get hooked on her and before I know it, there are panties in our shower and flavored coffee brewing in the kitchen."

Travis laughed. "No worries here. Falling in love is the last thing I'm ever going to do."

Kenny raised his glass towards Travis and clinked with him. "That's why you're my hero."

"Dear, I was so worried about you I had to call again."

"Momma, I'm fine."

Her mother paused a second. "Is that a jukebox I hear in the background?"

"Uh, yeah."

"Are you in a bar? Do you know the statistics for young women who are murdered after visiting bars in big cities?"

"I'm fine," Meredith repeated, more firmly this time. "I'm over twenty-one, remember? And besides, I'm not doing anything illegal."

It was only illegal if she *paid* him.

"Still, I wish you wouldn't have gone to Boston. Caleb is still pining for you, you know."

Meredith sighed. Breaking up with Caleb had been the right thing to do, even if he had taken it pretty hard. In an odd way, she was sure her former home ec teacher, Mr. Galloway, who'd lain in the Deluxe 2000 casket in the back of the hearse, would have approved. At least he hadn't rolled over in the cherry box when she'd told Caleb she was moving on. "It's over between us, Mom. I really don't care what Caleb thinks."

"Honey, he still loves you. Why he could hardly get through Lester Hewitt's funeral, he was crying so hard. Reverend Wilkins had to call a time out so Caleb could pull himself together."

"We're not engaged anymore. He'll meet some-one else." She'd known Caleb since kindergarten and when he put on a dark suit and held out a box of Kleenex with that mixture of compassion and charm he had, he was nearly irresistible to women.

"Not in his line of work."

"Morticians get out. They have, like, casket con-ventions or something."

"Still, he says he'll never meet anyone like you."

"I'm not having this conversation."

"J.C. Henry called this morning. He needs to know when you'll be back to fulfill your duties."

Meredith had dropped a letter in the mail slot at J.C.'s office the morning she left, resigning her position as Miss Holstein. Apparently, J.C. wasn't going to let her off that easily.

"I'm not having *that* conversation either. I told you, I don't want to be Miss Holstein. Tell him to find another cow girl."

"You used to want to be."

"I was different then." When Meredith had signed up to compete in Miss Holstein, it had been on a lark. She hadn't expected to win; she'd only done it to do something, *anything* different from what she was doing right then. A beauty contest, even if the prize was wearing a cow suit for a year, was definitely out of the ordinary for Meredith Shordon's life. It had been her first step toward independence.

And then she'd gone and won the damned thing. She'd tried to tell J.C, the event's organizer, they'd picked the wrong girl, but he wasn't having any of that. Finally, she'd given in and accepted the hooved crown, figuring she'd find a way out of her bovine obligations afterwards.

Five hours later, Rebecca had called and Meredith had ditched it all—the crown, the sash, and most of all, the damned udders.

"I don't see how you could change overnight," her mother said. She let out a sigh, then switched gears. "If you won't come home, then at least take care of yourself so I don't have to go out there and claim your body from some alley somewhere."

"Momma, that isn't going to happen."

"Take your vitamins. Maybe I should have Dr. Michaels send you a prescription for antibiotics. It is cold season, you know."

"I'm fine. I haven't coughed once since I arrived." She took a sip of margarita. Tequila would kill anything in her anyway.

Her mother let out a frustrated sigh. "Promise me you won't talk to strangers."

She'd already broken that rule. But for a good reason. Hearing about Caleb—and the life that waited for her in Indiana if she didn't find one here first— just reinforced her determination.

She said goodbye to her mother, flipped the phone shut and glanced over at Travis Campbell, who was chatting with his friend.

As she took a step closer to him, years of her mother's neurosis flooded her mind. She didn't know this man at all. She could be wrong about him. Could she even trust her instincts?

The last time she'd done that, she'd been the one girl at day camp who thought the shiny plant with three-leaf clusters was cute and picked some for a bouquet. She'd spent the entire week in the infirmary, covered from head to toe in pink calamine lotion while everyone else canoed and caught fireflies in itch-free comfort.

Travis Campbell wasn't poison ivy. Still, he could be toxic to her in other ways. And she knew a little dab of pink lotion wasn't going to be enough to rid her body of all she'd felt when he kissed her.

She already knew she'd be back for more anyway. Her body still simmered with unanswered desire. Meredith closed the distance between herself and Travis and figured if she didn't take a risk now, she'd never do it.

"Sorry about that," she said, arriving at his side again. "Phone call I had to take."

"The reluctant boyfriend?" He arched a brow.

"No." She ran a hand through her hair. "I'm not exactly on his friends and family list right now."

"Business then?"

"No. I'm not really in the kind of business where my cell phone would be ringing off the hook."

"And what business is that?"

"Well, for a few weeks, I'm working at a gift baskets shop, helping out my cousin."

"A temporary gig? And where will you be after that? At Hallmark, recommending a good thank you card?"

She shook her head. "I'm going back to Indiana."

"Why?"

"Because that's where I live." For a second, it sounded so sad to picture herself going back home. It was the only place she'd ever lived and yet, despite the honking horns and congested streets, she liked Boston. As clichéd as it sounded, she now knew how a bird felt after living in a cage too long. Boston held something Heavendale never had; it felt as if the real Meredith was somewhere here, waiting to be found among the crowded neighborhoods and the slim saplings that peppered the sidewalks, as if Mother Nature was bound and determined to punch through the concrete.

But once she returned to Heavendale, would she be able to go back to the life she'd left? To Petey's? To being Miss Holstein? Or would she find herself displaced and lost in the town where she'd lived all her life?

And be worse off than when she'd left?

Meredith shook off the maudlin thoughts. She was only after one thing right now. Travis. The rest could wait.

Sheryl Crow had segued into the Dave Matthews Band. Across from them, a couple danced in the space between the jukebox and the tables. Another pair was making out at the table beside the juke.

"So, I'm a what, few-weeks stand for you?" Travis asked with a teasing grin. "You're going to love me and leave me?"

Her gaze hit his, hard and direct. "I will leave you, Travis Campbell, but I won't love you."

He grinned. "You think so?"

"I know so."

"Have this pretty planned out, don't you?"

"Down to the last contingency."

"No, you haven't. I'm a contingency you haven't counted on. Me. And what *I* might want from *you*."

She'd deal with that, and what he meant— later. For now, Meredith had one goal and a short timeline. Rebecca could have the baby early or Meredith's own obligations could come knocking, and Meredith would be back on her way to the cornfields before she had a chance to work a life transformation. She was afraid if she left Boston too early, she'd slip back into that complacent life she'd led before and end up married to Caleb, passing out Kleenexes and grave-site plans for the rest of her life.

"So," she said, drawing in a breath, "shall we get started?"

Travis took a look around the bar, filling up now that the hour was getting late. "Now?"

"No time like the present." She smiled. That was exactly how a city girl would act. Confident, sure ... and ready anytime.

Travis, though, shook his head, deflating her confidence balloon a little. "Nope. No can do. You want to do this, you need to do it right." He trailed a slow, sure finger along her lower lip, teasing her with a taste of what had been there earlier. Need tingled inside Meredith for more, for a firmer touch, for... anything. Travis traced her lips, then drew back, leaving her feeling like something had been half-started between them. "You want to do this right, don't you, Meredith?"

She gulped. "Oh, absolutely." If doing it right meant more of that kind of touch, she'd do it right many, many times.

"Good. Then I'm going to make damned sure you get what you asked for."

And with that, Meredith knew she was no longer in charge of her destiny. Not tonight.

Cordelia's True-Wealth-is-in-Your-Friends Oysters Rockefeller

4 tablespoons parsley
2 shallots
4 tablespoons celery leaves
1-1/4 pounds fresh spinach leaves
1/2 cup butter, softened
1/2 cup fresh white breadcrumbs
Salt and pepper
Tabasco, to taste
Rock salt or kosher salt
24 fresh oysters on the half shell
2 tablespoons Pernod or other licorice-flavored liqueur, optional
Lemon wedges, optional

Just because you aren't wealthy doesn't mean you can't live like those who are. It's all a matter of perceptions, dear, starting with your own. If you see yourself as rich, well then, you are. Just don't go acting that way with your Visa too often. The banks don't quite see the fantasy the same way, silly gooses.

Preheat your broiler. Then chop the parsley, celery leaves, shallots and spinach, nice and fine. Melt the butter in a pan and cook the shallots first, then add the spinach and the other veggies, just long enough to soften them up for the next step. Sort of like how you'd soften up a man to ask him for a really big favor.

Add the breadcrumbs and cook for another few minutes, melding those flavors like a happy little group (not at all like one of those society parties where you have the parsleys over here and the spinaches over there; how I despise those cliques). Season with salt, pepper and as much Tabasco as your mouth can take.

Now, nestle those pretty little oysters in a bed of rock salt on a baking sheet. Spoon the stuffing onto the oysters. If you're feeling decadent, drizzle each with a little Pernod. Then pop them under the broiler, a couple spaces below the top so you don't end up with a three-alarm fire instead of a gourmet treat.

Be sure to watch them, instead of tending to your company. I know, it's hard to be a proper hostess then, but believe me, when guests taste this, they'll be friends for life (of course, some may just be mooching for the free oysters; kick them off your Christmas card list right away, dear). Serve with lemon wedges and martinis.

And lots and lots of good friends.

Chapter Five

The naked woman stood tall and proud, breasts thrust forward, generous hips tilted back, emphasizing a roundness even J. Lo would envy.

"That's not natural," Maria said. "No one looks like that."

"Apparently Mrs. Kingwood does," Candace said. "Her husband said he gave us her exact dimensions. Scaled down to a manageable size for a piece of candy, of course."

Meredith readied the cellophane wrap for the Kingwood female form, made for them by a local chocolatier since naked women were out of the range of Gift Baskets to Die For's talents ... and the shop's candy mold collection. "Why do you suppose he'd want her cast in chocolate?"

"Apparently he never outgrew his fascination with hollow Easter bunnies." Maria winked.

"That's just... weird. A chocolate replica of your wife? I mean, what's he going to do with it?"

Maria raised a brow. "Let her melt in his hands?"

"I am not even going to entertain that with a response," Candace said, laughing nevertheless.

"My dears, this one takes the cake. *And* the cake stand. Is that woman *naked?*"

All three women turned toward the voice. A small elderly woman stood in the doorway of the kitchen, a tiny pink pillbox hat on her salt-and-pepper hair, set slightly askew, perfect for the matching Jackie O-style suit she wore. She had to be close to seventy-five, Meredith guessed, but she wore pale cream pumps and hose, her appearance as precise as the First Lady who'd inspired her look.

"Good morning, Ms. Gershwin," Candace said. She indicated Meredith with a wave of her hand. "This is Rebecca's cousin, Meredith. She's come to work with us while Rebecca is home on bed rest. Meredith, this is Ms. Gershwin. She owns the antique shop next door."

"Cordelia Gershwin," the woman said, taking Meredith's palm in her own, "of the Gershwins, but not *the* Gershwins."

"Meaning, she comes from money, not show tunes," Maria said.

"But I have a distant cousin whom we suspect was a member of the royal family," Cordelia said, releasing Meredith's palm with a wink. "I could be a princess in disguise."

Maria laughed. "You already are the queen on our street."

The older woman's bright coral lips spread across her lined face in a wide grin. "You girls are too sweet by half. Must come from working around all that chocolate." She motioned toward the naked torso. "Speaking of which, what is that?"

"A chocolate version of one of our customer's wives," Maria said.

Cordelia raised a brow at the perfect ten shape. "Are you sure she's the wife?"

Maria chuckled. "We don't ask the questions. We just melt the Ghirardelli."

They finished assembling the basket, complete with the chocolate missus in the center. They surrounded her with candy flowers peppered over a green-tinted coconut base. While they worked, Cordelia grabbed a cup of coffee and watched their progress, amusement clear on her face. "Quite the ... odd creation," she said, admiring their finished product.

"What's weirder is he's sending this to himself for Sweetest Day," Maria said. "Mrs. Kingwood is out of town."

"Oh, I almost forgot!" Candace said. "Speaking of Sweetest Day, something arrived for you today, Meredith." She crossed to the opposite counter and picked up a clear glass vase filled with cranberry roses and baby's breath. The roses had just begun to open, releasing their sweet fragrance into the room. "Here."

Meredith took the vase, inhaling the sweet, heady fragrance. For a second, she wondered if

Travis had sent them. Was he even the type to send flowers? Or did his idea match that of the boys she'd known back home, where romance meant letting her have first dibs on the bowling ball selection at the Heavendale Bowl-a-Rama?

Clearly, none of the men in her hometown had ever opened up a romance novel.

She'd left the bar last night while she was still able to walk and think, handing Travis her cell phone number and receiving a promise of a date for tonight Anticipation had been singing inside her, ever since she'd woken up.

Or maybe it had just been the shock of finding Rebecca's beagle at the end of the bed, licking her toes like rawhide bones.

"So, tell us, dear," Cordelia said, peering over her shoulder and making no secret of her curiosity. "Who's Caleb?"

Disappointment plummeted to the bottom of Meredith's stomach. She took a step forward and read the card attached to the plastic holder. "My one and true love," she read aloud, "though miles may separate us, even death can't keep my heart from beating for you. Forever, Caleb."

"That's uh, sort of poetic," Maria said. "Almost Shakespearean, if you leave out the reference to being dead."

"That's Caleb's specialty," Meredith said. "Working a reference to the hereafter into all his correspondence."

"How ... er ... romantic."

"He's a mortician," she explained.

"As in, he sees dead people?"

"As many as there are in Heavendale, considering we have a population of three thousand. We don't exactly have a high turnover rate."

Maria choked back a laugh. "Rebecca said you and she came from a small town, but she didn't say it was that small."

"Everything about my life was small... until I got to Boston."

Cordelia peered past them, out the plate glass of the front of the shop. A nattily dressed couple in their mid-forties waited under the brightly striped green awning of Remembered Pasts Antiques. "Oh, dear. Time to open," she sighed. "I suppose I'd best get next door."

"You sound down this morning," Candace said. "Everything all right?"

Cordelia brightened, straightened her pillbox hat and adjusted the little purse on the crook of her arm. "Perfectly fine. Why wouldn't it be?" Then she was gone, off to her little shop.

Maria draped an arm over Meredith's shoulders. "Well, it's a damned good thing you came along. Things around here were getting pretty boring now that Candace and I are both engaged and Rebecca is working on baby number two. With you, we have a new mission."

"A mission?"

"Yep. We're going to show you the town and help you get out of that small-town life."

Meredith hadn't expected Maria and Candace to accept her so readily, or for their immediate friendship to leave her feeling choked up.

In Heavendale, she and all the other kids had been stuck with each other from grade school on up. Friendship wasn't so much a necessity as a require-ment, following math and before recess. With the nearest town dozens of miles away, there wasn't much worry about anyone running to a better party or finding a new cow-tipping gang.

But here, Meredith was sure Maria and Candace had a thousand other people to choose from besides herself. And yet, they wanted to be friends with her— and not because they shared the same smell on their shoes.

"I'd love that," Meredith said. "Do you think we could start with my clothes?"

It was, of course, the most obvious place where she didn't fit in. It had taken her about five seconds after landing at Logan to realize she wasn't quite city-girl material in her homespun *Country Woman* attire. What was fine for the county fair wasn't good for the city of Boston.

"What's wrong with your clothes?" Maria glanced down at Meredith's outfit. "You look nice."

"That's the problem." She lifted the long paisley skirt that hung past her knees. "I look like a quilt."

"You've come to the right women to fix that," Maria said. "If there's anything we love to do, it's shop."

Candace nodded. "Shopping is the city girl's therapy. Probably a lot more expensive than a session with Dr. Phil, but it sure looks better than some bald guy in a suit."

Larry Herman was holding court in the conference room again. He stood at the head of the faux cherry table, palms down on either side, and stared down his two-member team, assembled on either side of the oval table.

Travis had no idea why Larry bothered to hold these theatrical meetings every morning. No one in the office took him seriously. He was their boss, yes, but beyond that, Travis and Kenny had little use for their department manager. As the cousin of the owner, Larry had a secure position as vice president of Belly-Licious Beverages and a superiority complex that added a fashion *faux pas* touch to his middle-age paunch and balding head.

Everyone knew he was bald, though he tried really hard to disguise it. A lifetime member of the Toupee of the Month Club, Larry had a collection of hairpieces even Cher would envy. Unfortunately, despite sixty months of "real" fake hair, Larry had yet to hit on a set of strands that matched his own strawberry blond, or what was left of it.

"I need a miracle, men," Larry said, nodding as he spoke. October's ash blond hair fluttered with the movement, as if it were waving agreement. "A miracle with No-Moo Milk."

"It's Monday, Larry," Kenny said. "We're flat out of miracles until Friday."

"Ha ha. Very funny. We don't have until Friday. We need an ad campaign for No-Moo Milk by Thursday at five."

"We? Or you? Last I checked, *you* took the meeting with your cousin, leaving us sitting outside his office like a bunch of truant kids," Travis said. "You weren't thinking of stealing our ideas and passing them off as your own again, were you?"

Larry let out a short, dry, nervous laugh. "Why would I do that? We're a team here. There's no I in team."

"There's no recognition either. At least not in your idea of a 'team.'" Travis leaned back in his chair. The faux black leather crinkled with the movement and the base squeaked in protest.

"Listen, you guys go to bat with me on this and I'll be sure to put in a good word for you with the boss."

As the head of both marketing and research and development, Larry's motto was that it was "everybody's ass" on the line. When it came to taking care of asses, though, his was the only one he ever worried about.

Travis had woken up Monday morning determined to turn over a new leaf of his personal life. While he was in the woods of change, he figured he might as well rake up a few new things at work, too.

Like Larry's hair, which could use a comb and a can of Ronco spray-on color.

"We busted our butts on Choco-Carrot Juice," Travis reminded him. "And you were the one who ended up with a company car and your own parking space."

Larry's laugh was almost a choke. "I tried to get something for you guys—"

"You call a subscription to *Dog Fancy* a bonus?" Kenny asked. "Larry, I don't even own a dog."

Larry shrugged and put up his hands. "You might someday. I'm only thinking of your future."

Travis muttered a few choice words under his breath.

"Anyway, we need to make No-Moo Milk the leader in the beverage industry. If we can get people to buy that instead of real milk, we'll corner the market."

"And put a lot of farmers out of business," Travis said.

Larry waved his hand. "They'll still have cheese. Now, give me something on No-Moo Milk that will convince those mustached lunatics to buy it, and I'll take care of you both."

"Mustached lunatics?"

"Yeah, those idiots in the dairy ads who are always talking about how good milk is for you." Larry snorted. "Like a synthetic product that's chemically fortified isn't more nutritious."

"And it's up to us to make them see the error of their ways." Travis shook his head and vowed to crack open the classifieds the minute he got home. He'd had enough of Larry, his hair fetish, and the insane products he worked with. Now that he was sober, Travis Campbell had a hell of a lot less enjoyment for his job.

He'd get the hell out of here, just as he and his brother Brad had vowed long ago. Their jobs were a joke, a way to pay for beer and dates. Now that Travis wasn't funding either for a while, he could afford unemployment. Either way, it was better to be poor and sober than drunk and working for Larry and his hair one more day.

Brad, who worked in R&D for Belly-Licious, had developed No-Moo as a lark, a sort of *ha-ha* back at Larry, who was lactose intolerant but refused to admit it. Everyone in the office suffered after one of Larry's daily "I can still eat ice cream" trips to Dairy Queen.

Brad and Travis had had a big laugh about the test product, thinking there'd be no way anyone would take Brad's chemical version of nature's finest beverage seriously.

Clearly, they'd been wrong.

"Travis, I can see that look in your eyes. Don't you even think about letting me down on this one."

"Larry, don't you find it even remotely disturbing that we're trying to encourage people to *not* drink milk, one of the healthiest natural beverages around?"

"Uh, no." Larry lowered himself into the claw-footed chair at the head of the table and crossed his hands over his notepad. "Now, who's got an idea?"

Kenny looked at Travis. Travis looked at Kenny.

"This is what I pay you two for, in case you forgot."

"No offense, Larry, but that No-Moo Milk tastes like my grandmother's toilet water." Kenny shook his head. "How the hell do we sell that to people?"

"Old ladies can be very convincing salespeople. That Clara dame worked wonders for Wendy's." Larry said. "I can see it now." Larry spread a hand across an imaginary billboard. "Where's the No-Moo?!"

Travis groaned.

"What, you guys have something better? Something *before* payday?"

Kenny glanced at Travis, then back at Larry, then did a damned good job of avoiding Travis's gaze. "Well... we do have one ace."

"An ace?" Larry's eyes brightened behind his tortoiseshell rims. "What kind of ace?"

Travis suddenly knew what Kenny was talking about. He remembered the conversation in the bar, his brilliant idea last night that no longer seemed so brilliant, not in the light of day. "Kenny—"

"A woman from Indiana," Kenny went on. "A *farmer's* daughter."

Larry's grin spread from sideburn to sideburn. "That's not a woman, that's a focus group."

"Larry, she's a nice woman." Travis shook his head and gave Kenny a glare. "We shouldn't use her."

"Travis, might I remind you that she's using you?" Kenny said. "*Quid pro quo*, as I always say."

"Since when do you speak Latin?"

"Since my ex got her alimony upped. Remember?" Kenny leaned in close to Travis and lowered his voice. "I'm asking you this as a friend in debt and in need. I need this job and whatever raise I can squeeze out of Larry if No-Moo Milk is a success."

"Come on, Kenny, this is wrong."

"And since when did you grow a conscience, pocket-book boy?"

Since he'd met a woman who seemed damned determined to make sure he didn't think with anything remotely conscientious. But he kept that to himself.

As Kenny had said, all she wanted from him was a little *quo*. And he'd be a fool if he didn't exact some *quid* while he was at it.

Maria's Time-for-a-Change Seafood Lasagna

2 tablespoons olive oil
1 small onion, diced
1 clove garlic, minced
1/2 cup fresh mushrooms, sliced
2 14-1/2 ounce cans stewed tomatoes, cut up
1/2 teaspoon dried oregano
1 tablespoon tomato paste
Dash salt and pepper
1/2 cup peeled, cooked shrimp
8 ounces crabmeat
1/2 pound scallops, sliced
3 tablespoons butter
3 tablespoons flour
1-3/4 cups milk
1 cup shredded mozzarella cheese
1/4 cup dry white wine
8 ounces lasagna noodles, cooked and drained
1/4 cup grated Parmigiano Reggiano

I know, it looks lot of ingredients, but trust me, the results are worth it. Besides, when did you ever meet a lasagna you didn't like? Preheat the oven to 350 degrees and get ready to cook.

The dish, not the man. Not yet. Save him for later.

Sauté the onion and garlic in the olive oil, then add the mushrooms. Cook until everything is as weak as your resolve to be a good girl. Add the tomatoes, spices and paste. Simmer for twenty minutes, then stir in the seafood and remove from the heat.

Mmm ... bet you can taste the blend of flavors already. That's pretty much what you're doing with your life and new look, isn't it? Blending something new with something old, hoping for a result he'll find irresistible?

In another saucepan (don't worry, that's what a good-looking man is for, to get sudsy with you and help with the dishes), melt the butter, then add the flour. Stir in the milk a little at a time with a whisk, cooking until it's as thick and bubbly as your desire for more. Add the mozzarella and stir until it's melted. Finally, add the wine.

Oh, *yeah*. It looks good enough to eat as it is, doesn't it? Trust me. Layer one sauce, then the other on the lasagna noodles, repeating one more time. Top with the Parmigiano. Then bake it uncovered (doesn't everything look better naked?) for a half an hour.

It says this recipe serves six to eight. But honestly, I've never been able to stretch it past two. And with a good-looking man sitting across the table to indulge with, why the hell would you want to invite anyone else over anyway?

CHAPTER SIX

Meredith sat in the waiting area of an upscale hair salon in Harvard Square during her lunch hour and instead of eating the Subway wrap in the bag beside her, she chewed on a big regret.

That she'd answered her cell phone. Again.

"Are you eating your vegetables, dear?"

Meredith knew no matter how bad her mother got, she was still her mother. And she did this all out of love—a love that sometimes suffocated her like a two-ton comforter, but still, love. "Yes, I am."

"Because if you don't, you'll get constipated and when you get your plumbing backed up—"

"Momma, this is not the time."

"I'm just saying a girl's gotta keep her plumbing in good condition. Don't want those pipes freezing when you're a married woman."

"I'm not getting married."

"That's not what Caleb says," her mother sing-songed over the phone. "A little birdie told me he has plans."

"We *had* plans. We're no longer engaged. It's over."

"Oh, pshaw. Temporarily. When you start eating more fiber, you'll come to your senses again."

"My diet has nothing to do with how I feel about Caleb."

Martha harrumphed. "It's all that smog. I tell you, it isn't good for your brain. Why I can practically hear your brain cells dying from here." On the other end, her mother started the water for the dishes. It was nine-fifteen in the morning. If there was one thing Martha Shordon excelled at, it was sticking to a schedule. Breakfast dishes soaked until nine-thirty, then they were washed, dried and back in the cabinet before ten.

"All my brain cells are intact," Meredith said, then wondered for a moment if they were. Was this idea completely insane? It would be so easy to go back home, to settle back into the complacency of Heavendale that had surrounded her with the thickness of one of her grandmother's wedding-ring pattern quilts. "I'm doing great," she said as much to reassure herself as her mother.

"Your voice sounds a little hoarse. Are you catching a cold?" Her mother didn't wait for an answer. "Chicken soup. That's what you need."

Next it would be an onion poultice. Meredith had some particularly ugly memories of onions and childhood. "I'm fine," she repeated.

"Don't forget to take your vitamins, either. You get too low on your Bs and before you know it—"

"I will. Give Dad a kiss for me. I have to go now."

A pause, then a sigh. "Meredith, what should I tell Caleb?"

Undoubtedly, telling her mother not to say anything would backfire. 'Tell him I've moved on. And I'm happy now."

"You don't sound happy. It must be a cold," Momma insisted. "You're not acting like yourself at all. I'll send you some Campbell's. I'll put that on my list for the Kroger store."

Meredith bit back her first response. As well as her second. "Thanks, Momma. That would be great."

"I knew you'd come around. You always were my good girl." Back in the sunflower-yellow kitchen in Heavendale, her mother turned off the water and let the egg-coated plates soak. "Once you're back home where you belong, everything will be back to normal. You'll see."

Meredith hung up her phone and knew one thing for sure. Soup or not, it was going to be a long while before she went back—if ever—to who she was before.

Across the waiting room of the Hair and Gone Salon, a slim, redheaded guy waved Meredith over to a booth. "Your turn. You're with Elona," he said, gesturing toward a black chair on a rotating pedestal. "I'll warn you. She's a little quirky, but she works a miracle with a pair of shears." Then he was gone, tending to the appointment book and phones.

A miracle. Hopefully she'd find one of those here. And be able to afford it.

Meredith took a seat in the chair and pulled out her ponytail, releasing her long blond hair and letting it swing against her shoulders. Now or never, she told herself. City women didn't run around with straight blond hair that had all the shape of a burlap sack. They styled their hair, used products that cost twelve times the value of the ingredients list and added colors until they forgot what shade they'd been born with.

That was a hairstyle. What she had on her head right now was glorified straw.

This haircut would, she hoped, trim off that cornfed look and add some pizzazz to her look. Help her become someone besides Meredith Shordon, the girl everyone could predict with the accuracy of a ticking second hand.

It hadn't helped that she'd lived with practically every resident in the town in her back pocket, like overstuffed tenement housing in Siberia. Mrs. Billings, who had little to do but look out the windows of her small ranch on the corner of Elm and Grave Streets, could give an FBI deposition on Meredith's birthdate, her first day of school and the time Sheriff Coultrey caught Meredith and Caleb making out in the parking lot at Petey's.

A new haircut wouldn't quite get rid of all that, but it was a start.

Elona hurried into the booth, spouting a greeting and an apology in one quick, long sentence. A tall spike of a woman with short black hair, black high heels and a shimmery turquoise dress that looked almost plastic, Elona started by draping a neon tie-dyed cape over Meredith's khaki capris and pale blue T-shirt. Then she laid her palms on either side of Meredith's shoulders and peered at her in the mirror. Elona had even tinted her eyelashes in a bright mascara to match her dress.

Meredith had asked for someone who could give her an adventurous look. Clearly, she thought, taking another glance at her wild-child stylist, that had been a mistake.

"So, honey, what can I do for you today?" Elona asked.

Meredith inhaled the scent of citrus shampoo and the too-sweet smell of a perm from the booth next door, then closed her eyes and clasped her hands in her lap. The stone in the opal ring her grandmother had given her pressed against her palm, a reminder of the persona she was leaving behind, the girl who looked about as sexy as a mule in a miniskirt. "However you want. Just make me look sophisticated."

"Did you hear that girls?" Elona squealed. "She's letting me be in charge. When was the last time that happened?"

"Can we keep this between us?" Meredith asked. "I just want a cut that makes me look like ..."

"Yourself?"

"No! The complete opposite."

"The complete opposite?" Elona spun the chair around so that she was now facing Meredith. "Now, honey, why would you want to do a thing like that?"

"Because I look like—" Meredith didn't finish the sentence. The dishwater hair and lack of style spoke for themselves. She pointed at the pictures ringing the walls of the salon. "I'm from Indiana. And I look nothing like those women."

Elona studied Meredith for a long second, tipping her head right, then left. "The girls think you're perfect as you are. Of course, you could use a trim here," Elona reached forward and touched the ends of Meredith's hair, "and a bit of bangs and—"

"No! I want more. I want..." Meredith pointed again at the wall, at a photograph of a slim blonde with a pixie cut that framed her face in a slash of angles. To Meredith, she looked like the personification of Boston. "That."

"Oh no. No. No. That's all wrong for you," Elona said. "Girls, we have a tough case here." The salon hummed with activity around her, but as far as Meredith could tell, there was no answering voice to the African-American hairdresser. Who the heck was she talking to? Who were these girls? The ones in the booths on either side? And where did they get off, discussing her as a "tough case"?

Meredith jerked her head around. "Listen, this is my first real style and it's a pretty traumatic thing. I'd appreciate it if we could keep this event between us."

"Oh, I'm not talking to anyone outside of here," Elona said, her spiky black hair standing out around her head like a halo on the Grim Reaper. Meredith felt a flash of panic at being stuck with a stylist who looked like she'd been sent through a shredder. "I'm talking to my girls." She held up a pair of brass scissors and a matching comb. "Meet Bella and Luna."

"You *named* your styling tools?"

"Hey, the Marines do it with their guns. And I make beauty, not war with these. Ain't that right, girls?" She smiled at the duo.

Oh God. I've put the fate of my head into the hands of a full-blown Loony Tune.

"Okay, now let me look at you one more time," Elona said. She spun the chair around, cupped Meredith's chin and tipped her face right and left. "Nice heart-shaped structure. Deep blue eyes. A natural blonde, not something I see every day. Not too fine, not too thick. Hmmm ..." Elona closed her eyes and continued her "hmmm," turning the thoughtful sound into more of a low-pitched hum.

Oh no. Humming was a bad sign, particularly with closed eyes. Meredith wanted to bolt from the chair but the hairdresser had a dang good grip on her chin. "Uh, Elona?"

"Shh ... don't interrupt. I'm waiting for Brigitte to tell me what she thinks."

"Brigitte? What is that, your hairspray?"

"No, silly. Brigitte Bardot, one of the goddesses of hair."

"B-B-But she's like living on the other side of the world or something, isn't she?"

"Good thing, too. I wouldn't have been able to consult with her in person. Do you know how hard it is to get one on one time with celebrities? Take a number and get in line, lady, Miss Bardot is too busy for the likes of you," she said, affecting the voice of what Meredith envisioned as a burly guy in a tank top. Clearly one of Sybil's—i.e., Elona's—many personalities. Elona raised the cutting implements over Meredith's hair. "Now. Let's give you your new look."

Meredith put up a hand. "Are you sure you know what you're doing?"

Elona laughed. "Of course I do. And even if I didn't, Brigitte is here, in a way, to guide my hand."

Panic flashed in Meredith's gut. She glanced around, at the mounted posters of happy clients with stunning haircuts. From his station at the front desk, the redhead sent her a thumbs-up and a grin. Maybe Brigitte *had* been channeling her energies into this place from wherever Miss Bardot was right now.

What if Elona was wrong today, though? And standing on the other side of her psychic door wasn't Brigitte ... but Cyndi Lauper?

"I'm not so sure I want to do this." Meredith started to rise out of the chair.

Elona put a firm hand on her shoulder. "Trust me, honey. We're going to take the country right on out of you."

Elona had spoken the magic words. Meredith still wasn't so sure she wanted the spirit of a distant Hollywood celebrity having any input on her hairstyle, but if that's what it took to make her look like anything but herself, then she was willing to take a chance.

After all, wasn't that what she'd vowed on her trip to Boston? To take more risks? To stop being as scared of risk as a cat around a weedwacker?

She inhaled and closed her eyes again. "My head is yours."

"Hear that, girls? She's going to let us cut. Now do your best."

And with that, the first snip was made, sending tendrils of the old Meredith fluttering to the floor. Somewhere above her head, Meredith was sure she heard Bella and Luna laughing with glee.

Elona's Appearance-Is-Everything Crab Soufflé

4 tablespoons butter, separated
3 tablespoons flour
3/4 teaspoon salt
7 tablespoons milk
2/3 cup whipping cream
4 eggs, separated
2 6-1/2-ounce cans white crab meat, drained
1/2 cup dry bread crumbs
1/2 teaspoon onion powder
1/4 teaspoon paprika

Now, honey, you know if you make something that looks good, it's gonna take all the attention away from anything else in your life that's going wrong. Start by preheating your oven to 350 degrees. Then take one tablespoon of the butter and use it to grease a 1-1/2-quart soufflé dish.

Melt the rest of the butter in a pan, add the flour and salt and mix well. Can't you just hear Julia Child talking to you? Now I know she passed already to the other side, but I tell you, she's there, over your shoulder, helping you get this just right Add the milk gradually, stirring constantly, then bring it up to a boil and cook until it's as thick as a good shampoo.

Beat the egg yolks in a separate bowl. Don't be dumping them all in at once with the hot stuff; you'll get scrambled eggs instead of crab soufflé. Add a little of the sauce mix at a time, mixing it slow. Then add the bread crumbs, crab meat, onion powder and paprika.

In a whole other bowl (I know, but ask Julia, if you want to be a great chef, you have to dirty a few bowls), beat the egg whites until they've got stiff but not dry peaks. It's an art, just like cutting hair. Fold a little bit into the crab mixture to slacken it, as Julia would say, then fold in the rest. Gentle now, honey, don't want your peaks to fall.

Spoon it into the soufflé dish, pop it into the oven and bake for 45 to 50 minutes or until you can slip a knife into the center and it comes out looking as clean as a brand-new perm rod.

Don't wait to eat. Your new life is waiting for you and if you're pokey, you risk your soufflé deflating and your dreams escaping. Just ask Julia; she'll tell you the God's honest truth (because right now, she's got His ear).

CHAPTER SEVEN

Meredith's life had been ruined by a mullet. Elona had pronounced her hair "outstanding" and apparently Bella, Luna and Brigitte had concurred. But all Meredith saw staring back at her from the wall mirror had been a fluffy, longer version of the 80's mullet, with layers on the top of her head and straight lengths of hair running along the sides.

Her life was over.

"Oh, don't you love it? Brigitte thought it would bring out your eyes." Elona eyes beamed with pride at her handiwork.

"It's ... it's ..." And then Meredith couldn't get out another word. She buried her face in her hands and started to sob.

"You don't like it?"

Meredith shook her head.

"But... but it's perfect for you."

"It's perfect for Duran Duran," Meredith cried between her fingers. She planned on never leaving this seat, never facing the world again. Or at least until her hair had grown out and resembled the look she'd had an hour ago.

In other words, she was staying here until the old Meredith grew back.

"Oh, honey, it's not so bad. Wait till you get home and play with it. Make it your own." Elona gave her a pat on the shoulder. "It's a big change. A lot to get used to."

"I look horrible." The words, muffled by her tears and her hands, came out more like "I wook how-wibba."

Elona came around to the front of the chair and gently peeled back Meredith's hands from her face. "No, honey, you don't. The girls agree with me. You'll see. Just get used to it."

Get used to it? Maybe in eight weeks, when her hair had grown out and she'd gone from a mullet to a shag. All her life, she'd had the same style—long, straight and plain. It may have been boring but at least she hadn't looked like an extra member of REO Speedwagon.

"Here, dry your eyes," Elona said, handing her a tissue. "And look again. It's not as bad as you think."

Meredith did as Elona said. She lifted one end of her hair, then the other. The haircut still looked like an overgrown mullet but it had ... possibilities.

"It's a big change," Elona repeated. "You'll love it soon, trust me. Brigitte is never wrong."

Meredith wasn't so sure the input of a star who wasn't even in the same country, never mind the same room, should be trusted, but she paid Elona anyway, because the guilt at not paying would have plagued her for the rest of the day, bad haircut or not.

And besides, Meredith had to admit that Elona was the expert and maybe the fact that she'd just had her first haircut in a decade had sent her spiraling into some weird crazy feelings of regret. Maybe tomorrow she'd wake up and miraculously find herself with Cameron Diaz's hair.

Meredith glanced again in the mirror before she left Hair and Gone. It was going to take more than a night's sleep to make her look like Cameron Diaz.

When she got back to the shop, Maria and Candace assured her they loved the haircut and that it was perfect for her face and her new look. The clothes they'd bought the day before were sassier and hipper than anything Meredith had ever owned, and once she put on one of the new outfits she had stored out back, she could at least stop sobbing.

Maybe, in time, she'd be able to stop wearing waterproof mascara. But until her hair grew out, she wasn't taking any chances.

Six hours later, she stood on Rebecca's front stoop, clutching her purse, and waited for Travis Campbell to come and pick her up. She wore the new outfit she'd changed into, a dark blue skirt and silky pink T-shirt. She'd fiddled with her hair until she was afraid she was going to go bald, all to no avail.

No matter how much she strove for City Girl, Meredith was sure she came off looking more like Country Gone Wrong.

A silver convertible slid into the parking space in front of her. Travis sat behind the wheel, his dark hair a bit windblown from the topless ride.

Heat smoldered within her at the sight of him. He was more man than any man she'd ever met before, certainly sexier than the boys who'd been in her high school.

They *had* been boys. Inexperienced in the world, and in knowing what made a woman tick.

Travis was a M-A-N.

He parked the car, slid out of the seat and came around to face her. "I wasn't sure you'd be here."

In jeans, with a battered black leather jacket over a white T-shirt that stretched across the planes of his chest, Travis looked like an ad for sex.

Oh, Lord. This was more than she'd bargained for. Meredith let go of her purse. It hit against her hip, the strap tugging against her shoulder, a dead weight reminding her of what was inside. Was she up to this? Could she really go through with it?

Besides, would Travis even want to sleep with a woman who now looked like the long-lost third member of Wham!?

He took a step toward her, reaching up and touching her hair. "I like this," he said, lifting the ends and releasing them in a flutter against her neck.

"You *like* my haircut? I thought it was awful."

He tick-tocked a finger at her. "Never argue with a man who's telling you that you look beautiful."

"But—"

"But nothing. It's a wonderful change." He touched the ends again, allowing the tendrils to slide through the first two fingers of his hand like silky ribbons. Beneath his touch, her hair felt a thousand percent feminine. Sexy. Like a weapon she could use for seduction.

From somewhere in the ether, Meredith swore she heard Brigitte Bardot whisper, "I told you so."

"And best of all," Travis went on, still toying with the ends of her hair, "it lets me see those eyes of yours." He tiptoed his touch up her cheek to circle her gaze. "Those eyes, that say so much and hide even more."

Heat quivered in her belly, snaking through her veins. "I'm not hiding anything."

"Oh yes, you are, Meredith. But telling me would mean getting close, and you don't want to do that, do you?"

Oh she wanted to get close right now. Very close. Skin-to-skin close. But not the kind of close he meant. The kind where she opened her heart and let him in. That would mean a relationship and where Meredith came from, there was only one reason for a relationship.

A ring.

She didn't want one of those. And she didn't want any loose ends left here in Boston when she returned to Heavendale. "No, I don't want to do that," she said finally.

"Uh-huh." A smile crossed his lips. "Then we're perfect for each other because I'm the last man on earth who should have a relationship with a woman."

She opened her mouth to ask him about that, then shut it again. That would be going down the very road she'd vowed not to take. Nope. Meredith was only interested in the highway. None of those traditional detours for her.

She pushed a smile to her face. A wind gusted past and tangled in her hair, whipping it against her cheeks. "Well, shall we go to a hotel?"

Get it over with, quick, before she changed her mind.

His smile widened. "A woman who says shall," he said softly. "No, we won't be going to a hotel right now."

"But—but—" That was the agreement. That was all she wanted. Not to look at him and think how nice he'd look sitting on a porch swing beside her, sipping lemonade and complaining about the summer heat but meaning something else.

He took a step closer, his hand reaching up to brush the hair out of her face. "Don't be in such a rush, Meredith. Savor the anticipation."

She stepped back, breaking the contact. He was messing up the plan. "I don't need to be wooed, Travis. You don't have to make me anticipate anything."

He shook his head. "Sorry, but I have other plans for you."

"Other plans?" The words came out in a squeak.

"Do you trust me?"

"Trust you? I don't even know you."

He pressed his right hand against her abdomen. Heat raced through her, as if he'd tossed a match into her gut."Here, Meredith. That's where you find trust."

"That's also where you'll find the chicken I had for dinner."

"Chicken? When you're in Boston?" He shook his head. "Seems a shame, when you're surrounded by the best seafood in the world."

"I stick to safe meals. You can get food poisoning from undercooked shellfish."

"And salmonella from chicken and trichinosis from pork." Travis took her hand and tugged her toward his car. He leaned forward and opened the passenger's side door for her. "Come on, live a little dangerously, Meredith."

"I am living dangerously. I'm meeting you and asking you to ... well..."

Unwrap a little foil with her? Hop in the sack and do the horizontal mambo with her? That sounded too crass, so Meredith let the words trail off.

Travis grinned. "I never do that on an empty stomach."

She slid into the seat and looked up at him. His eyes were such a deep green, like roasted spearmint leaves. "If you eat a full meal first won't you get stomach cramps?"

He laughed as he shut her door, then came around the car and slid in beside her. "It's not swimming, Meredith. You're okay to enter the shark-infested waters with me anytime."

That was an image that only inflamed the heat inside her. Swimming with him. Naked. Water running down that hard body, sluicing between them.

Meredith reached forward and flipped the air conditioning on, in lieu of a cold shower.

Travis put the car in gear and pulled away from the curb.

"Travis, I didn't ask to be wined and dined," she said a moment later, as they wound their way out of Cambridge and through the downtown streets of Boston. "You don't have to do this."

"I'm giving you a taste of the city. Isn't that what you want?"

"Well, maybe a small taste since it is my first time here. And then—"

"And then we'll get to tasting what you wanted. I promise."

His grin sent another shiver of heat through her, despite the cold air blowing on her skin. And, damn him, it also gave her a little thrill of anticipation and joy that he'd planned something, rather than rushing off to the first Motel 6 he found that had left the light on.

Damn him, she thought again. He'd gone and put penguins in the chicken coop of her plan. All she wanted was an end to her virginity, not a date who showed up every Friday night with a spray of mums and a bottle of zin ... and an expectation that the Friday nights would never end. She'd had that with Caleb and it had been a dead end.

Literally.

City women didn't settle down with morticians into wedded bliss. They lived their lives without much care for consequences or other people's opinions. And they didn't need a full stomach to do it.

Clearly, Travis had no intentions of following her plan. Well, she'd just have to get him back on track— if she had to drag him there herself.

A few minutes later, they were in a part of Boston that Meredith recognized as located not far from Gift Baskets. Travis zigzagged along the small streets, then parallel parked along one so narrow, Meredith couldn't imagine it fitting more than one car at a time. Buildings on either side abutted each other like conjoined twins centered by a cobblestone road and stone sidewalks.

Meredith got out of the car and pivoted on the sidewalk, taking in the sights and sounds. Everywhere she went in Boston, it seemed as if each area was unique unto itself, sprinkled with its own flavor. "Where are we?"

"Quincy Market, home of Faneuil Hall Marketplace."

From down the street, she heard the raucous sounds of a party spilling out of a bar. "It's very different from what I'm used to. I've never seen so many businesses in one place."

"Actually it used to be a lot more like Indiana than you think. Quincy Market started out as an open-air food market back when the Puritans arrived."

"I can't imagine that."

"Just a block or so away at Haymarket Square, they still have the food market on Fridays and Saturdays. The charm of the marketplace, though, is all in the food. Almost every taste for every kind of person." He grinned and gestured toward a long, tall masonry and glass building. "There's a great restaurant here that I want to take you to. The Salty Dog."

"Salty... Dog?"

"Sailor's term, not canine cuisine."

She smiled. "That's a relief. I had to wonder if we were dining on dog biscuits tonight."

Travis chuckled. "Usually it's my exes who are sending *me* the dog biscuits. And more often than not, I suppose I deserve them."

Again, another comment that begged Meredith to probe a little deeper, to ask a little more. She glanced at him and wondered how other women could find him so horrible. Had they not seen the Travis she'd seen in Slim Pickin's?

Or was she so blinded by her goal that she was missing some fundamental flaw in Travis's character?

Meredith reminded herself that it didn't matter. She didn't need a saint to help her shed her virginity. And, she suspected, a saint wouldn't be much good at it anyway.

They walked along the street and then crossed it to enter the bustling marketplace. Dozens of shops lined the glass fronts of the building. Ann Taylor, Coach, Crate & Barrel.

Meredith made a mental note to come back here again. With more time and her Visa card.

She and Travis strolled along close enough to touch, yet he didn't take her hand, nor did she take his. Her fingers brushed against his when her arm swung forward and an ache of want for the feel of his palm in hers surged through her.

No. She wouldn't go there. She wasn't here for hand-holding. *Especially* not hand-holding. Her experience in Boston was designed to give her more independence, more confidence. Not more dependence on anyone.

"Where we are used to be the edge of Boston Harbor," Travis said as they walked along, as if he, too, wanted to change the subject from the simmering heat that ran between them.

"Really? But I thought the water is still quite some distance from here."

The lights were coming on as twilight turned to dusk. Christmas lights twinkled in the trees in the center of the plaza area while tall black poles with clusters of globe bulbs illuminated the brick and stone walkways. It cast everything with a magical glow, something that might have had Meredith feeling romantic.

Had this been anything other than what it was.

"As Boston grew," Travis went, "they brought in dirt and created more space. Quincy Market was the commerce center." He gestured down the end of the marketplace, toward an impressive white stone building with three wide columns supporting the large overhanging roof.

They built all this from nothing?"

He nodded. "It's amazing how you can change something from simple to elaborate when you want to."

"It's beautiful," Meredith said, spinning in place. And it was. The buildings were bustling with sound and people, the music carrying from each door adding a festive air. The entire place seemed rich, infused with flavors, as if she could taste it and ingest some of that city life.

People strolled from shop to shop, laughing and chatting, their conversation sparkling as much as the lights overhead. Benches peppered the cobblestone walks, a few decorated by bronze figurines seated as silent companions to those who visited.

"Sometimes simple is better, too, though," Travis said. "It's busy here in the city. And noisy. A lot of people leave it for the country."

Meredith laughed. "I can't imagine why. If I lived here, I'd never leave."

He laughed. "You'll feel differently after a while. The grass is always greener on the other side of I-93."

Had he always lived here, in Massachusetts? And what would make anyone want to leave? Meredith wondered again about Travis Campbell and bit back the urge to get to know him more.

They arrived at a small restaurant, its bright blue canopy and matching umbrellas heralding the outside cafe-style tables. True to Travis's word, the name "Salty Dog Seafood Grille & Bar" circled the logo in the center of the awning. The scent of the ocean drifted from the kitchen, along with steam and the citrusy smell of lemon.

"Do you want to sit outside?" he asked.

The weather was still warm and Meredith nodded, not wanting to be inside just yet, craving more of the magical environment around them.

They waited a few minutes before being seated at one of the tables along the edge of the restaurant's outdoor seating area. Meredith propped her chin in her hand and watched the people come and go. Coffee, cookies and seafood scents carried on the air with the hum of conversations. An elderly couple sat silently on one of the black benches, holding hands and watching the shoppers come and go.

For a second, Meredith felt a twinge of envy for the old couple. To sit like that with someone after fifty years of marriage, hands clasped, with no need for conversation.

Or, had they simply run out of things to say to each other after all those years? Was it like those last few dates with Caleb, where it seemed they'd run through every subject and had nothing left to fill the long silences except small talk?

"Tell me, Meredith," Travis said, drawing her attention to him. He'd lowered his menu to the table, his hands flat on top of it. "Why did you choose me? Was I the first warm male body in the bar?"

She smiled. "There were other men there."

"Okay then, the first warm male body that wasn't drunk?"

"No. Well... yes."

He cocked a grin at her. "That's not exactly the best way to stroke my fragile male ego."

"I doubt anything about you is fragile." The words, so much bolder than anything she'd ever said to a man before, were out before she could stop them. A thought, vocalized, and all because she hadn't been able to tear her gaze from his biceps.

"My, my Meredith. You're not always the shy farmer's daughter, are you?"

"Until a few days ago, I was." She stirred at her water with the straw. The lemon slice danced with the ice cubes, swirling a flash of yellow into the clear liquid.

"What changed a few days ago?"

"Me mostly. I got on a plane to Boston and decided to change my life."

"And I'm part of that plan?"

She thought of the condoms in her purse, of the vow she'd made to change everything about herself, from her clothing to her virginity, and nodded.

"You didn't answer my question. Why me? Did I win eenie-meenie-miny-moe against Kenny?"

She laughed. "No, not at all." Meredith toyed with her silverware for a moment, then decided answering him was only fair. "When I saw you in the bar, smoothing things over with the bartender for Mike, calling him a cab, calming him down about his dog ... You seemed like a nice guy."

He snorted. "You don't know me that well."

"Yet."

His gaze met hers. Something smoldered in those dark green depths, something she'd never seen before when a man looked at her. Something that scared her, and excited her, and told her the roller-coaster she'd boarded had twists and turns she couldn't see.

Travis swallowed and looked away before Meredith could figure out where the next bend might be on the ride. "Listen, you're a nice girl," he said. "You really don't want to get involved with a guy like me."

"Why?"

"Because I'm not the kind of guy a girl like you deserves."

She let out a gust and pushed her menu to the side of the table. "Why don't you let me decide that? I'm tired of everyone else choosing what's good for me. All my life, everyone has told me what decisions to make and I've gone along with it. Because I'm a good girl." She air-quoted that with her fingers. "Well, I'm tired of being the good girl. Now I want someone who can teach me how to be *bad*."

When she said the words, she caught his gaze again and left no doubt of her meaning. Ever since she'd met Travis Campbell, she'd wanted him, and the more he pulled away, the more she wanted to reel him back in, like a stubborn bull that refused to be penned. He was the right man for what she wanted. She knew it, deep in her gut and deep inside the parts of her that had lain as dormant as onions in a cellar until the night he'd walked into Slim Pickin's.

"Meredith, Boston is a city that... well, that does funny things to people. It's not like New York or LA or hell, Dallas. People here can get swept up in the quirkiness of the place and do things they'd never do anywhere else."

"Are you saying I'm not thinking straight?"

"Yeah."

"You're wrong. I know exactly what I'm doing *and* what I want." She took in a deep breath and decided she'd prove that to him, and herself. Meredith got to her feet, skirted the table and stopped beside his chair. Before she could think twice, she cupped Travis's face with her hands, drew him to her, and kissed him.

She didn't kiss him like she'd kissed Caleb. Or any of the fumbling boys who'd taken her to school dances and football games. She let her instincts guide her, allowing those primal calls she'd always ignored to be heard. Her tongue darted in to meet his, tasting and teasing, asking him to come out and play. When he did, a grenade launched itself in her pelvis, turning on switches she hadn't even known existed.

It was exactly the kind of move a city girl would make. And exactly the kind of thing shy, predictable Meredith Shordon would never do.

That knowledge sent a fire rushing through her veins and yet at the same time, it was chilled by a chaser of a question. Would changing herself so drastically leave her even more lost in the end?

From behind her, she heard the whispers of the other diners, the gasp of some woman a few feet away and knew she'd gone a little too far. At least in a public place.

Before she ended up straddling him in the middle of the restaurant, Meredith pulled back. Her mother's words, "Indiana girls are good girls," echoed in her head, like drums beating a warning of impending danger.

"Now who's not thinking straight?" she said to him, determined not to let her mother's warnings or her Indiana roots show. Her voice sounded husky and sexy, filled with everything stirring deep inside her.

"My, my," said a voice over her shoulder. "Most people do that *after* they have the oysters."

Meredith's the-Heat-Is-On Steamers

1 tablespoon butter
1 teaspoon garlic, minced
1 pound clams, soft-shell, cherrystone or littleneck
1/4 cup white wine
Clarified butter for dipping

It's already steaming in the kitchen, so be sure to get a bite to eat to keep up your stamina. Start by rinsing the clams thoroughly in cold, running water. Soft-shell clams can hold onto that sand like some mothers try to hold onto their daughters, so scrub well. You may even need to soak them for a while in salted water to encourage them to let go. Drain, rinse again, then it's time to cook.

Preheat the saucepan, melt the butter and cook the garlic—but don't burn it. It's hard to lose track of what you're doing, especially with a man who looks like him around, but pay attention, just for a few minutes. Add the clams, just enough to cover the bottom. Too many and they'll stack up on each other and make it hard for each one to open up. Give them a stir, then add the wine. Cover and let it steam.

If you have nothing else to do, feel free to kick up a little steam in the kitchen yourself with that gorgeous guy who's doing everything in his power to resist you. I'd put a timer on, though, because those clams will be done in four minutes. Take out any clams whose shells are open .. .just begging to be eaten.

Any stubborn ones that didn't open should be discarded.

Serve with clarified butter and a little of the leftover juice. The best way to eat them? Dip, take a bite and then kiss him ... then repeat.

Many, many, many times.

CHAPTER EIGHT

The waitress's interruption had been both a blessing and a curse for Travis. Meredith was making it impossible to stick to his resolution and yet at the same time, he wanted nothing more than to forget the whole damned plan, especially when she had her lips on his.

Wasn't that where all his trouble had started, though? Between the beer and the women, Travis Campbell had somehow lost his way. The best answer to finding the path back was to suspend all bad behavior until he got his head clear.

Of course, his head was reeling now, filled with lusty images of Meredith Shordon and the education she wanted him to give her.

The waitress left after they placed an order for a large basket of steamers. Meredith, now safely on her side of the table again, asked for a glass of wine, Travis stuck to Coke. And stuck to his side of the white table top, keeping his thoughts on everything but the woman sitting across from him, the curve of her breasts teasing him through the V of her pale pink T-shirt and her unbuttoned leather coat.

Work. He'd think about work. And how getting to know Meredith—and probing into her thoughts—could help him get that promotion he was after.

Yeah, that worked. Sort of.

"Tell me about Indiana," he said.

"You don't need to get to know me. I'm not interested in a relationship."

"It's small talk, Meredith, not a marriage proposal."

"Well. .. good." Was it his imagination or did she look a bit disappointed?

The woman was a contradiction, that was for sure. Clearly, as desperate as she was to shed that Midwestern upbringing, a part of her still clung to those values like a security blanket.

Despite his baser self, that intrigued him.

"It's good for me, too," he said. Kept him on track and reminded him he'd made a thirty-day deal not to get involved with a woman, if only to prove to himself that he could live without wine, women or both together.

"If you're uncomfortable with me using you for sex—"

"Not at all," he lied.

"Good." But her storm-blue eyes seemed to send a very different signal.

Who was Meredith Shordon? And why did she keep saying she wanted one thing when she was so clearly not that kind of person?

"Tell me about where you come from," he asked again.

"Indiana is boring," she said after a moment "Lots of green nothing and a few farms."

"There are cities there, I hear." He grinned. "Even a state capital."

She chuckled. "There are, but not where I live. My town boasts a whopping three thousand people, and that's only in the summer."

"When all the snowbirds return?"

"Exactly."

"So what do you do for fun out there?"

She toyed with the stem on her wine glass, sending the zinfandel swirling a little against the clear goblet. "Well... compare our hogs."

He blinked. "As in Harleys?"

"No." She laughed again. "In Heavendale, we're strictly interested in the four-hooved kind. Virtually everyone is a member of 4-H," she explained. "The height of excitement is a blue ribbon at the state fair for having the honor of owning the world's biggest, and laziest, hog, or managing to get your sow to give birth to a record-breaking farrow, meaning a big litter of piglets."

He took a sip of his soda. "You don't seem the piglet type."

"I'm not."

When she didn't elaborate, curiosity nudged him closer. He leaned forward, waiting until her gaze met his a second time. A pretty shade of pink that mirrored her wine bloomed in Meredith's cheeks, like lightly dusted apples. "What type are you?"

She looked away, investing her attention in straightening her silverware. "The type that doesn't want to spend my Friday nights mudding in Bobby Reynolds's four-wheeler and my Saturday afternoons at Petey's Pizza Parlor serving pitchers of Bud to the men's athletic league."

"And so you came here to Boston, seeking more?"

"A lot more," she said softly, and the tone in her voice reignited the slumbering fire inside his gut.

The waitress came by and dropped off their basket of steamers. She checked on their drinks, asked them if they wanted another appetizer, and altogether lingered so long that the heat between Travis and Meredith subsided again from High to Low.

With that, Travis's better sense returned and he reminded himself he wasn't here to have sex with her—unfortunately—but rather to save her from making a reckless decision, something he knew way too much about, and to help him find a way to market the impossible to Middle America.

"What are these again?" Meredith asked, gesturing toward the covered basket sitting in the middle of the table.

"Soft-shell clams with drawn butter for dipping." He lifted off the bowl on top, picked up one of the opened clams and held it out to her. "Otherwise known as heaven on a plate."

Meredith gave him—and it—a dubious glance. "They look kind of... slimy."

"Not at all. Try one. You'll see."

She arched a brow and picked up the clam, careful to only touch the shell with the tips of her fingers, then put it back down into the pile, clearly not ready for steamers yet.

"What's the matter, don't you trust me?"

"Well... no."

He chuckled. "Good. Because I wouldn't trust me either, except when it comes to seafood." He reached for a second one, slipped the clam meat out of the shell with his fork, then dipped it into his dish of butter before popping it into his mouth. The taste of salt and fat hit his palate like a gift.

"I don't know ..." She gave the clams another uncertain glance.

"Here." He took his fork, scooped out the clam meat from the shell, then swirled the plump tan morsel in the warm, clarified butter. Then he moved forward, holding the fork outside her mouth. His gaze met hers and asked her to do the impossible.

Trust him.

The air between them stilled, caught in the crossfire of a budding desire and the first tentative steps each was taking toward the other.

Then Meredith smiled, leaned toward him and opened her mouth. When she parted those soft pink lips and took the bite with white, perfect teeth, Travis almost groaned. His mind flashed images of her mouth on him, giving his body the same delicate attention she had given to the ocean's finest.

Oh, damn. He was crazy if he thought he could keep his hands off her. If he thought some silly resolution he'd made while still in the throes of a hangover would stand up against a real woman.

A real woman who wanted him to go to bed with her. A virgin, no less.

Every man's fantasy—on his own personal queen-sized platter, anytime he wanted it.

Oh, boy. He was in trouble now.

"Oh God, Travis," Meredith said twenty minutes later, the words almost a sigh. "I had no idea it would be this good." A contented smile spread across her lips.

"I told you so."

"Mmm." She closed her eyes, clearly reliving the entire experience. "You were so right. I'll have to listen to you more often."

With her looking like that, satisfied and happy, and just waiting for him to take the lead, Travis nearly sprang out of his seat and finished what Meredith had started earlier, consequences be damned. Instead, he reined in his hormones, picked up his fork and speared the last steamer from their second order. He dipped it in butter before holding it out toward her.

"You're letting me have the last one?" she asked.

"I'm not hungry anymore." For food at least. For watching her give him that smile again ... That appetite he suspected would never be quenched.

Meredith opened her mouth, accepting the edible gift, and sighed again after she swallowed. "*Nothing* in Indiana tastes like this."

"Too many cows spoiling the epicurean experience." Travis grinned.

She dabbed at her mouth with her napkin, then replaced it neatly in her lap, the primness of her actions—and all its contradictions to the way she'd behaved earlier—a turn-on he hadn't expected. "Does all seafood taste this good?"

"Everything I've had does."

She looked down at the dish, now just a pile of empty shells and leftover juice. "Can we do this again sometime? Soon?"

"Anytime you want." *Tonight, in my bed. Tomorrow morning, after breakfast. Preferably naked next time.*

Meredith cupped her chin in her hand and smiled at him. "Well, I guess that makes two things I'm craving in Boston now."

"Two?"

"Uh-huh." The twinkle in her eyes left no doubt what one of the two things was. "And I want to get as much of both as I can before I have to return to the land of beef and pork."

Oh God. Travis waved a hand at the waitress. "Uh, check please."

Around them, the restaurant and the market-place plaza hummed with activity but Travis barely noticed. His attention stayed riveted on Meredith, on the woman he'd tried so hard to avoid and now couldn't seem to stay away from.

Her hair, now freed by the new cut to frame her face, trailed along her jaw and neck. He wanted to reach forward and brush the tendrils back, then lower his mouth to the delicate flesh along her throat, to taste the sweet skin there, working his way down along the edge of her breasts, taking first one in his mouth, then the other, giving each equal attention. Then he'd kiss a path along her waist, slipping past her hips, down, down, down to—

No. No. *No!*

That was *not* why he was here.

Hadn't he agreed to her crazy proposition to protect Meredith from herself? What was he thinking? That was like asking the Big Bad Wolf to be Little Red Riding Hood's Sunday school teacher.

"So, are we going back to your place now?" Meredith asked, moving her empty glass to the side.

Leaving more room for the wolf to come across the table and devour her in one easy bite.

"Don't you want to get to know me a little first?"

She shook her head. "Not particularly."

"Don't get me wrong, Meredith. What you're offering me is pretty much every man's dream ..."

"But..." she prompted when he didn't finish.

"But I can't quite figure out why you're doing it or why I'm even hesitating on taking you back to my bed and tearing off that little pink T-shirt right now." His voice dropped into a growl. "And everything else."

A flush of crimson showed in her cheeks. Miss Meredith Shordon wasn't as unflappable as she liked to think.

"You're not like any woman I've ever met," he said. "And I find that intriguing."

"What kind of women have you been meeting?"

"Not the memorable kind, that's for sure." He rubbed at his temples. Well, they'd been memorable, but not in a good way.

The waitress slid the bill onto the table. Meredith grabbed it before Travis could and slipped forty dollars inside the leather folio.

"Why are you paying?" he asked, covering her hand with his own.

"Because this isn't, technically, a date."

"It isn't? We're alone. Together. Talking about ourselves. Sounds like a date to me."

"Fine." She slid one of the twenties out and put it back in her purse. "Then we can split the tab."

"Quite the modern woman, aren't you?"

"I'm trying." Meredith fingered the stem of her empty wineglass and looked at Travis. "Why aren't you dating memorable women?" she asked again.

Travis let out a sigh that seemed to weigh more than the cobblestones that paved the marketplace. "It's complicated."

She reminded herself that she didn't need to get to know this man. She didn't want to get close to him. But something about that sigh and the way he said the words touched a common thread inside her heart. "What do you mean?"

He rubbed his head again before speaking. "I know you think I'm some ... Well, I don't know what you think I am, but trust me, before a couple days ago, I wasn't that kind of man."

She circled the rim of the delicate goblet. "That makes two of us turning over a new leaf in our lives."

"Well, mine's more like raking out the dead debris and hoping like hell there's something better than a shriveled up pile of manure underneath it."

She laughed. "You couldn't be that bad."

"I'm not Exactly Clark Kent."

"Well, I'm no angel myself."

He shook his head, a smile playing at his lips. "I disagree. I look at you and I can practically see the halo glowing around your head."

She directed a finger at his chest. "That's because you haven't helped me shed it yet."

"And what if I said I thought it would be wrong to do that?"

"Wrong to go to bed with me?"

"Yeah."

There he went, throwing a huge cog into her plans again. Five minutes ago, he seemed ready to head off to the nearest flat surface and give her the tour of Boston no one talked about in the Dummies guide. But now, he had blocked those vibes, as if he'd thrown a switch to "off."

"I'm not underage or wanted by the FBI," she said. "I'm not a nun or a married woman. There's nothing wrong with sleeping with me."

"Oh, I think there'd be many things that would be right about us going to bed together," he said, his grin seductive and teasing all at once, the switch back at on, then just as quickly, flicking off, "but..."

"But I'm not your type?"

He let out half a chuckle. "You, Meredith, are as far from the kind of woman I usually date as lemons are from chocolate cake."

"I'm the lemon, I take it?"

"Oh no. You're the cake. And I'm not so sure I should be, ah, let's say ... licking the frosting."

She studied him for a long moment. Here was a man who made no bones about his own checkered past and yet, he wouldn't sleep with her because he was worried about *her* honor? There was more to Travis Campbell than she suspected even he knew. More depth. More morals.

More man.

And for a girl who vowed she wouldn't get involved with him, she was suddenly feeling very tender and very involved.

He rose, slipping a twenty over the bill to accompany hers. "Let me bring you home."

"So soon?"

"I'd better do it before I forget all those pretty little resolutions I just made."

She stood and crossed to him, standing within an inch of his chest. "And what if I tempt you to throw those resolutions into Boston Harbor? Like our own little personal tea party?"

"Don't," he said, his voice low and hoarse. "Remember, I'm a weak man."

"Oh, I don't think so, Travis," she said, walking a finger slowly up his chest and taking a small thrill from the rise she saw in his eyes. "I think you've got all the strength I need."

Then she turned on her heel and walked out of the restaurant, leaving a whole lot of farm girl behind.

Travis's Not-Much-of-a-Cook Shrimp and Bacon Bites

16 cleaned, cooked shrimp, medium size
1/3 cup chili sauce
8 slices bacon

Hey, I'm a bachelor who lives on Cheerios and Papa Gino's pizza. What'd you expect? Crème brulee? This is as fancy as I get without calling for delivery.

Still, it's a nice way to tempt a woman, especially one who has eyes the color of a stormy sky. Start by mixing the shrimp with the chili sauce. Cover and refrigerate for a few hours. Can't think of a way to fill those hours with the woman by your side? Then you must be married.

Cut the bacon strips into halves and cook them until they're limp, not crisp. The *bacon* is limp. Don't be getting any wrong ideas here. Wrap each shrimp in a bacon piece, then secure with a toothpick. Broil until the bacon is crisp and the woman you want to impress is dying for a bite.

Take turns feeding each other... but watch out for the toothpicks. If you get too distracted, you could end your evening in the emergency room.

Trust me, that's no way to get a second date.

CHAPTER NINE

Travis had never noticed how small the interior of his convertible was—until Meredith Shordon sat in the passenger's seat. It felt as if the walls of the car were closing in, bringing them nearer together, edging her fragrance, her skin, her very presence closer to him.

Tempting him.

The word "virgin" danced around his head with images of sexual positions heretofore untried by most of mankind. Damn his hormones. Damn the testosterone that coursed through his body, hot as lava, inflamed by Meredith's innocence and gimme-gimme-gimme mouth.

He shouldn't. He was sure he'd go to hell, or at least purgatory, for defiling someone so pretty and nice and well... Midwestern. She had none of those hard city edges about her, just a calm purity that seemed a lot like a daisy in a field of nettles.

"Do you remember how to get back to my cousin's house off of Mass. Ave.?" Meredith said, breaking the silence. Since they'd gotten into the car, he hadn't exchanged much more than small talk with her, because every time she opened her mouth, he started watching her lips move and watching her lips move led to thoughts of other parts of her body moving...

That path to hell seemed awfully short right now.

"Yeah. I even know a shortcut." He banged a quick left and pushed on the gas. The rev of the six cylinders beneath the hood was a weak echo of the horsepower itching to be let out beneath his own hood.

Damn. Damn. Damn.

What had been his plan again? It went beyond sex, that he knew. But damned if his brain would picture anything other than a firm mattress and clean sheets.

Oh yeah. Work. The job he hated but needed because the phone company—and Kenny's ex—liked to be paid on time. He needed Meredith's input on No-Moo Milk and then he'd be able to save Kenny's butt and his own at Belly-Licious Beverages, maybe even with the added bonus of displacing Larry Herman from his blood-borne pedestal.

"You're awfully quiet," she said. "Is it something I did?"

"No." He paused. "Yes."

"I'm sorry. I'm just not used to being in a city and sometimes I—"

"There, like that," he said, waving at her. "You're apologizing, for God's sake. No one around here apologizes."

"They don't?"

"Hell no. They cut you off in traffic, then flip you the bird like it was your fault for being on the road in the first place. They sell you shoddy merchandise and give you crap about returning it because then maybe you'll back down and they won't have to eat the loss. They connive to get your promotion then screw you on your review so you'll be stuck in the mail room until you're sixty-five."

"That's what it's like here?"

He let out a gust. Now he'd done it—taken out years of annoyances and irritations on her for no reason other than the fact that she was here and he was caught up in some stupid denial plan. "Not really. I'm just... frustrated right now."

"Oh." She paused a second, then noticed the death grip he had on the steering wheel and the rigid set of his chest. "*Oh.*"

"Yeah. It's *that* kind of 'Oh.'"

"We could—"

"No, we could not. Not now. And I'd appreciate it if you would never mention the word sex again because my hold on my hormones is ... Well, let's just say you don't make it easy for a guy." The numerous lights on Massachusetts Avenue slowed his progress and kept them together in the car.

Kept her closer. Kept reminding him that all he had to do was take a left or a right and he could avoid taking her home altogether and instead take Meredith off to the closest hotel.

Travis tightened his grip on the steering wheel and shut down his peripheral vision. Hell, if a good workhorse could do that, so could he.

"But that's exactly what I'm trying to do," Meredith said. "Make it easy for you. No strings, no expectations."

"Well, that's not right." He didn't know where on planet Earth it wasn't, but it wasn't.

"Are you sure there's nothing wrong with you? I mean, I have read *The Sun Also Rises*. I know men can have issues with their ... manhood and not want to tell the truth."

Travis bit back a laugh. "Trust me, I have no issues with my manhood."

"Would you rather be plowing a different kind of field?"

"What is that supposed to mean?"

"I was trying to be tactful and ask you if you ..." She arched a brow. "If you were more of a guy-guy than a girl-guy."

"A guy ..." It took a second before the synapses in his brain started firing and he made the connection. "Trust me. I'm a hundred percent American male. And I only put my tractor in female ... ah, fields."

She smiled, then reached across the car to lay her hand on top of his. Her touch ratcheted up his temperature what felt like ten degrees and sent the peripheral vision plan down the tubes. He'd have never made a good workhorse, that was for sure.

"Good," Meredith said, her voice as tempting as a warm blanket. "Then you can fulfill your end of the bargain, right?"

At that moment, he pulled up in front of her cousin's house. He stopped the car, parked it and turned off the engine.

She was his for the asking. Heck, he didn't have to ask—she was doing all the asking. And yet, some leftover morality, probably instilled in him by the nuns that had taught him how to read at Sacred Heart Elementary School, kept him from saying a word.

Meredith was too sweet, too vulnerable and too nice for the likes of him. The best thing he could do was convince her that her plan was crazy and that the smart plan for her was to get back on a plane, head back to farm country and settle down with a man who'd treat her right.

If she'd just cooperate, it would be a whole lot easier for him to do that.

"Well?" she prompted.

"You're asking too much of me, Meredith."

"I don't understand. Don't you like me?"

"I know I'm some kind of idiot for turning you down, but—"

And then, the need to kiss her—to do much more than that—reached its boiling point again and Travis opened the door, scrambling out of the car before he could break his own promise and his vow to keep Meredith from the depravity she was asking for. Both conveniently available in the car's backseat.

Meredith didn't let him escape. She got out and came around to his side of the car, her skirt swishing against her legs, the volume of that sound seeming a hundred decibels higher than the hum of traffic a block away.

"I am going to kiss you, Travis Campbell, and when I'm done, then you can tell me if you're still confused."

And then she did just that, leaning in and first brushing her lips against his, then pressing harder and firmer. He threw his objections out the window and came right back at her, his lips meeting hers and his tongue dipping in to taste the sweet inside of her mouth. She let out a little mew and melted into his arms.

Desire roared in his head and he forgot everything he'd intended earlier. Meredith fit perfectly against his body, her lithe curves pressing against the hard planes of him like they'd been carved from the same piece of wood.

His hands cupped her chin, thumbs tracing along her jaw, asking her to open wider, to allow him more of her. She obliged and then wrapped her arms around his back, drifting her hands down to trace along his waist, teasing along the line where his shirt disappeared inside his pants.

Travis nearly groaned. His hands dropped down her throat, along her shoulders, and then finally to

the one place he'd seen all night and not touched—
the soft twin peaks covered by the silky pink shirt.
His thumbs rolled over the tips, noting the sensa-
tion of lace beneath the satin fabric, then returned
to cup her perfect breasts in his palms. She mewed
again and pressed her pelvis to his, stoking a fire
that was already raging.

"Get your friggin' hands off her or we'll do it for
you."

Travis jerked away from Meredith and wheeled
around. Two men stood behind him, their faces set
in angry masks that seemed to glow beneath the street
lights. No, not men, mountains of male hormones
with bulging Popeye arms beneath white tank tops and
open, battered denim jackets. Their faces were shaded
by John Deere ball caps, giving them a menacing look.

Travis kept Meredith behind him with one arm,
then stepped forward, putting himself squarely
between the twin Mr. Everests. "Who the hell do you
think you are?"

"We're your ride to the preacher," the bigger one
said, pointing a finger at Travis's chest, "because if
you're doing *that* to our baby sister, you better have
a ring in your pocket, buster."

"A preacher? Are you nuts?" Travis said. Then
the words sank in. *Baby sister.* These two hulking
giants were Meredith's *brothers?* What the hell did
they feed men in Indiana?

"These two very rude individuals," Meredith
said, stepping around Travis and inserting herself
between the three men, "are my brothers, Ray Jr.

and Vernon." She gestured from one to the other. "And they're leaving."

"Nope. No can do," said the smaller of the two, smaller being a misnomer since Travis suspected the six-foot-three man weighed in around two-fifty. "We're here to keep an eye on you." He gave Travis a glare. "Seems a good idea, considering you got a deer tick on you."

"Travis is not a deer tick and for your information, Vernon, *I* was the one who kissed *him*."

Vernon scratched his head beneath his cap, the tractor logo riding up and down before settling back into place. "Seems to me he was the one doing all the fence crossing. And when a coyote wanders onto your property—"

"You either shoot him or chase him off with a bigger dog." Ray Jr. gave Travis a look that left no doubt which option he voted for.

Meredith stepped up to her elder brother and poked him in the chest. "Get back, Ray Jr." To Travis's surprise, the huge man took a step back at his little sister's touch. "I do not need babysitting. I'm an adult."

"Right. You're acting like a two-year-old," he said. "Running off like that, leaving everything—and everyone—behind. You need to go home with us. Rebecca can get on without you and you know it."

"I think you should leave Meredith alone," Travis said. "She—"

"And we think you should go away, deer tick," Vernon said, taking a step forward. Ray Jr. moved in unison with him, two soldiers marching to blot out the enemy. "Now."

Travis started to protest, ready to take this to the mat if need be. Then Meredith laid a soft hand on his arm. "Go ahead," she said. "I can handle them. They are, after all, my brothers."

Travis's gaze went from her to the Hulk twins. They hadn't moved any closer, but seemed to have multiplied in size as if the mere act of inhaling made them bigger. He thought he could maybe take down one, but two...?

And besides, they were Meredith's flesh and blood. Getting into a fistfight in front of her, he suspected, wasn't the best way to endear himself to her. "Are you sure?"

"They may seem menacing," she said, "but really, they have my best interests at heart."

Travis didn't comment on what those best interests might be since they seemed to come attached to a preacher and a courthouse, but did as she asked, leaving Meredith outside her cousin's house and in the meaty paws of Tweedle-big and Tweedle-bigger. "I'll call you."

She stood on her tiptoes and pressed a lingering kiss to his lips. "If I don't call you first."

Ray Jr. blanched and started to sputter admonishments but Meredith just put up a finger of warning and started up the stairs to her cousin's house. Her brother backed off, looking like a sulky puppy.

When he was sure she was going to be okay, Travis got into his car and left. Meredith could definitely handle Ray Jr. and Vernon better than he could— and do it without her fists.

For the second time that night, he thought about the contradiction of this woman from Indiana. She said she wanted things to be so simple, and yet she was anything but.

And her kisses ... Well, they were more than he'd expected, too. They led him down a path he'd vowed to avoid, if only long enough to figure out who Travis Campbell was and why he was more often on the receiving end of a pocketbook than a pillow.

He turned right onto the Mass. Ave. connector, heading toward the highway and home, instead of going left, which would take him toward the bar where Kenny undoubtedly was seeing how far he could stretch the limits of his Visa and his charm.

As Travis eased onto I-93, his cell phone jingled. He flipped it open, half expecting Kenny to be on the other end, about to badger him into coming to the bar. "Hello?"

"Whatcha doing on the nineteenth of November?"

"Brad?" His younger brother's voice was nearly drowned out by the festive sounds of a party behind him. Laughing, clinking glasses, a popping champagne cork and several congratulatory shouts.

"I did it," Brad said. "I proposed to Jenny. We're doing it up right, and I need a best man."

"You're getting married? *You?*"

"Hey, everybody's gotta settle down someday."

"Yeah, but not you. You're ..."

"Not the commitmentphobe I used to be." There was the sound of giggling, then a loud lip smacking as Brad kissed someone. Jenny, Travis presumed. A nice woman, whom he'd met several times in the two years she and Brad had been dating. Still, the news that Brad was getting *married* came like a Mack truck at his head. "This beauty has got my heart but good," Brad added.

"But we swore—" When they'd been kids, it had been a solemn oath. The kind you never broke. A blood oath, he went to add, but didn't.

"Trav, I was twelve. Who knew how I'd feel at twenty-eight? Besides, there's no guarantee I'll turn out like Dad."

"There's no guarantees either way, Brad. That's why we decided not to take chances."

There was a long moment of silence, punctuated only by the ongoing celebration on the other end. "Never expected you, of all people, to rain on my parade, Trav."

"Brad, it's not that. It's just—" What? How could he explain? That he felt betrayed because his brother had broken an adolescent promise? That he couldn't celebrate something that filled him with a sense of dread as surely as the opening of a Stephen King movie? That he'd give Britney Spears better odds on her next love match than he would any of the Campbell boys? "I'm happy for you, Brad. Really I am." He worked up a little enthusiasm into his voice.

"Yeah. Sure. I'll send you an invite. If you have time, maybe you can make it." Then Brad clicked off, returning to his party and leaving Travis in a convertible filled with regrets and words he couldn't take back.

Ray Jr.'s Keep-Your-Claws-to-Yourself Crab Salad

1 pound fresh cooked crab meat
1/2 cup mayonnaise
2 tablespoons lemon juice
3 tablespoons sour cream
Salt and pepper
Cayenne pepper to taste

Want to work out a little frustration? Well, this ain't the dish to do it. For that, you gotta get yourself a punching bag or a bale of hay and have at it. This is for protein, which gives you muscles and energy so you can kill the next man who comes within ten feet of your baby sister.

Pick through the crab meat and make sure there aren't any shells. The last thing you want to do is end up needing the Heimlich, just when you're about to pulverize someone. Kind of ruins your credibility as a menacing threat.

Mix the other ingredients in a separate bowl, then add the crabmeat. Make it as spicy as you want with the cayenne. Hell, I don't care if you add so much you're howling at the moon. It's your damned tongue.

Eat it plain, on bread, don't matter to me. Just eat it fast so you can get to back to dragging that city boy away from your sister. 'Cause he definitely spells trouble.

CHAPTER TEN

"You can just get right back on the Mass Pike and drive back home because I don't need watchdogs." Meredith said, turning around when her brothers followed her up onto Rebecca's porch. She parked her fists on her hips and tipped her head up, eyeing them.

"Sorry, Mer, no can do. This is direct orders from Momma and you know how she gets if we don't do what she says. Besides, we have a standing invite to stay at Aunt Gloria's, for as long as we need to."

Meredith let out a muttered curse. "I don't need, or want, a keeper."

"Seems someone needs a leash at least," Vernon muttered, cocking his head in the direction Travis had gone.

"Do I ever interfere in your lives?"

"Well..." The two brothers looked from one to the other.

"I didn't think so. I would appreciate it if you would kindly stay out of mine." She turned on her heel, intent on heading into Rebecca's house. With her brothers staying next door, her plan had been shot with more holes than an archery target.

"Caleb is real broken up, Mer," Ray Jr. said. Meredith paused midstep. "He ain't been the same since you dumped him."

"He'll get over it."

Ray Jr. laid a big palm on her shoulder, the width and breadth of his grip nearly encompassing her entire clavicle. "You used to be soft-hearted, sis. You changed that much since you got here?"

Something sharp ricocheted around her chest. "I want something different from what I've always had, that's all."

"I can understand that," Vernon piped up from the sidewalk. "The boys at Petey's damn near banned me from the bar when I started drinking Coors Light instead of Bud. Said I wasn't a real man anymore. I gotta tell you, though, that mountain stream stuff they say ain't no bull—"

"This isn't about a beer commercial," Ray Jr. growled.

"Hell, I know that." Vernon ran a hand through his mop of brown curls. "Just making a point."

"You don't understand. Neither of you do." Meredith pivoted toward her eldest brother. "I don't want to work in Petey's the rest of my life and be married to Caleb and go to church every Sunday and make a Jell-O cake every July fourth for the Heavendale town picnic. I want more than that."

Ray Jr. shrugged. "Then get another job. Marry another guy. Buy a different cake mix. What's the problem?"

Meredith let out a gust. "Don't you see? I don't want any of that! The farm life. The Sunday picnics, the boy-next-door romance. I want..." She swept her arm out in an arc, gesturing toward the rush of traffic passing by on the distant highways, the bright lights of the bustling city that twinkled so bright, they blotted out most of the night sky. "This."

"So move to Indianapolis. It's a city."

"Maybe I will," Meredith said. "Later. For now, I want to be here. Tasting all Boston has to offer."

"You were sure having a taste earlier," Vernon muttered. "Surprised you didn't choke, what with his tongue that far down your dang throat."

Ray Jr. jabbed him in the arm and gave him a shut-up glare. "Meredith says she wants to stay. We'll let her do that." He gave his sister one last look. "For now."

She let out a gust. "What are you going to do, Ray Jr.? Hogtie me and throw me in the back of the truck if I don't come home before curfew?"

He grinned. "If it comes down to that we'll do what it takes to protect your honor."

The very thing she was so desperate to get rid of.

To do that she was clearly going to have to get rid of her brothers first.

A little while later, Meredith went inside her cousin's house and found Rebecca on the sofa, eyes closed, surrounded by a little girl's paradise of Barbie dolls, miniature stilettos and teeny garish outfits that would have made Yves Saint Laurent turn over in his grave. Meredith slipped off her shoes and went to tiptoe past Rebecca and up the stairs to the guest room. The last thing she wanted to do was rehash the appearance of her brothers. With any luck, they'd go home instead of staying next door and making her life a living hell.

"I'm awake," Rebecca said. "Just playing possum."

"Possum?"

"Emily was up a few minutes ago, making a good case for playing all night instead of sleeping. I told her if I was asleep she couldn't play, so I'm asleep." Rebecca shut her eyes and feigned sleep again.

"Impressive. You should be in movies."

Rebecca smiled and opened her eyes. "I know. Oscar-worthy, isn't it?" She sighed and pushed herself into a sitting position, her belly leading the way. "I suppose I should get all these toys picked up now. Considering I've been waiting two hours for my husband to come help me. I think he's lost forever in the den."

"Working?"

"No. Watching the Patriots. As long as it's football season, Jeremy is invisible. He loses all his peripheral vision to the television."

Meredith bent over and started putting some of the dolls into the big plastic bin marked *Barbies*. "Sounds like my father. My mom can barely get him to come to the table when Notre Dame is playing."

"You don't have to do that," Rebecca said, raising herself into a sitting position. "I can manage."

"And you can go into labor right here, too. I'm here to help."

"You're a guest, not a slave."

"Rebecca, this isn't a hotel. And you aren't my maid."

Rebecca smiled, relief clear on her face. "Okay, but only because you insisted." From the sofa she made a three-pointer toss of a Barbie doll into the bin. "I take it from the look on your face that Vernon and Ray Jr. found you. They stopped by here earlier looking for you."

"Oh yeah, they found me. Me and Travis. Together."

"Oh. How ugly did it get?"

"Well, no broken bones. Just a lot of manly glares and puffed-up chests."

Rebecca laughed. "Typical older brother stuff, huh?"

"I told them to butt out and let me be a grown-up.''

"Good for you!" Rebecca sent her a high five from across the room. "You do know they went over to my mom's for the night, right?"

Meredith nodded. "I was hoping they'd get the hint and go home."

Rebecca laughed. "They're Shordons. No one in this family gives up easily."

"I know. It's one of those traits, passed on down along with Great Grandma's family baby teeth necklace."

"Eww. That still exists?"

"Yep. And growing by the year. Keeps the Tooth Fairy pretty busy."

"That's what I need to do." Rebecca stuffed a pillow beneath her back and settled into a more comfortable position. "Steal that necklace, put it under my pillow and in the morning, wake up to a mint." She grabbed an afghan off the back of the sofa and draped it over her legs. "Time for a hotter, and younger, topic. How was your date?"

"Perfect... and not."

"Did Travis turn into a werewolf when the moon came up?"

Meredith laughed. "No. We just didn't have the same idea of how the date should end."

"He didn't kiss you?"

"Oh, he kissed me all right." Meredith closed her eyes for a second, remembering that kiss.

"So what was the problem?"

"I wanted... more. But he made it clear there wouldn't be more, even if my brothers hadn't come by and interrupted my lame attempt at seduction."

"On the first date?" Rebecca's eyes widened. "Well, cousin, you do surprise me."

"You didn't think we girls who lived on farms ever... well, did those kinds of things?"

"I didn't think *you* did."

"Well, I'm changing." Meredith gestured toward her new haircut. "In more ways than one. And as long as I'm here, I want to experience all the city has to offer."

"Including Travis Campbell?"

"*Especially* Travis Campbell."

"Just be careful," Rebecca said, her voice softening with concern. "I don't want you to get hurt."

Meredith shook her head. "I'm not going to fall in love."

Rebecca smiled and tossed a couple more dolls into the bin. "You can't control that."

Which was exactly what Meredith was afraid of but she didn't say it. She would *not* fall in love with Travis Campbell or any other man in the city of Boston. She'd get what she wanted, then be on her way. Guys did it all the time—why couldn't she? "Barbie managed not to fall in love with Ken. Hey, she's even on her own now."

Rebecca chuckled as she stacked up a pile of Jeremy's books on the end table. "Yeah, she probably dumped him because he was always leaving her with a messy townhouse." As she finished with the books, she picked up a package sitting beside them. "I almost forgot. This came for you today."

Meredith took the small box and glanced at the return address. "Perkins & Son Funeral Home."

Meredith put the box to the side, unopened, and started tossing Barbie's extensive shoe collection into a smaller bin marked "Shoes."

"You aren't going to open it?"

"It's from Caleb. We're over. Done. He just can't take the hint."

"You told him?"

"Many times. He's a nice guy, but being engaged to him was like being wrapped in top-grade satin."

"Suffocating, huh?"

"Yeah."

"So there's no chance of resurrecting the relationship with the mortician?"

"Nope."

"It's as dead as—"

"A doornail," Meredith finished, laughing.

"And you wouldn't date him again, even if..."

"Dr. Frankenstein himself set us up."

Rebecca laughed. "We are mean. You said he's a nice guy and here we are, making dead jokes."

"The sad part is, Caleb would appreciate them. He's a big aficionado of death humor."

"And Travis?"

"He's, ah, very different from Caleb." Meredith tried to keep the smile from her face but didn't succeed. She had enjoyed her time with Travis, and the steamers at the Salty Dog, more than she wanted to admit. She was already looking forward to seeing him again.

"Just be careful, cousin."

"I am." Meredith reached into her purse and held up the package of Trojans. "I bought protection."

Rebecca's face softened. "Condoms don't protect your heart."

That was exactly what Meredith was afraid of.

Travis's Can't-Get-Her-Off-Your-Mind Baked Cod

1/4 cup breadcrumbs
1/8 cup parmesan cheese
1 teaspoon parsley flakes
1/2 teaspoon dried dill
1 pound cod fillets
Ranch dressing

Okay, so I'm not Wolfgang Puck. I may keep my meals simple, but lately my love life is as complicated as the latest IRS tax code.

Preheat the oven to 350 degrees. Mix the breadcrumbs, cheese and spices and put on a paper plate (if you have a kitchen that has more than six utensils and two coffee cups, you might have a pie plate and can use that. Me, I'm lucky to have some Dixieware laying around). Dip the cod into the ranch dressing, then into the breadcrumb mixture, shaking off the excess.

Yeah, that was tough. When you're mind is elsewhere, the last thing you want is something complicated in the kitchen. Put the fish on a foil-lined baking sheet and bake for 10 to 15 minutes, until it flakes with a fork or, hell, looks done enough to eat.

If that's not enough to get her off your mind, then you have worse troubles than learning how to cook.

CHAPTER ELEVEN

"So," Larry said the next morning, "did you convince our little Midwestern test market to come over to the No-Moo dark side?'

"No." Travis poured himself a cup of coffee and averted his eyes from the bright blond toupee on Larry's head today. Apparently he was going for the white-gold overall look because he'd matched his belted polyester pants to his hair.

At least *something* on Larry matched his wig. From his station by the doughnut box, Kenny shot Travis a grin filled with mirth.

"Might I remind you, Travis, that we launch No-Moo Milk on the first and we still don't have a definitive ad campaign?"

"You don't have to remind me. I'm the one working with the graphic designers on the ad conceptual."

"Executing *my* ideas, you mean."

"Uh, yeah. Whatever." Travis took a sip of his coffee and tried not to choke. Larry's ideas included buxom Swedish twins in fake cow-print bathing suits with smiles on their faces hoisting a glass, plus a naked supermodel wearing nothing but a few strategically placed bottles of No-Moo, with the words "Where's the Moo?" running across her abdomen.

Advertising Federation award winners they were not. In fact, Travis was quite sure they were the kind of ideas that would get them sued or worse, on Bill O'Reilly's show, defending both misogyny and cow-ogyny.

He was about to tell Larry where to stick his bottle of No-Moo but then remembered the e-mail from Brad this morning. "Don't let me down, man. I need the money. I'm about to become a married man," his brother had written.

Talk about pressure.

And talk about betrayal. A double one at that. He and Brad had always talked about walking out of Belly-Licious Beverages together someday to launch their own company. And most of all, of enjoying the single life until they were past collecting social security.

In short, of never ever turning into their father. The autocrat who kept insane work hours and married women as frequently as most people changed their toothbrushes.

"I'll have her in here," Travis said, ignoring the war in his gut that told him he was crossing some moral boundaries with Meredith even as he tried to uphold a pledge to his brother. "You can count on me, Lar."

Kenny raised a brow in surprise, but stayed mute.

"Knew I could, Travis." Larry gave him a bone-shattering clap on the shoulder and shot him a toothy grin as if they were now old buds. "How about tomorrow at four? I'd like to have her in the focus group room, let the ad people watch her reactions behind Big Ike."

Big Ike, the one-way mirror that saw everything in the focus group room and felt a lot like being a peeping Tom. For a second, the thought of Larry and his toupee watching Meredith drinking No-Moo Milk, her pretty pink lips curved around the glass, her slim legs crossed at the ankle, revealing a hint of what lay beneath her skirts, her newly styled hair teasing around her chin and cheeks ...

It made him want to tear Larry's eyes out and feed them to the foxes in the Franklin Park Zoo.

That would probably *not* be the best way to keep his job. Or secure Brad's future at Belly-Licious.

"So, now that you've mentioned the Midwest pixie we met at Slim Pickin's," Kenny said after Larry had left the room, "how are you doing with your new and might I add, very stupid, no-touch policy?"

Travis laughed. "I'm surviving."

"Suffering is more like it. You look like you didn't sleep at all last night."

He hadn't, but he wasn't about to admit that to Kenny. He'd tossed and turned, dreaming of Meredith, of taking that pert, sweet mouth of hers and letting it venture into uncharted territory. They'd had a damned good thing going until her brothers interrupted. A good thing he'd continued in his mind, soon as he'd turned out the lights and climbed under the covers. His thoughts had drifted back to Meredith like a fish to a dangling lure—he couldn't resist her and he wasn't putting up much of a fight even trying.

And if he wasn't careful, he'd end up hooked like a two-hundred-pound tuna.

But when he closed his eyes, he thought of her kissing him, of how she'd started out soft and gentle, then quickly moved into aggressive territory, asking without any words for what she wanted. Heck, she didn't even have to ask. His body was running down the same thought paths. He wanted to kiss her, to undo the flimsy fasteners that kept her body covered from his eyes, then run his fingers and his mouth down her body, taking time to taste every inch before carrying her to his bed and—

Whoa, cowboy. Better reign those thoughts back in before he broke his own self-imposed waiting period. Thinking about her late at night was one thing, but continuing the thoughts in broad daylight could get him into more trouble than he wanted.

Plus, it could hurt Meredith if he slept with her. He had a feeling that no matter what she said, she was the kind of woman who wanted a dog and kids and ranch on a cul-de-sac. Despite all he had done wrong in his life, a deep-rooted sense of conscience in Travis didn't want to commit that particular sin— not against her. She deserved more, whether she wanted it or not.

Not to mention that getting wrapped up in a woman right now would undoubtedly—as it always had before—distract him from his job. That was something he couldn't afford, as Brad's e-mail had reminded him.

"Tell me again," Kenny said, wagging a jelly-filled in his direction, "just why the hell are you doing this?"

"Doing what?"

"Waiting thirty days before you have sex again?"

Travis let out a sigh, and realized when he did that for the first time in a long time he could face the sunlight in the office without wincing. Clearly, not being hungover had its advantages. Like clear-headedness, and a weird enjoyment of the morning that he'd forgotten. "Because I'd like to try a relationship built on minds, not bodies."

Kenny had been taking a sip of coffee when Travis answered him and now spewed half a sip over the smooth faux cherry surface. "That's bullshit!"

"No, I'm serious."

Kenny pressed a hand onto Travis's forehead. "Are you sick? Or did Olivia knock a few of your brain cells onto our bathroom tile? If she did, I'm calling the cleaning lady and having her save them for reinsertion. Because that is crazy talk, man."

"Hundreds of men have real relationships every day, Kenny."

"Hundreds of men besides you. You are the king of no commitment. Didn't you tell me once that you wouldn't settle down, even if Britney Spears attached a Hummer to your left hand and dragged you to an altar?"

"That still holds true." And it always would. Travis was a Campbell and Campbell men did not make good boyfriends or husbands, despite what Brad was planning. He knew, as surely as he knew that Kenny would blow his 401k plan on a pair of shapely legs and a whispery laugh, that he was his father's son.

And that alone was enough to convince him any woman in her right mind would be smart to stay away from him and an altar.

Kenny shook his head. "Travis, Travis, Travis. Have you learned nothing in the four years we've been roommates? The minute you start dating women for their minds"—Kenny let out a snort—"is the minute they start getting those ring-bearing claws into you. Next thing you know, you're driving around in matching Volvos and picking up organic produce after work on Friday night."

"I'm just working on getting my head straight for a little while, that's all. No wedding bells for me." All Travis wanted was some time to figure out why every day seemed so screwed up; why the bachelor life he'd once loved had lost its allure.

And why everything he'd thought had been so clear had become fuzzy, as if his entire life plan had had a few too many rum and Cokes.

Kenny rose and poured himself another cup of coffee from the carafe on the sideboard. "Long as your head doesn't end up on the other side of a long white aisle, we'll be square."

"It won't."

"If it does, I'm coming after you. My brother Tony has a tractor trailer that can out-pull Britney's Hummer any day."

"He's out there. Again." Vernon stood at the entrance to Gift Baskets early Tuesday evening, looking like a bouncer for anyone who got out of line with the chocolate cookies.

"He is?" Meredith strained to look past her brothers, but their imposing bulk all but blocked the view through the plate glass windows. Maria and Candace had said they didn't mind the male-dominated view, but Meredith was mortified.

The two had even made friends with Candace's three-legged dog, Trifecta, who was relegated to the front glass partition of the shop. She had sidled up to Ray Jr., fallen asleep under his tender attention, and was now snoring happily at his feet.

Travis strode up the sidewalk to the entrance. Vernon moved to block the door. "She don't want to see you," he said.

Meredith slipped in beside her brother and gave him a sharp elbow beneath the ribs. He let out a surprised *oomph* and defensively moved to the left. "Hey!"

"It worked when I was nine, it works now." Then she turned to Travis and despite her intentions not to get involved, not to feel a thing for him, a smile curved across her face at the sight of him and something hot and liquid ran through her.

He must have come straight from work because he still had on a suit and tie, the dark blue a perfect contrast for the forest green of his eyes and the cocoa brown of his hair.

"Hi." Her voice went soft and quiet, as shy as an eighth grader with a crush on the new boy at school.

"Hi." His tone was equally low and private, as if they were the only two in the shop.

But they weren't, a fact made very evident by Ray Jr.'s loud and annoyed throat clearing. "She ain't art, you know. You don't need to be staring at her."

"Yeah, she ain't a Pee-casso. Take a picture or move on." Vernon moved forward, his frame menacing.

"I'm here to take Meredith out. And neither one of you two is going to stop me." Travis looked like an ant standing up to a pair of gorillas, but still he stood his ground.

"Nope. She has a man."

"I never liked that man," Vernon muttered. "Any man who never wears shorts has got a screw loose somewhere."

"Hush up, Vernon. Meredith is still spoken for and we aren't going to let her throw her life away on some smooth-talking city boy."

"Spoken for?" Travis said. "I hate to be the one to break this to you guys, but it is the twenty-first century. Meredith can date whomever she wants, whenever she wants."

"Not if we have anything to do with it."

She elbowed her brother again. Harder. "You two have nothing to do with it. This is my life, not yours."

"Ow. Why do you always have to do that?"

"Because it always works." She shouldered her way past the two of them to stand on the other side, near Travis. "Now, the only people I am answering to while I am here in Boston are Maria and Candace. If they say it's okay for me to leave early, then I'm leaving."

"Shop closes at six," Maria said, glancing at her watch. "And hey, look at that. It's six-oh-one. Time to go home. Or wherever." She grinned.

Across the room, Candace nodded her agreement, stifling a smile of her own behind her palm.

"There. It's quitting time for me. And quitting time for the Shordon Sentinels." Meredith swung around, grabbed her coat off the rack by the door, then headed out the door, grabbing Travis's hand and pulling him with her before her brothers could stop her.

After his sister had taken off like a ten-point buck who'd heard a baying hound, Ray Jr. turned to his brother. "Well, hot damn. We're going to have to do something about that girl. Momma is going to beat our butts if we don't."

"Probably cut us off at the dinner table, too," Vernon said, his mouth downturned. "A man's got to eat."

"We got to get us some duct tape." Ray Jr. rubbed his chin. "That'll fix this. Duct tape fixes about anything."

Vernon nodded. "Man's best friend, next to his rifle."

"You can say that again."

"Man's best friend, next to his rifle."

Ray Jr. shook his head. "Sometimes, I wonder if there was something defective in your genes."

Vernon craned his neck and peered down at his Levis. "They look okay to me. Getting a little loose, but I expect that'll change once we get back home to Momma's cooking again." He grinned, clearly proud of his pun.

"Either way," Ray Jr. said, ignoring the joke, "we aren't getting any home cooking 'til we get Meredith away from that pretty city boy." He opened up the door to the borrowed pickup and swung his body inside. "So hold onto your hat, Vernon, because we're gonna have us a round-up tonight."

Meredith's Sometimes-What-You-Want-Is-Sweet-and-Sour Shrimp Stir-Fry

2 teaspoons vegetable oil
2 cloves garlic
2 cups broccoli, chopped
1 red pepper, sliced
1 carrot, sliced
2 tablespoons water
1 pound medium-size shrimp
8 ounces mushrooms, quartered
2 tablespoons sweet and sour sauce
2 teaspoons sesame oil
1/4 teaspoon ginger
2 cups rice, cooked

Just when you think things are going down a sweet and tasty road, they take a detour. The best thing to do? Make something yummy to eat and indulge in so many calories you forget why you were upset in the first place.

Heat a wok or skillet over medium-high heat. Add the oil, then the garlic. Drop in the broccoli, pepper and carrot, stirring for a couple of minutes, just to get them cooked a bit yet leave them as crunchy as you'd find them in your garden.

Add the water, then cover and cook for two minutes. Long enough to wonder about those mixed signals he's been sending out and whether you should just give up on this man and find one who will do what you want—when you want to do it.

Add the shrimp, mushrooms, sauce, oil and ginger and stir-fry until done, about another three minutes. Probably not long enough to come to any major life decisions. But definitely fast enough to get the food out of the pan, onto some rice and into your mouth so you can start eating and stop thinking.

Because if you try too hard to figure out what a man is telling you, you'll end up as confused as a cucumber growing in a field of zucchinis.

CHAPTER TWELVE

"I think I love shrimp more than steamers," Meredith said a few hours later as they walked along the path that curved around the waterfront at Castle Island. There wasn't really a castle there, Travis had told her, just the stalwart concrete buildings of Fort Independence, one of the bastions used by the British to protect Boston Harbor back in the 1600s—until the newly patriotic Americans ejected them in the next century.

Meredith loved the quiet of the walkway, after the busier park area that had been populated by residents who were Rollerblading, biking or walking, each enjoying the last bit of evening air and the spectacular view of surrounding Boston Harbor before heading in as eleven turned to midnight.

Travis had taken her to dinner at a cozy little seafood restaurant on the waterfront, then driven her throughout the city, showing her Chinatown and the North End, before finally bringing her here, to end their date in privacy. Neither of them felt the late hour and they walked along, their bodies brushing against each other from time to time, rekindling the fire between them.

"I could be wrong," she continued. "Maybe I need to taste them both again."

Travis laughed. "Already craving seconds?"

She turned to look at him, his features seeming carved out of marble in the encroaching moonlight. "And more."

"Meredith—"

She could hear the "but" in his voice, as clearly as if he'd put up two hands to ward her off. "What is it, Travis? You keep coming around, taking me out, making me think you want... more, and then as soon as I try to get close to you, you put up that Do Not Disturb sign."

"I want you to disturb me ... and I don't." He grinned. "I'm a typical guy. Don't know what I want."

Virtually everyone had gone home, leaving them alone in the deep shadows of the old fort.

"Well, I know what I want." Meredith took a step forward, grabbing at his shirt and hauling him to her, the frustration having reached a fever pitch after an hour of sitting across from him, eating another seafood delicacy and dreaming instead of tasting the same sweet flavor on his lips, not on her own. Every time she got close to her goal, something—or someone—interrupted, and she was tired of waiting. Of letting someone else call the shots.

"*I want you*," she said. "I don't know how much plainer I can make that."

A couple strolled by them on their way back towards the parking lot, walking a dachshund on a leash, but Meredith barely noticed them. She hardly heard the wash of the tide coming in, going out. All she saw was Travis. He had everything she needed to transform herself from country girl to city woman.

And he wasn't giving it up.

"Don't you feel the same?" she asked.

"Of course I do. What do you think, I'm made of stone? That I haven't noticed how gorgeous you are or how sexy you look in that little skirt? I just don't want to hurt you."

"You *aren't* going to hurt me." His tie crumpled under her grip. "I told you, all I want is a one-night stand. Nothing more. No strings, no calls in the morning. No expectations."

"All you want is sex?" he asked, a harsh, husky edge in his voice that bordered on a growl. "You want me to screw you and then walk away? Is that it?"

"Yes." She nodded, then swallowed. "That's all."

"Fine." He swooped forward, taking her in his arms, his mouth not kissing her this time, but conquering her, demanding more than she'd ever given before, the kiss hard and severe. A jolt of need rushed through her and she surged forward, clawing at his back.

Yes, yes. This was it. *This* was what she wanted. Mindless, hot, passionate.

His hands came up between them, cupping her breasts, his forefinger and thumb almost pinching at her nipples through the fabric of her shirt and the lace of her bra. Immediately, she went hot inside, as if he'd hit a switch—

But then the switch turned another way, as he bent down, pressing against her, lowering her to the ground, his body on hers, long and hard and lean, just the way she'd asked.

No. Wait. This isn't it. It isn't right.

She couldn't figure out what was wrong. She reached up, rubbing at his back in a soft, slow circle, trying to send a signal, even if she didn't know what signal she wanted to send. But he didn't listen. Instead, he grabbed one of her arms and thrust it to the hard bulge at the front of him.

His kiss deepened, tongue sweeping in, tasting every inch of her, dueling with her own, then slipping in and out, in and out, a preview of what was to come. It wasn't like the other kisses. Every other time Travis had kissed her, she'd felt...

Special.

And now, she felt...

Like a sex object.

It was ... awful. Hot tears stung at the back of her throat.

Suddenly, Travis jerked away, getting to his feet. "There. Is that what you wanted?"

She wanted to say no, to tell him it was the exact opposite of what she wanted, but realized that was crazy. She had, after all, asked him for a one-night stand. Nothing more. And a one-night stand didn't kiss her with all the care of a jeweler handling a diamond. A one-night stand didn't make love to her with sweet slowness and the care of someone who knew her body, and her soul, inside and out.

A one-night stand gave her what she asked for, then walked away.

"Of course," she managed. Her body, which didn't have the feelings that her mind did, had yet to return to simmer. Her breath came in short, fast bursts, the memory of what they had just been doing still coursing through her, echoing in her mind, her veins, her limbs.

As the feelings ebbed, a heavier one took their place, sinking to the pit of her stomach and weighing an awful lot like—

Disappointment.

Travis shook his head, let out a breath that was more of a curse, then turned to walk back down the path. She ran up to him and grabbed his arm.

"Why did you do that?"

"To give you a taste of what you want. Love you and leave you. Goddamnit, Meredith, isn't that what you asked for?"

Put that way, it sounded harsh, cold. Like the plot of a B-movie that went straight to video. She jerked her head up as if the words didn't bother her. As if the way he'd kissed her earlier hadn't left her with tears in her eyes and a sad lump in her chest. "Of course."

"You're lying to yourself," Travis said. "And you're lying to me." He shook his head. "And I tried like hell, but even I'm not enough of a jerk to ruin your life on purpose."

"You wouldn't be ruining my life."

"Oh, so I'd be expanding your horizons if I screwed you and left you?"

She turned away. "That's crass."

"That's the truth, Meredith. It's what you want. What you came here for."

"I want..." She shook her head and turned away, facing the ocean. The wind off the water whipped at her hair, plastering it to her face. "All I want is to be different."

"Why?" Travis came up behind her and wrapped his arms around her waist, all traces of the hard edges from earlier gone. "Why do you want to be different, Meredith? You're pretty perfect the way you are right now."

It would be so easy to tell him, to confess how boxed-in she felt, how every minute in Heavendale made her feel like she was suffocating in one of Caleb's deluxe caskets. But she didn't. That would mean opening up to him, building a bridge. And if there was one thing Meredith didn't want to leave behind in Boston, it was any bridges.

So instead she faced him and turned the tables. "Why are you so intent on *not* sleeping with me? Are you saving yourself for marriage or something?"

He laughed. "Hell, no. I'm not even the kind of guy who gets married."

"Bachelor for life?"

'That's the Campbell son motto." A shadow passed over his face, but he didn't elaborate.

"So why am I the one woman you decided to be virtuous with?"

"Because you're different, Meredith. And I happen to like that about you, whether you like it or not. And Lord help me for saying this, but I don't want to have *that* kind of sex," he gestured toward the grass, "with you."

Her heart betrayed her by melting a little. She shouldn't like him for foiling all her plans and especially not for making her care.

He tipped her chin up, so her eyes met his. "I don't want to see you give such a precious gift to a guy who doesn't deserve it."

"But— "

Her sentence was jerked off and buried in a flurry of wool. Meredith opened her mouth to scream, but she was jerked back so quickly, the wind rushed out of her. She fought against the confinement, causing the wool to slip a little below her eyes.

A Fighting Irish blanket. The blue-and-gold wool of Notre Dame smelled faintly of deer and woods, and Cecil Montgomery's hound dog, Boomer. Meredith's burst of fright gave way to a double dose of annoyance.

"Get off me, Ray Jr.!" But her voice was a mumble against the fabric.

"We're doing this for your own good, sis." Her brother's deep voice sounded in her ear. "You got him good, Vernon?"

"Yep, but he's fighting like a raccoon caught in a 'lectrified fence." Vernon chuckled. "Damned good thing we brought the tape."

Meredith struggled against the confines of the blanket, to no avail. Ray Jr. had been smart enough to tuck both her elbows out of lethal rib range as he'd wrapped her in the blanket. Now, he held her in place with one arm while wrapping a length of yellow rope around her, securing the Notre Dame prison in place.

Then he lifted her up and tossed her over his shoulder like a sack of seeds and hauled her towards his truck. She fought against him, pounding on his back with her mermaid legs. All futile efforts.

"Put me down or... I'll tell!"

Yeah, that was good. Scream at him like she was a two-year-old who's only out was running to Momma. Way to assert her new, independent-city-girl persona.

He ignored her and chugged along the sidewalk, her body bouncing against his shoulder, surely leaving bruises and internal organ damage.

Meredith jerked her head backward, managing to loosen the blanket and get it off her face. She looked around for a helpful bystander, a nosy cop—anyone who could get her out of her brother's well-meaning clutches—and saw nothing. It was after midnight in October and people with any sense at all had already gone home. She was on her own. "I said, put me down!"

"Not till you come to your senses. We got a thousand-mile drive back. Plenty of time to think about it." He balanced her with one hand, then lifted the handle on the door and plopped her onto the torn brown and white vinyl seat. He pushed down the lock button, then shut the door. She knew, from experience, that even if she could get the blanket off, she couldn't open the door. Cecil had never gotten around to putting a new handle on the inside passenger door so you either had to climb through the open window like one of the Dukes of Hazzard or navigate over the massive stick shift and out the driver's door.

Considering she was currently a human burrito, neither option, Meredith suspected, would work.

Still, Meredith struggled against the blanket, working her elbows to loosen the rope and nudge it down. A millimeter. Whoa. Some progress. Clearly there was a reason why Angelina Jolie got to play *Lara Croft: Tomb Raider* and Meredith carried hot pizzas for a living.

She whipped her head around and saw Travis. Vernon had him down on his knees, arms bent behind his back. Vernon's towering height and seventy-pound advantage, coupled with the element of surprise, had clearly outmatched Travis. In his mouth, Vernon had a roll of gray tape.

Oh no. No telling what could happen now. The only book that had ever been required reading in her house was *1001 Uses for Duct Tape.* Travis had little hope of escape.

"What the hell do you two think you're doing?" she screamed at Ray Jr. when he climbed in the cab and immediately put the truck in gear.

"Protecting your virtue."

Still no one around to witness the event. Castle Island was a relatively remote place, a peninsula encapsulated in darkness. As Ray Jr. pulled the truck forward, Travis was lost in the shadows. "You can't leave him there."

"Don't worry. Vernon didn't buy the name-brand tape. Your city boy will get himself loose." Ray Jr. grinned. "Eventually."

"I don't want you interfering in my life or protecting me from anything." She struggled against the blanket, but with her weight on top of the ends, it was impossible to pull it free. When she tried to buck forward and off it, her knees slammed into the dashboard. Pain sent stars shooting through her head. Once her vision cleared, she went back to trying to work the rope down.

"Sorry, sis, but we have to, like it or not." Ray Jr.'s features went from apologetic to enjoyment at getting her back for all those elbows in his ribs.

Meredith turned around, looking for Travis in the inky darkness. Instead, she saw Vernon make a running leap into the back of the pick-up, the roll of duct tape ringing his wrist. He tapped on the glass divider to the cab. "Let's make dust. That ram ain't going nowhere."

"Vernon, I am going to kill you!" Meredith wrestled against the blanket more, but got nowhere.

Ray Jr. stepped on the gas. The tires squealed as he rushed out of the parking lot and down the street, abandoning Travis on the walkway in the shadow of the old fort.

From the back, her middle brother roared with laughter. He'd come in first place in the hog-tying competition at the Indiana State Fair when he was eleven. Apparently, he hadn't lost his touch. Or his penchant for wreaking havoc.

"Why are you two doing this?"

"Cause Momma told us to."

"You are almost thirty years old, Ray Jr. You can stop doing what your Momma tells you."

"Not if I want to eat tomorrow. And you better do what she says, too, or you'll get the hundred-dollar lecture."

Momma's dollar lecture was a quick, five-minute, "do you think we live in a barn, shut the damn door" kind of talk. Ten dollars netted a half-hour talk, about the importance of washing after using the restroom or disinfecting the door handles efficiently. At a hundred dollars, they got the full-blown, all-night affair, filled with lines about "how could you throw your life away" and moaning wails of despair from Martha that her children would be end up homeless, strung out on drugs and wearing the same clothes for more than two days in a row because they'd missed curfew.

"Rebecca needs me. I can't leave."

"Aunt Gloria said she'd be glad to step in and cook," Ray Jr. said.

"Aunt Gloria? She can barely make a peanut butter sandwich."

Ray Jr.'s face bunched up in a grimace. "I know. But she and Momma talked and they made up their minds."

Meredith wanted to scream. This was exactly what she had run from Heavendale to get away from. Other people deciding her life. Other people telling her what was best.

"I'm not going home. Period." Meredith wriggled more against the rope and blanket bindings. This time, she was rewarded with the rope dipping to waist-level, leaving her less of a burrito and more of a messy taco.

"J.C. said—"

"I don't care what J.C. or Momma or Caleb or anyone has to say. I'm done letting other people run my life. Including you." The anger at what they had done bubbled inside her and she gave another jerk against the blanket. This time, it loosened and she was able to push one arm out, then the other, yanking the Fighting Irish off and to the floor. "Now take me back to Travis or I'll tell Momma about that night you took Cecil's truck up to Strawberry Hill."

"You wouldn't."

"I certainly would."

Ray Jr. scowled, still driving. "Mer, I can't let you go. Not till you come to your senses. Momma said you were acting crazy. I mean, you ran off one day. And now, you won't come home. She says you don't even answer your phone and when she does talk to you, you say crazy things about how it's over with Caleb."

"It *is* over with Caleb."

"I thought you loved him."

Meredith let out a sigh. This was going nowhere. Why did everyone in her family think they knew her better than she knew herself? "You know that pet rabbit you used to have?"

"You mean Whitey?"

"Yeah. You had him for years. Fed him, took him out of his cage and pet him once in a while."

"Even showed him at the 4-H Fair a couple years in a row. Whitey got a blue ribbon one year."

"Then he died, remember? And you buried him out back and never got another rabbit. Why?"

"Well, cause I don't really like rabbits. I like dogs. At least you can teach 'em tricks."

"Exactly."

Ray Jr. took a left, sending Vernon swaying in the back of the truck. "What the hell does that have to do with Caleb?"

"You kept feeding Whitey and taking care of him because he was there. You'd had him for a long time and you didn't know anything else. But then, when he was gone, you realized what you were missing out on by having just a rabbit and not trying any other animals."

Ray Jr. scratched his head with one hand, leaving the other on the steering wheel. Cecil's truck bumped along the road, its shaky exhaust leaking fumes everywhere it went. "Meredith, it's late and I'm tired. What are you saying? You don't want a pet rabbit? Or is there some deeper-meaning crap here I'm supposed to get?"

Meredith let out a gust of air. Ray Jr., as much as he tried, was like all the rest of them. He didn't understand her and he never would. "Never mind."

"Well, you can deal with whatever the hell it is you're talking about later. We're supposed to hold onto you until you're home and in your Miss Holstein costume."

"I am not putting that thing on." She shuddered at the thought of the black-and-white cow print out-fit. "Ever."

"You have a contract. J.C. showed it to me."

"I don't care. I told him I resigned and I had to go out of town—"

"And he told you he needed his Miss Holstein at the Tractor Pull this Saturday." Ray Jr. pushed the brim of his ball cap up a little higher on his fore-head. "Who's gonna ride on the front of Big Green?" he asked, referring to the giant tractor that led the Bovines-n-Beans Parade each year.

"Annie Wilson can do it. She was last year's Miss Holstein." And looked better in the cow costume, too. Annie had filled it out in ways Meredith never would.

"Everybody needs you, Meredith. You can't stay here forever."

Guilt washed over her. They always needed her, as if she was the one in the family that everyone had pinned their hopes on. The donkey at the never-ending family birthday party.

But it was her turn now, and she refused to feel guilty anymore. "Rebecca needs me too, Ray Jr.,"

Meredith said. "And *I* need some time away from Heavendale."

Ray Jr. didn't say anything else on the long ride to Rebecca's house and didn't slow down enough for Meredith to clamber out of the window. She was stuck, riding along in Cecil's truck, waiting for an opportunity to escape. It came too late, when he parallel parked the truck between Aunt Gloria's and Rebecca's. She climbed out of the window, refusing Ray Jr.'s offer to open the door for her.

"Are you going back to get Travis?" she asked her brothers.

Vernon chuckled as he climbed out of the back and leaped onto the pavement. "Eventually."

"You two need to take care of what you did. If you don't, I won't go home with you." She crossed her arms over her chest. "And if you try to kidnap me, I'll scream holy hell the whole way back to Indiana."

"Oh, all right. Let me grab a snack and then we'll head back over there." Vernon tossed a nod at Ray Jr. "You got her?"

Ray Jr. nodded and watched his younger brother lope up the stairs and into Aunt Gloria's house. "I don't get it, Meredith. I thought marrying Caleb and being Miss Holstein was everything you wanted."

She looked at Ray Jr., his hat in his hands, standing on the concrete sidewalk, in his thick-soled work-boots and faded Levi's 505s. He was the mirror image of their father, from his sun-kissed skin and his sandy hair to his view of the world. To Ray Jr., the smell of freshly cut hay and the sweat of a hard day's work were the essence of heaven.

"I want more than that," Meredith said. "I want something that makes me feel alive. I'm finding that here, in this city."

He studied her for a long time, then shook his head. "I dunno, Meredith. Seems to me you were pretty alive back in Indiana. And you could breathe a hell of a lot easier there, too."

"I didn't fit in there," she said. "And I didn't realize how much I was missing until I got away from Heavendale."

"Seems to me that's running away from your troubles, 'stead of facing them. Doesn't make them go away. You think stirring up a hornet's nest is gonna make things better?" Without waiting for an answer, he plopped his hat back on his head and headed up the stairs and into the house.

Leaving Meredith holding the blanket and wondering whether she should have done what Ray Jr. did.

And just got a damned dog instead.

Travis's Can't-Forget-About-Her-If-You-Try Oyster Stew

32 oysters, shucked (reserve juice)
1 tablespoon lemon juice
1-1/2 cups heavy cream
1 cup milk
Salt and pepper
Cayenne pepper, to taste
1 tablespoon chives, chopped

That woman has your blood—and everything else inside you—running at a fever pitch. Time to eat something that's simmering as hot as you are. Maybe it'll take your mind off her.

Yeah, right. Might be better off throwing yourself face-first into a glacier.

Put the oysters, their liquid and the lemon juice in a pan and cook for two minutes over low heat. In a separate pan (hey, the extra dishes are something to do while you're trying not to think about her), heat the milk and cream, just to a boil. Add to the oysters.

Season with salt, pepper and cayenne, then sprinkle with chives. Eat immediately, preferably while watching a good, manly boxing match. Avoid any show with blond women who have pretty blue eyes and making love on their minds.

CHAPTER THIRTEEN

For the second time in a week, Travis found himself down on the ground with a throbbing headache and wondering if dying might be the easiest way to solve the problems in his life.

It would certainly be cheaper than therapy.

And a lot easier to come by than a pocketknife and a third arm.

He wriggled against the duct tape binding his arms together for the twentieth time since Meredith's psychotic brother had hogtied him and left him for the seagulls, or worse, tomorrow morning's tourists. With no one around at this late hour, and the only sound coming from a biting night wind off the water, Travis was left to his own devices.

He tried to rub his ankles together and loosen the tape that bound his legs together but got nowhere. His wrists had about a centimeter of wiggle room.

Travis twisted to the left and managed to get his cell phone unclipped from his belt. He jerked and flipped, nudging the phone until he could get it around and press one of the speed dial buttons with his nose. He aimed for Kenny but ended up with his mother.

"Travis? Why are you calling me this late, dear?" she said, answering on the first ring, which meant she probably hadn't been asleep.

"Sorry, Ma. I was ..." He couldn't say he'd dialed the wrong number. "I was just thinking of you."

"Is everything all right? You're not in jail, are you?"

There was his mother, always thinking the best of him. In the background, he heard the theme music for *Law & Order* coming from her wide-screen TV. "No, I'm not in jail."

"Good. Did I tell you about your cousin Richard? He was arrested for bigamy. Can you believe that? I swear, the men in this family. They're either not marrying, or not staying married, or marrying women with all the choosiness of fleas on a dog. And then, your Uncle John—"

"Ma, I really don't have time for a family rundown right now," Travis said. "Can we catch up later?"

His mother paused, clearly not happy at having her gossip interrupted. "Have you talked to your father?"

"No." And since his father's number wasn't on his speed dial, there was no danger of that particular conversation tonight.

"Well, I think you should. Brad's getting married, you know, and we're all going to be together at the wedding. It would be nice if you mended a few bridges."

Travis shifted to get more comfortable. In the distance, he could see the white bow light of a passing boat on the water. "There aren't any bridges to mend."

"I swear, you're just like him. Stubborn as all hell."

"Ma, I'm kind of busy right now." Travis moved again but found the words "comfortable" and "concrete" didn't go together very well. "Can I talk to you later?"

"As long as you promise you'll support Brad's marriage. He's your brother, and he deserves that at least."

Travis sighed. "I will. I promise."

"And you'll be there, in a tux and with a date?"

"I'll be there." Assuming he could free himself from Vernon's idea of a good time, he would.

Finally, he seemed to have made his mother happy because she said good-bye and went back to watching one of the hundred different incarnations of *Law & Order* on her television in her condo in Miami.

On his third attempt, Travis managed to rhino-dial Kenny. He lowered his head beside the phone and waited for his roommate to answer.

"Call 9-1-1," Kenny growled after three rings, "because this line is busy."

"Kenny! Don't hang up!" Travis said. "I'm in a bind. Literally. And if you don't get your ass over here and help me, I'm going to be devoured by seagulls. Or worse, end up as a sex toy for some gigolo with a tape fetish."

On the other end, Kenny told someone to put that thought on pause, he'd be back. "Can you repeat that, Travis? There was a tongue in my ear. I thought you just said you were taped up."

"I am. I'm out at Castle Island, about halfway down the path to the fort. Just get out here and bring a sharp knife."

Travis swore he could hear Kenny laughing even after he'd hung up the phone.

When Kenny showed up a few minutes later, he started laughing the minute he rounded the corner and saw Travis on the ground. Travis raised his head off the pavement and saw the stubborn outline of a female standing a few feet behind Kenny. Under the soft glow of the streetlight, he could tell two things: she was blond and she was mad.

"Don't tell me you've crossed over to the light side of S&M," Kenny said, still chuckling. "Or in your case, the dark side of glue guns and tape."

"It's a long story. One I'll never tell you if you don't help get me out of this." Travis jerked his chin in the blonde's direction as Kenny bent down and started working on the tape with a pocketknife. "Is that your date?"

"Yeah. That's Delia. Though, after your untimely... interruption, there's been no dealing with Delia, if you know what I mean. She's the kind of woman who likes to see things to completion."

Kenny released Travis's wrists and moved down to his ankles.

Travis sat up and ripped off the remaining tape, wincing when it took half the hair on his forearms with it. "I could have waited. Maybe."

"I'd much rather owe Delia later." Kenny paused in sawing through the gray tape and grinned at Travis. "For a guy with hairless wrists, you're not so bad looking."

Travis glanced down and let out a groan. A two-inch wide white stripe ringed both of his arms near his hands. "Aw, shit. How am I going to explain this at work tomorrow?"

Kenny tore the tape off Travis's jeans and released his ankles. "Don't worry about it. Just tell Larry your date got a little kinky. When his sense of morality is offended, his toupee always leans a little to the right." Kenny rose and slipped his knife into the back pocket of his jeans. "Now, if you wouldn't mind driving back to the apartment, I need to work on apologizing to Delia in the backseat."

Momma's Get-Better-and-Get-Home Corn and Crab Chowder

1 tablespoon vegetable oil
2 tablespoons butter
1 clove garlic, minced
2 potatoes, peeled and diced
1 onion, chopped
2 celery stalks, chopped
1 green pepper, diced
1 bay leaf
Dash each of salt and pepper
1 tablespoon Old Bay seasoning blend
3 tablespoons flour
2 cups chicken broth
4 cups milk
3 cups corn kernels, scraped from the cob
8 ounces cooked lump crab meat

Your baby is sick! Move fast on this one, because there's nothing like a good chowder to make her feel like her old self. Heat the oil and butter in a deep pot, then add the garlic and sauté. When it's as nice and fragrant as the air back home, add the potatoes, onion, celery and green pepper.

Season with salt, pepper and Old Bay. Cook for five minutes, then sprinkle with the flour and stir for a couple of minutes until the flour is cooked (raw flour isn't good for your sick girl). Add the broth and stir some more. Next, pour in the milk. Keep on stirring; don't complain to me about your arms hurting, this is, after all, for your ill daughter.

I mean, she *has* to be sick. What else can explain the way she's been acting? She's simply not herself, that's all there is to it. A little of Momma's cooking and she'll be back to normal in no time.

Once the chowder boils, add the corn and crab meat and simmer for five minutes, then taste it. Adjust your seasonings as necessary to make it perfect for your loved one's overall health.

Serve it to her with love and a big napkin. And if she tells you she's just fine, don't believe her. Instead, send in reinforcements as needed.

Chapter Fourteen

Kleenexes, a hot water bottle, three cans of Campbell's chicken noodle soup, a bottle of Vick's VapoRub, a package of Hall's cough drops and a can of Lysol disinfectant spray stared back at Meredith from inside the box. Marked on the included note were the words, "From home, with love and worry."

"Are you sick, dear?" Cordelia asked from beside her. Maria and Candace had left on sales calls, leaving Meredith alone to run the shop. It was still early in the morning and everything was quiet in the little set of stores located off of Atlantic Avenue. Cordelia, as had now become her morning custom, had stopped in the gift basket shop first, to share a cup of tea and, Meredith thought, find a bit of company.

Meredith sighed. "No. My mother thinks I have a cold. So she sent me some get-well items."

If her mother thought she was deathly ill, that could work in her favor. *Too ill to travel*, she could claim. Why hadn't she thought of that yesterday?

After last night, she and Ray Jr. had talked again and he'd agreed to a truce, thereby buying her some time. She'd dangled every bit of blackmail in her arsenal over his head... and it had worked.

Never underestimate a baby sister.

"Oh," Cordelia said with a smile, holding up the hot water bottle. "She's one of *those* mothers."

"Those mothers?"

"I had one when I was a child. Every sniffle meant a call to Doc West. Every cut was a chance to parade out the entire contents of the first aid kit. I loved my mother, but she was a suffocator."

Meredith laughed and closed the lid on the package that had arrived at Rebecca's that morning just as Meredith was leaving for work. She hadn't had time to open it then, and, half afraid Caleb might have included something morbid that would scar Rebecca's four-year-old daughter for life, she'd taken the box with her to work. "It's good to know I'm not the only one."

Cordelia patted her hand. "Our mothers love us, in their own way. You'll survive. I did." She withdrew her palm and straightened her little hat. "Though I thought she might have a heart attack at my wedding."

"Why?"

"Well, my true love, Richard, God rest his soul, worked in refuse. He didn't actually collect the trash, just processed the paperwork, but that made no difference to Mother. She never did touch him, not even so much as a hug at Christmas or a kiss on the cheek for his birthday, as long as she lived."

Cordelia lowered her voice and moved closer. "Between you and me, it was just as well. Mother, who avoided germs like the plague, always had a cold and my Richard, who couldn't care less, never got the sniffles."

"Your mother and mine could have been twins, even cut out their Lysol coupons together on their spic-n-span kitchen tables," Meredith said. "What a shame about her and Richard, though."

Cordelia waved a hand in dismissal. "The loss was all hers. My Richard was the best man I ever knew. The good Lord took him from me last year and," she sighed, "my life has never been the same."

"I'm sorry," Meredith said, laying a palm on Cordelia's frail, thin arm.

"I miss him so much," she said, then drew herself up as if she'd lingered enough on self-pity. "The shop's just not the same without him."

"You worked together?"

She laughed. "Oh no! Richard and I in the same room, eight hours a day? That's how murder-suicides happen. He was manager of the South Boston landfill, but he was also an antique curator. The man could spy a Stickly in a sea of Hefty bags from a thousand paces."

Meredith chuckled. "Now there's a talent."

"You betcha." Cordelia patted the box. "Your mother will come around. Or, she won't. Mine never did. I just learned to love her for loving me." Cordelia sighed. "Though I do miss her chicken noodle soup."

Meredith reached inside the box and withdrew one of the cans, handing it to Cordelia. "It's not quite the same, but it'll do in a pinch."

Cordelia's wrinkled face softened and her pill-box hat slipped a little from its jaunty position on the top of her silver bun. "You're a sweetie. All you girls are. If I'd ever had children ..." Her voice trailed off. She brought the red and white can to her chest and shook her head. "Thank you. Now I must get back to my shop."

Then she was gone, the little bell over the shop door tinkling as she headed to her own store in the next building.

Meredith had just stowed the box from her mother beneath the counter when she saw Vernon and Ray Jr. heading into the shop. "Even though we decided to call a truce, I am never forgiving either one of you for what you did," she said.

"What? It was just a little duct tape." Ray Jr. put out his hands in a who, me? gesture, the sleeves in his cut-off red flannel shirt shifting with his bicep muscles as he did.

"A *little* duct tape? I know you guys and I know you never do anything halfway." Meredith shook her head and pushed through the glass door into the kitchen with Cordelia's empty tea cup in her hands, muttering as she put it in the sink. She tied on a bright white cotton apron, then pulled out ingredients for cookies and set up the mixer to begin baking the day's orders. Her brothers followed her, taking up stations on either side of the stainless steel counter.

"Besides, when we went back there, he was already gone," Vernon said. "Couldn't have done that good of a taping job if he got out that quick."

Meredith didn't care if Travis had escaped as fast as Harry Houdini. What her brothers had done went beyond a prank. She pointed at the door. "You two get in the truck and go home before I climb in the back, find Cecil's shotgun behind the seat and shoot you both."

"You don't even know how," Vernon said.

Meredith wheeled around and faced the younger of her brothers. He was now sporting a Patriots ball cap, Patriots T-shirt and even had the matching bandana hanging out of the back pocket of his Levi's, as if he'd been captured by a bunch of tourist aliens and whisked up to their souvenir mother ship. "I do too. I went skeet shooting with you guys last summer, remember?"

"And she whipped our asses, too," Ray Jr. muttered. "Cost me fifty bucks and a whole damned box of clay pigeons."

"Oh, yeah. I remember." Vernon shuffled in place.

"Never bet against your baby sister," Meredith said, wagging a finger at him. "And never tape up her date and leave him to the vultures."

"There ain't no vultures in Boston," Vernon said.

She grabbed the large metal mixing spoon on the counter and marched over to her brother, bringing her five-foot-four height straight up to his six-foot-two chest. As she spoke, she tapped it against his chest. "Vernon Estel Shordon, if I ever catch you within ten feet of Travis, I will kill you. I love you, but I'll *still* kill you."

Vernon took a step back, a sheepish look on his face. "We were just trying to help."

"Help who? You? Momma? Not me. This is not what I want. I like Travis. I didn't ask you to tape him up." She turned to look at Ray Jr., who was smartly keeping his mouth shut. "Now if he breaks my heart, fine, I'll let you two have at him. But until then, let me live my life. Please."

Vernon let out a sigh. He took off the hat and dangled it in his hands. His blond hair stuck up in a wave, then flattened against the rest of his skull where the hat had rested. "What are we gonna tell Momma?"

"Tell her I'm fine. I'm taking my vitamins, not going outside with my hair wet and eating my broccoli."

"That's it?"

"That's it." She turned toward the cabinet of dry supplies and pulled out flour, sugar and baking powder, laying the containers on the counter.

"But—" Vernon waved his hand over her, indicating the new haircut, the blue cowl-neck shirt and short black pencil skirt she wore today, hidden beneath an apron now. "What about all... this?"

"You tell her I'm fine," she repeated, returning to the cabinet for chocolate chips, "and I won't tell Dad you took off your Fighting Irish hat. You know how he feels about Notre Dame. And Notre Dame traitors."

Vernon looked down at the Patriots cap in his palms. "I... I only wanted to fit in."

"Who are you kidding?" Ray Jr. said. "We already went to two games at Foxboro Stadium. Vernon even bought one of those damned foam fingers. Waves it all over Aunt Gloria's den, even when we're watching UFC fighting. If he don't keep that finger to himself, I'll show him where he can stick that thing." He gave his younger brother an annoyed look.

Vernon spun towards Ray Jr. "And I'll show you where you can stick your nose that keeps getting in my business."

"Will you two cut it out?" Meredith said. "I swear, it's like you're still five years old."

"He started it," Vernon grumbled.

Meredith rolled her eyes, grabbed a Tupperware container from the counter and thrust it at them. "Have some cookies and call a truce."

"Cookies?" Both men brightened, took up seats on the bar stools and dug in. Within seconds, the dozen chocolate macadamia nut cookies she'd baked a couple days earlier had been reduced to a pile of crumbs. "Got any more?" Ray Jr. asked.

Meredith smiled. Finally, a trump card. She'd about run out of blackmail. "There are more cookies where those came from *if* you keep giving Momma good reports." She knew she'd never get her mother off her back on her own. And if she didn't get some help from her brothers, Momma would likely send out reinforcements.

Then things could get really ugly.

"Are you bribing us?" Vernon asked.

"Heck, yes," she said.

"Good." He grinned. "I like bribes I can eat."

Ray Jr. dipped a finger into the container and picked up a few crumbs, then licked them off and pointed at Vernon. "Long as you keep your damned foam finger out of my cookies, we'll get along just fine."

Travis was *not* going to call her, whether or not he'd promised to deliver Meredith to Larry this afternoon.

If he called her, Meredith would think he was interested. And only an idiot—or a masochist— would go back for more. Meredith might be a nice woman, and a beautiful one who did something funny in his gut every time he looked at her, but he preferred to live out his life with the rest of his body parts intact and not connected to each other.

With Tweedle-Dee and Tweedle-Dum around, he didn't think that would be happening. They clearly intended to see him in a body bag while Meredith got hitched to whomever they had stashed back on the farm.

But as his day wore on and nine turned to ten, then eleven, Travis had to admit he wasn't good for much of anything. Not when he started doodling Meredith's name on a pad in the middle of a meeting and lost his train of thought somewhere between images of her lips and her eyes.

Or when he went to the break room to pour himself a cup of coffee and got so distracted, he ended up with a Styrofoam cup full of half-and-half. Or when he reached for a donut and took a big bite out of the napkin instead.

"If you don't get laid, I'm going to kill myself," Kenny said, poking his head into Travis's office. "Just watching you is making me hurt."

Travis gestured to Kenny to come in and take a seat, "I don't want to call her."

"What, you're going to let a little duct tape get in the way?"

"A *little* duct tape?"

"Okay, maybe a half a roll." Kenny laughed. "On second thought, Meredith might not be your best choice, especially not with the Rambo twins for brothers. So how about we go to Slim Pickin's after work tonight and see what we can see?"

Travis thought of the clearheaded feeling he'd had the last few days, the difference he'd noticed in himself. Granted, he wasn't always excited to see the man who greeted him each morning but at least he did so without toasting his own image with a Tylenol cocktail. "I don't know..."

"Oh, come on, Trav. There are a lot of other women in Boston besides that one. And they're all just waiting to meet a man with an endless bar tab."

"Something you know from experience?"

"Have Visa, will date." He grinned.

"I'm not drinking, at least not right now."

"Then watch me have fun while you sip diet sodas and moan about your lack of a life." Kenny rose and headed for the door. "Trust me, pal, it won't be long before you're bellying up to the bar for a brewski."

That was exactly what he was afraid of, Travis thought as Kenny left his office. He didn't want to return to the life he'd had before, ending up on the floor after a good purse walloping, unable to remember the name of the woman he'd kissed the night before.

He didn't want to do anything foolish, either, like rush down the aisle and get committed to the marriage asylum.

Travis glanced at his phone. Despite everything, he missed Meredith. Until her brothers had come along, they'd had a really nice time on their dates.

A time he wouldn't mind repeating.

Maybe Kenny was right. Maybe he was starting to become a fan of S&M.

Brad's Aren't-You-Tempted Coconut Shrimp

Canola oil, for frying
1/2 cup breadcrumbs
1/2 teaspoon salt
1/4 teaspoon cayenne pepper
1-1/2 teaspoons Chinese five-spice powder
1 cup shredded coconut
1 egg
1 pound large shrimp, peeled and deveined

Getting used to the idea of marriage is a lot like getting these shrimp into the hot oil. You have to do a little prep work and yeah, you might get burned, but in the end, you have something delicious and memorable. So at least give it a try, will you?

Heat two inches of oil over medium-high heat. In a pie plate, toss the bread crumbs with the salt, cayenne and five-spice powder. In another dish, lightly beat the egg. Add the coconut to a third dish. Dip the shrimp in the bread crumbs, then the egg, then the coconut.

Fry for five minutes, until crispy and golden. See? That wasn't so bad. You lived through it *and* gained culinary skills. Marriage is a piece of cake after this.

CHAPTER FIFTEEN

Travis had caved. He'd gone by Brad's office and found his brother engaged in a quiet, private conversation with Jenny, his voice low and happy as he spoke into the phone, his back to the doorway.

A pang had slammed into Travis's gut. He'd forgotten why he wanted to see his brother, turned on his heel and went back to his own office, and had his phone in his hand a few seconds later. He told himself he was only calling Meredith to help his brother's career, not because of some weird feelings of longing when he'd heard the way Brad talked to his fiancée.

Now, three hours later, he stood in the lobby of Belly-Licious Beverages, handing her a laminated visitor badge. "Tell me again why I'm here," Meredith said.

All Travis had told her was that he wanted her input on a new product at the place where he worked. He couldn't tell her any more than that or he'd taint the results.

Travis leaned in close to her ear. "Because I promised you a lobster dinner afterwards." He grinned, then led her down the corridor to where Brad and Larry wait.

"That's not an answer."

"Because I need a favor." He opened the door and gestured for her to enter the room.

But she stood there, stubborn, arms crossed over her chest, which only served to thrust her perky breasts outward. If they hadn't been standing in the hall outside the unadorned focus group room, with Big Ike flanking the far wall, and Larry and his toupee-of-the-day watching and drooling on the other side, Travis might be tempted to do something about that. Surely kissing her wasn't out of bounds.

It was going further than kissing that got him—and Meredith—into trouble.

Yet, she wanted trouble, and gave him a look that reminded him he had yet to cause enough havoc in her life.

"I need a favor, too," Meredith reminded him. "And you haven't come through yet."

He let the door shut again. "I have reasons for that." And last night, he'd been confronted with two more reasons. Two reasons that might be armed and dangerous the next time they tracked him down with Meredith in his arms.

Vernon and Ray Jr. were like loose cannons, off creating their own special brand of justice, punishments from Home Depot already included.

Meredith frowned, her arms dropping to her sides, and turned away. Somehow she managed to look beautiful, vulnerable and disappointed all at once in the little black skirt and bright blue shirt she was wearing. "Maybe I should find someone else."

The thought of someone else taking her to bed, of another man running his fingers along her luscious, delicate body, then taking the one thing no one else had had yet, nearly drove Travis insane with jealousy. He barely knew Meredith, and he couldn't lay any claim to her. Hell, he had no right to lay claim to anyone, much less a woman like her.

But damn it all, he wanted to anyway. He wanted to protect her and to take her to bed, all at the same time. "Don't," Travis said. "Just don't."

She spun back. "Why? I'm through waiting for men who are going to disappoint me in the end. I came here for a change, Travis. Not more of the same."

He started to ask her what she meant by that when the door opened and Larry strode out of the room, his professionally whitened smile broad. "Well, you must be Meredith. Travis, you sneak. You didn't tell me she was so beautiful. Holding out on your boss again." Larry gave Travis a quick grin, then turned back to Meredith and thrust out a hand. "I'm Larry Herman, vice president of Belly-Licious Beverages."

Meredith's small palm nearly disappeared inside his beefy one. "It's nice to meet you."

"Nice of you to come in and be a part of the focus group for our newest beverage." He widened the whiteness of his grin. "You could help change the future of liquid choices for everyone."

"Such a big responsibility for a little Midwestern girl like me."

Larry didn't catch the hint of sarcasm in Meredith's voice, but Travis heard it and bit back a smile of satisfaction. She had already seen through Larry and wasn't going to fall for his flattery.

Larry gave her arm a little pat, a touch that treaded the line between condescending and consoling. "You're exactly the kind of audience we hope to reach. So, are you ready?"

"All I have to do is drink something?"

"That's it. Then we'll give you a special Belly-Licious beer cozy just for coming by." Larry winked and his grin spread even further. If Travis leaned forward, he could have counted the number of teeth in Larry's mouth. The man must be a dental hygienist's dream.

"I can hardly wait," Meredith said, her voice as flat as the floor. They followed Larry into the room and over to a small table set up directly beside Big Ike. Meredith flashed Travis a look that said "you owe me" before taking a seat in the gray vinyl office chair and pulling it up to the table. "I'm the only one here?"

"You're part of a very special focus group." Larry put one hand on either side of her chair. "Remember, the future of beverages rests in your mouth." He gave the seat's padded top a tap, then backed away and disappeared through the small side door.

"What is this all about?" Meredith asked Travis.

"I can't tell you. It might skew the test results. And we need you to be *honest.*" It was the only hint he could give her. He didn't want her to rave about No-Moo just because she knew him. Even Travis wouldn't sink so low to market something that people would hate.

Especially people like Meredith.

For a second, he wanted to scream "Stop!" to put a halt to the whole thing and tell Larry to go to hell. Then he checked himself.

This wasn't a big deal. Nothing could go wrong, despite the dread churning in Travis's stomach. Meredith was just here to offer her opinion. If he knew anything at all about her, he knew she'd be honest.

And nothing bad could come of that, could it?

Meredith turned around in the chair, draping her arm over the back. "So, you're using me ..."

"Just like you're using me."

She nodded. "Good. Long as we're clear on where we stand."

"We are," he said, and for some odd reason, disappointment weighed heavy on his chest. He turned away and headed for the small door.

Why did he care? Wasn't this what he wanted? The kind of relationship Travis Campbell had perfected over the years?

No involvement. No commitment. No expectations of phone calls in the morning or diamond rings after six months together. No plans for three-day weekends away and meeting the parents.

He took his life, and his dating, one day and one night at a time.

Any man in his right mind, and especially a Campbell man, should be thrilled that a woman like Meredith wanted nothing more out of him than a good time in bed and a kiss good-bye.

Then why did he keep resisting? It wasn't the stupid thirty-day waiting period. Travis knew that was an excuse, not a valid reason. There was more going on inside him than just some silly promise he'd made after a bad go-round with a Coach purse.

But figuring that out would require self-analysis. There were two things Travis avoided like the plague: spinach and looking inside himself. Both had the nasty side effect of turning his stomach.

"Hey, Trav," Brad said, entering the observation room from the hallway and pulling up a chair to the conference table where Larry and Kenny sat. His younger brother had lighter hair and a more boyish roundness to his face, and favored business casual in his attire. He was the studious one, the one who worried about his grades, made it home in time for curfew and never got a speeding ticket. He was, as their father often told them, what Travis could have been, had he put in a little more effort.

"How's Jenny?" Travis asked.

His brother grinned at the mention of his future wife's name. "Picking out a wedding dress and curtains. I think I need a second job, or a raise." The last he directed at Larry, who made it a point to ignore him.

"We're ready," Joe, the disconnected voice from the control room, announced over the loudspeaker.

Travis took the seat opposite his brother and turned in the swivel chair to face Big Ike and watch Meredith.

Larry leaned to grab the microphone sitting in front of him. "Go ahead, Meredith, and try out our drink. There are some cookies there if you want a treat to go with it. Mark your thoughts on that sheet on the clipboard."

Meredith picked up the floral printed Dixie cup filled with No-Moo Milk and took a tentative sip. She paused, as if deciding whether it was good or bad. She took a second sip, swallowed, and paused again. "Well... it's, ah, pretty good," she said. "I guess."

"I told you she'd love it," Larry crowed.

"Pretty good isn't loving it," Brad said. "It's a onetime purchase with no recommendation to buy."

Larry scowled at him. "Give her a second. For God's sake, Brad, don't you even believe in your own product?"

"I never thought—" Brad began, then bit back the rest of the sentence. He caught Travis's eye, a mirror image to his own green. "Have her try the cookies with it."

"Good idea." Larry clutched the mike and leaned toward it again. "Meredith, why not try dunking a cookie in there? Think of it as a little late afternoon snack."

She looked over at Big Ike, clearly knowing they were sitting behind it, watching her. Her gaze traveled across the one-way mirror, and then paused, almost at the exact spot where Travis was sitting on the other side. He knew she couldn't see him through the special glass, but she knew he was there.

And he knew she was going to expect some payback. His gut roared to life with anticipation. A lobster and a dish of drawn butter just wasn't going to cut it.

Meredith picked up an Oreo from the dish in front of her and dunked it in the No-Moo, then took a bite. Travis watched her teeth sink into the dark cookie and he almost groaned.

He needed a cold shower. No, make that an ice-filled fanny pack—that he wasn't going to use anywhere near his damned fanny.

"It's ... okay with cookies," she said after swallowing. "Not bad."

"Did you hear that?" Larry said, rising and facing the rest of the men. "It's not bad. That's good enough for me. Let's get a quote from her and use it in our marketing. No, wait. I have a better idea."

Dread filled Travis's gut. Larry and ideas were as dangerous a combination as oil tankers and wrong-way drivers on speed. "What?"

"She's a hot chick," Larry said, and Travis had to clench his fist to keep from slamming it into Larry's jaw. "Let's make her our spokesmodel."

It seemed to take a year to get out of Larry's clutches. Meredith hated the man the instant she met him and had no idea how Travis, or his brother, stood working for a guy who so clearly fit the dictionary definition of jerk.

Brad had been a younger, more studious version of Travis. She liked him immediately and decided Travis's prediction about Campbell men being bad matches for women was wrong.

She'd be willing to bet a hundred single women in Heavendale would take Brad Campbell in a second. And the other three hundred would take Travis in a half second—assuming Meredith didn't beat them off with a two-by-four.

"So, are you ready for lobster?" Travis said as they left the Belly-Licious Beverages building and walked out to his car. Fall had definitely arrived, she noted, as the sun set along the horizon and a chill picked up in the air.

She shivered in her light leather coat, wishing she'd worn something warmer. The silky shirt she had beneath the coat did nothing to keep out the draft. Without a word, Travis removed his long black trench and draped it over her shoulders.

Something tugged at her heart when he did that, something she knew she shouldn't feel, but did anyway.

If Travis Campbell ever came to Heavendale, Meredith was definitely going to have to go beyond wood and arm herself with a steel girder.

"I don't want lobster," she said when they'd reached his car. Meredith stood on the passenger's side, Travis on the opposite. He hesitated, his thumb on the remote, about to release the locks. She thought of the tenderness in the way he'd draped the coat over her shoulders, the slight squeeze he'd given her arms before releasing her and then walking beside her as if he didn't feel the cold at all, and decided she wanted him even more now. "Take me to your apartment."

"Now?"

"No time like the present. You owe me, remember?"

"I thought you wanted—"

"I don't need any more seafood, Travis. Well, I might... later." She felt her face color but didn't care. She wasn't hungry for food and was tired of waiting for him to come around. If he didn't intend to go through with their deal, then she'd move on.

But as she looked across the car's roof at him, her gaze connecting with his, a shot of sadness ran through her at the thought of any other man taking her to bed but him.

And that's when Meredith knew she was in trouble. She'd started to care. To like Travis.

To build one of those damned bridges she'd been so determined not to leave behind. She sucked in a deep breath and with it, a new resolve to make this all temporary. No heart commitments. No promises. No expectations.

Those were the kinds of things that came with her old life. Not with who she wanted to be now. She wanted to be a woman who could go to bed with a man and not think about marrying him. She wanted to be able to have a fling, and then move on.

Even if moving on meant wearing black and white cowprint and riding around the Lincoln County Fairgrounds on the front of a tractor.

Travis hadn't flinched or said a word. His thumb still hesitated on top of the remote control, as if he'd been frozen there. Meredith circled the car, went up to him, grabbed his red diamond pattern tie in her fist and pulled him gently down to meet her mouth. "I want you and I'm not waiting one more minute."

Desire filled his gaze, widened his pupils. "I want you, too."

"Then show me." She gave his tie another little yank. "Kiss me. But kiss me the way you did..." she hesitated.

"The way I did when?"

If she said the words, it would mean asking him to show her he cared. To make this more than a one-night stand. It would be going against that whole nice argument she'd given him in the shadows of Castle Island when she told him she didn't care if he had sex with her and walked away.

Right now, she did care. Very much. Maybe because he had sacrificed his coat in the cold. Maybe because she was feeling needy and lonely being so far from home—

Or maybe she was kidding herself that she could be a love-'em-and-leave-'em girl.

The reasons didn't matter. All she wanted was for him to do what he had done so many times before. "Just kiss me, Travis," she said softly.

He smiled, then tipped her chin up with his finger in a soft move, wrapping his free arm around her. "Your wish is my command."

His mouth captured hers, softly this time, yet taking the lead. He moved his hand to cup her chin, tracing a line along her jaw with his thumb, while his fingers trailed a soft touch along the tender skin of her throat. His tongue played with hers, dancing in and out like a wild, native tango. Then, when she thought she could stand no more, he pulled back a little, taking her bottom lip with his mouth and nibbling at it, sending a roar of desire through her. Meredith moaned and arched her pelvis against his.

Travis's arms went around her waist, hauling her body to his. Against her pelvis, he went hard and the feeling of that—*that power* and that desire packed into one incredible place—sent a charge through Meredith. She reached up, tangling her hands in his hair, a slight kitten sound escaping her.

It had never been like this with Caleb. Never in the dark Embassy Movie Theater. Never in the back of the hearse, parked in the Hillside Cemetery. She had never felt this tidal wave of desire washing over her like hot lava. She tipped her head back, allowing him access to her chin, her throat...

Heck, anything he wanted.

But he didn't take it. He pulled back, releasing her, his hands moving up to capture her face in a move so gentle, she thought she might cry. She blamed the gush of emotion on the still-throbbing need running through her, the unanswered call sounding in the rest of her body.

"That's enough for now," Travis said with a grin. "You'll get me fired for doing anything more than that in the parking lot."

Oh yeah. She'd forgotten they were still standing in the employee lot of Belly-Licious. Likely the entire office staff, especially that sleazy Larry Herman, was watching from one of the windows above them.

She'd have to wait. Again.

"I only live ten minutes from here," he said, his voice low and dark and filled with everything simmering in her gut. "Seven if 93 isn't too busy."

"Can you make it in six?" she asked.

She could probably wait six minutes. She had, after all, waited twenty-seven years.

"For what we're about to do, I think I can make it in four." He thumbed the remote, took her to the passenger side, whipped open her door as soon as the beeps finished, then ran around to his side and had the car in gear and squealing out of the lot seconds later.

Finally, Meredith thought as they barreled down the road. Nothing was going to stand between her and losing her virginity now.

Meredith's It's-About-Damned-Time
Clams Casino

2 dozen cherrystone clams
Rock salt or kosher salt
6 tablespoons butter
1 shallot, finely chopped
1/8 cup fresh parsley, chopped
1/8 cup fresh dill, chopped
1/8 cup fresh tarragon, chopped
Salt and pepper
Tabasco, to taste
6 strips bacon, cut into one-inch pieces

You've waited long enough for this moment to come, so get the broiler roaring. You, of course, already are.

Open up the clams, loosen the meat from the shell, and set them atop the rock salt on a shallow baking dish. Mix the butter, shallot, spices and a few drops of the Tabasco. Put a little bit of this delicious—and *hot*—mixture on top of each clam, then top with a piece of bacon. Broil for about six minutes, until everything's crisp and sizzling.

Now you're *really* ready to cook. Find that man— and his bedroom—and go get what you came here for.

Chapter Sixteen

Nothing, that is, except a Massachusetts State Trooper with a stony face and a pair of aviator sunglasses. "Do you know how fast you were going, sir?"

Pretty damned close to the speed of light, Travis thought, but didn't say. "Uh ... seventy-five?"

"Eighty-four-point-five," the state trooper said, emphasizing each number with a tap of his pen against the lowered window. "That's miles per hour." He stared at Travis, or rather the opaque black of his sunglasses did, waiting for a valid excuse.

Travis didn't have one, at least not one he was going to share with a member of the state's law enforcement team. So he did the next best thing.

Kept his mouth shut.

Meredith sat beside him, hands in her lap, wisely doing the same. She looked a little nervous, as if she hadn't been on the receiving end of a ticket before. Travis had. More times than he liked to remember.

Another thing he needed to add to his never, ever again list.

The trooper snorted, then scribbled on his ticket pad and tore off the top sheet, thrusting it at Travis. "I hope it's worth it, wherever you're tearing off to," he said. "Because this is going to cost you an arm and a leg."

Travis glanced at Meredith. "I think it will be."

The trooper raised a dark brown brow above his sunglasses and the left side of his mouth curved up a quarter of an inch. He shook his head, then wagged his pen at Travis. "Take your time now, sir. Don't want to blow all your gas just getting home."

Then he turned, the smirk on his face wider as he hiked back to his cruiser and zipped past them and down the highway.

"You still have enough ... ah, gas?" Meredith asked, a mirroring smirk on her face as he pulled the car away from the shoulder and continued down the road.

Travis waved the ticket at her. "Watch it, or I'll ticket you."

"For what?"

"Distracting the driver."

"I just wanted to warm you up." She reached over, placing her palm against the black gabardine of his trousers and demonstrating her distraction skills a second time.

Travis groaned and grasped her palm, stopping her. "I'm going to hit something if you don't stop."

"How far away do you live?"

He glanced at the exit sign a few yards ahead. "A mile and a half."

"Too far," she said, biting her lower lip and sending a hundred different fantasies running through his mind.

At first, he tried to turn off the images in his head, then stopped himself. What the hell was he thinking? Meredith was a big girl—a woman—and she clearly didn't want him to protect her from anything.

All she wanted was his body. Since when had that been a bad idea?

Meredith pointed out the window, a devilish glint in her eyes. "There's a wide grassy place over there."

He chuckled. "I'm daring, but not that daring. Besides a bed will be a lot more fun."

"You promise?" She gave him one last stroke, then withdrew.

"Oh God, I'd promise you a trip to Nassau about right now. And a new car *and* the Hope diamond. Just name it and it's yours."

Meredith's smile widened with the power she held over him. She grabbed his hand, putting it on the steering wheel with her own. "Then drive."

Travis obliged. What was that reason he'd had about waiting a month? Stupid idea. What man in his right mind did that when he had a willing, very desirable *virgin* begging him to take her back to his bedroom?

As soon as the state trooper was out of sight, he risked a second ticket and sped the remaining mile and a half to his apartment, off of Broadway in Somerville, tires squealing as he parked the car, not even caring that he'd angled it into the lot so badly that the car took up two spaces. He jumped out, slammed the door and ran around to her side, being as chivalrous as a man in a damned fine hurry could be.

"Hold on a second," Meredith said, hesitating on the sidewalk.

Hold on? He was barely holding on to his sanity as it was. But he obliged her, standing beside her while she shaded her eyes with a palm and peered down the street behind them.

"Nope, no sign of my brothers. We're safe to sin." She grinned and bounded up the wooden stairs and into the renovated Dutch Colonial that served as a six-apartment building for young executives working in the Boston area.

A moment later they'd reached Travis's second-floor apartment. He slipped the key in and pushed the oak door open. Kenny wouldn't be home for hours—and if he was smart, he'd call before he arrived, just to be sure the coast was clear.

Travis paused inside the door, dropping his keys onto the small cherry table and kicking the door shut in one quick movement. Then he turned to her, lowering his mouth to her throat and kissing the sweet, delicate skin there. He inhaled the soft vanilla scent of her and thought he'd never met a woman who smelled so innocent.

Innocent.

He hesitated again. What was he doing? He wasn't a man with a lot of morals, but even *he* knew this was wrong. Meredith deserved more than losing her virginity to a man she barely knew.

Especially a man like him.

"What is it?" Meredith asked.

"We ... We shouldn't."

"Don't tell me you're getting cold feet. Again."

"Your first time should be special, Meredith," Travis said. "With someone you love."

She frowned. "You sound like my mother."

"Well, they say Mother knows best."

"Not mine." She shrugged off her jacket and draped it over the back of the chair in his living room. She stood before him in the same silky blue blouse and black skirt he'd had all those fantasies about earlier and Travis's good intentions fell to the floor.

The skirt hugged her hips, the black only serving to accentuate the slim curves. Her blouse peeked open, revealing a lacy matching bra beneath and a slight swell of absolutely perfect breasts. His mind, clearly not working in concert with his morality, provided him with a few quick and very lusty images of what Meredith looked like beneath her clothes.

To hell with good intentions. All they did was ruin all the fun.

Travis took a quick glance around at the organized, neat and good-smelling apartment. It was Thursday. The day the cleaning lady came, thank God. The chances of any disgusting signs of bachelorhood lying around were slim.

He'd have to give that woman a raise.

Meredith wandered around his living room, trailing a hand along the beige leather sofa, her heels making no sound against the plush pale carpet. "I don't want to wait for true love," she said quietly. "I don't want to wait for my life to start."

"What's wrong with waiting?" Travis said, coming up behind her. He couldn't believe those words were coming out of his mouth, but there they were, hanging in the air.

"*Everything*," she said, nearly shouting the words and wheeling around, spinning into his arms.

He looked into her deep blue eyes and wanted her like he'd never wanted anyone before. She was his, for the taking. All he had to do was lean forward, press his lips to hers and she'd head down that hall just as so many other women had before, and be in his bed, her naked body pressed to his, in seconds.

But the thought of Meredith making the journey others had, of taking her to the same room where he had been with women whose names he couldn't even remember, left him with a sick feeling in the pit of his stomach.

She may not want more, but God help him, for the first time in his life, Travis did.

He tipped a finger under her chin and forced her to look at him. "Don't take the first opportunity that comes along, Meredith. Savor every moment and taste things one at a time. It'll be that much sweeter when the time is right."

"Are you speaking from experience?"

He shook his head. "No. But after meeting you, I wish I were."

"Damn you, Travis Campbell." Her eyes misted and she jerked back. "Don't be a gentleman. Not now."

"I'm no gentleman, trust me."

"Oh yeah? Then prove it to me." She grabbed his hand and tugged him toward the hallway. "Take me to your bed and make me a woman."

"You already are one."

"You know what I mean." She stepped up to him, pressing her torso to his, wriggling a little against his pelvis. His body begged him to stop listening to his head. "Make love to me."

"I want to. Oh man, do I want to." He stood as still as he could, willing himself not to react, but that worked about as well as using Legos against an impending tidal wave.

"Maybe you just need some incentive." She released his hands and reached for the hem of her bright blue shirt.

He watched, every muscle in his body frozen, as she tugged the soft fabric up and over her head and threw it onto a chair. Then, when he thought he couldn't stand the anticipation for a half a second longer, she reached behind herself and released her lacy blue bra, letting it slip off her arms and drop to the floor.

Meredith had magnificent breasts, wine glass sized, and he knew if he touched one it would be firm and even in his palm, that the nipple would harden beneath his thumb and she would gasp at his touch, melting against him, releasing another of those quiet mews that nearly drove him insane.

"Do I need to go further?" she whispered.

"No. No." He blinked, but she still stood before him, half naked and more tempting than Aphrodite herself.

"Then quit telling me what I need to do and take a few orders from me instead." She grabbed his palms and placed them against her breasts. Unbidden, his fingers curled into place, cupping them with a natural touch as if he'd held her a hundred times before. "Make love to me, Travis Campbell, before I go insane."

Travis had scooped her into his arms and carried Meredith halfway to his bed before reason stepped in. Actually, reason didn't make an appearance at all. It was the vibration of her cell phone, clipped to the pocket of her skirt and thrumming against his pelvis, that jerked him back to reality.

"Your... your phone," he managed, pausing in the doorway of his bedroom. Eight feet away his queen-sized bed waited, made up with dark cranberry bedding and a quartet of down pillows.

"Let it ring," Meredith said, her fingers working on the buttons on his shirt.

The phone began to play a Bach Minuet, the classical music coming out in a tinny sound. "You really should get that. It could be important."

"I guarantee it's my mother and it isn't important." She yanked at his shirt and got the first tail out of his waistband.

Oh God. Eight steps and he could have her on the bed. In three seconds he could have her skirt up, panties off and be entering bliss. No U-turns allowed.

"You *really* need to answer that," he said, releasing her to the floor before she got a good grip on his belt because he only had so much willpower. And the better half of it he'd left back in the doorway.

"Fine," she said, in a tone that said it wasn't fine at all. She flipped open the phone and said hello.

Travis took that opportunity to take a step back and breathe. Actually, to remind himself to breathe in and breathe out because being this close to both Meredith and Nirvana made it damned near impossible for him to remember to do anything much at all.

"Momma, I'm busy right—" Meredith cut off her sentence, listening. "No. He *didn't*. I told him it was—" she listened again. "Momma, I don't need you to—" another pause. "Yes, I *am* wearing a coat when I go outside." Pause. "And yes, I do know better than to go out with wet hair." She sighed. "Momma, you have to talk to him. Stop him somehow."

Travis shrugged out of his shirt and draped it over Meredith's shoulders, easing her free hand into one of the sleeves, then holding the other while she switched the slim cellular phone to the opposite ear. All the while, he wondered who the "him" was that she was referring to and what she wanted her mother to stop him from doing.

It was none of his business, he reminded himself. Meredith had made it clear there was nothing between them but what they had been about to do in his bed.

And yet, as he helped her slip her slender arm into the too-big sleeves of his shirt, he felt a weird surge of protectiveness and God help him, *caring*.

He took one last glance at his bed and knew it wasn't going to get unmade. Not this afternoon.

While Meredith finished her phone call, Travis leaned forward and did up two of the buttons on his shirt. It was enough to give him some mental—and visual—breathing room.

At least it took his mind off of what he wanted to do on the Serta Perfect Sleeper just a few feet away.

Meredith hung up her phone and reclipped it onto her waistband. "Talk about a mood killer," she said, laughing.

"Probably a good idea," he said, taking a step forward and putting his hands on her waist. "I like you, Meredith," and as the words left his mouth he realized they didn't sound nearly as scary as they felt, "and I want... Well, this is going to sound crazy."

"Want what?"

"I've never said this before in my life and I'm sure that five seconds after you walk out my door, I'm going to kick myself for saying it, but," at this, he took in a breath, "I want to wait."

"Wait?"

"At least until we get to know each other better."

"You want to *wait*." Meredith stepped up to Travis, getting close enough to touch, yet not putting a hand on him. "Why? What are you afraid of?"

"Me? I'm not afraid of anything."

"Bullshit. I've never seen a man run from something so hard in my life." Now she did touch him, dancing a hand up his chest. "I'm just a woman from Indiana. How can I scare you?"

"You..." He started to say "you don't" then realized he'd be lying. She did scare him. Her and everything she came packaged with. "You're the kind of woman who deserves a man who's going to put a ring on your finger."

"I had a man who offered that. I didn't want it." She placed her second hand against his torso and in an instant the heat from her palms transferred onto his skin, as if she'd branded him as hers.

"What about you? What are *you* afraid of?"

He saw the surprise light in her eyes at him turning the tables on her. Her touch faltered and she stepped away, turning toward the windows in his apartment. He had a crappy view out the second floor of his living room, but she seemed to suddenly find the brick facade of the building next door and the metal stairs of the fire escape interesting as hell. "I'm not afraid of anything. Except..."

When she didn't finish the sentence, he came around to the front of her, planting himself between Meredith and the view he'd never cared about until now. For a second, he wished his apartment looked out over the Boston Gardens or a park or something serene and pretty. Anything but stark, hard brick that seemed as cold as his life had been before he met Meredith.

"Except what?"

A corner of her mouth lifted up. "We're a lot alike, aren't we?"

He blinked at the change in direction of the conversation. "Us? How so?"

"We both want to use people without caring about them."

The words hit him like a sucker punch from Mike Tyson. Was that how she saw him?

And was that how he really was?

She let out a gust and twisted away. "You don't want me. I don't even know why I'm here."

"I *do* want you." He touched her shoulder and turned her back toward him. "More than I've wanted anyone."

"Right. I'm just some boring Indiana girl with no experience. I'd probably be a good snooze in bed compared to the women you've been with." She jerked her head away, but not before he saw a shimmer in her eyes.

"Is that what you think?" Travis circled around Meredith, until the two of them stood before the full-length mirror mounted against his wall. She couldn't hide her face from him if she wanted to now. "You're wrong, Meredith."

"Am I?" She jerked off his shirt, the two buttons he'd done up popping off and scattering against the wood floor, clicking and rolling under the bed. "Then why didn't *this* make you want me?"

Then she turned on her heel and strode out of his room, grabbing her clothes and leaving his apartment without even bothering to put them on.

This was why he needed to swear off women. Because he couldn't please them when he was being a jerk and he didn't make them any happier when he was being a gentleman.

What the hell did women want, anyway?

Candace's Leap-Before-You-Look
Coquilles St. Jacques

4 tablespoons butter, divided
1/2 pound mushrooms, diced
2 shallots, chopped
1 tablespoon fresh parsley, chopped
1-1/2 pounds scallops
3/4 cup dry white wine
1-1/2 cups cold water
1/4 teaspoon fennel seeds
Tabasco
3 tablespoons flour
1/4 cup heavy cream
Salt and pepper
Pinch nutmeg
1 cup Swiss cheese, grated

If you're going to make a major, life-changing decision, you need a fancy dish to help you do it. Preheat your broiler. In a saucepan, melt one table-spoon of the butter, adding the shallots, parsley and scallops. Cook for a minute, then add the wine and season. Bring to a boil, just like your great idea to up and run off, then turn it down to a simmer for two minutes— you need a clear head before you leap into a huge decision like that.

Remove the scallops and set aside. Add the water, then the fennel and a couple drops of Tabasco. Cook for a few minutes over high heat, bringing all the flavors together just like you're bringing all your life decisions together into one place.

In a separate pan, melt the remaining butter, add the flour and salt and pepper, then slowly stir in the cooking liquid from the other pan, the cream and the nutmeg. Bring to a boil, then simmer sauce over low heat for five minutes until thickened.

Place the scallops in scallop shells or on a pie plate. Cover with sauce and—yummy, yummy—top with cheese. Broil until it's as gooey and delicious as your new adventure promises to be.

CHAPTER SEVENTEEN

"We set a date!" The squeal of feminine joy rocked through Gift Baskets to Die For on Friday morning, interrupting the preparation of seven thousand orange marmalade thumbprints for the upcoming Halloween on the Harbor festivities.

In the little shop off Atlantic Avenue, cookies always took a back seat to news involving diamonds and men in tuxedoes.

Amid all that happiness, Meredith stood in the kitchen of the shop, deep in cookie dough, and felt something sharp hit her in the chest. She told herself it was only because she'd left Travis Thursday night without looking back and was now stupidly expecting ...

What? A phone call? A hot pursuit?

That wasn't supposed to be the plan. She had intended to love him and leave him. No pain, no heartache.

And especially none of that high school crush waiting by the phone stuff.

Yet her gaze lingered anyway on the cream-colored phone hanging on the wall. She shook herself, went back to the dough, and returned her attention to Maria. Meredith knew all about Dante Del Rosso, the restaurant owner who had won Maria's heart a few months ago. Candace had told Meredith the whole story over lunch yesterday.

"Congratulations!" Candace said, extending a quick hug before pulling the first batch of cookies from the oven. "When?"

"The third Saturday in June."

Candace slid the cookies onto a cookie sheet. "That's wonderful. I'm so happy for you."

Maria smiled. "Thanks."

"Ditto from me," Meredith added, now finished mixing the cookie dough. She dumped the empty bowl into the sink and washed her hands. "I met Dante yesterday morning when he stopped by to order some chocolates for his restaurant. He's quite the guy."

"He'd have to be, for me to choose him," Maria said, grinning. She turned to Candace, a hand on her hip. "Now that we've got a wedding date nailed down, it's your turn, Miss Procrastinator."

"I'm not procrastinating. Exactly."

"Well, what are you waiting for? Michael proposed over a year ago. He'd marry you tomorrow if you'd just put that dress on and find an aisle. Hell, at this point, I think the man wouldn't care if you walked down an alley and married him in a burlap sack."

Candace laughed. "No, I don't think he would. It's just..." She sighed. "I don't want the circus I had the last time I was engaged."

"Then don't have it." Meredith clamped a hand over her mouth. "Sorry. Uninvited opinion. I have a habit of doing that."

"Hey, giving your opinion is one of the few benefits around here. It's even better than our health insurance plan." Maria grinned.

"Meredith, what did you mean when you said, don't have it?" Candace said.

"Well... Why not just run off and get married in Vegas or something? Why have the big to-do?"

"Because—"

"Because other people expect it?" Meredith leaned against the sink and dried her hands on a towel. "That's how I used to be. Then I ran away. More or less."

"Well, we're glad you ran here because you make damned good cookies," Maria said, reaching for one of the thumbprint bases cooling on a wire rack. "Orders are up twenty percent for these."

"You know, you're right," Candace said to Meredith, taking a seat in one of the stools. She put her chin in her hands and thought for a second. "I should just do it. I mean, the wedding is really about Michael and me. If my mother and grandma want to attend a big wedding—"

"They can come to mine," Maria piped in. "Mamma's already invited the entire North End. We're going to have to rent out a concert hall for the reception. Or an airplane hanger." She laughed.

"Then that's what I'm going to do." Candace got to her feet, dusted off her hands on her apron and started putting away the containers of flour and sugar. "Soon as I can get a day off."

Meredith understood that craving for spontaneity and decided she'd help Candace, no matter what it took. "Listen, we have things under control here," Meredith said. "Don't we, Maria?"

"Of course we do. No big orders on the books. Halloween orders are just about all done and filled. I say it's time you got on a plane with that hunk of a man and married him."

"Just run off to Vegas and elope, huh?" Candace's eyes shone with a mixture of excitement and trepidation.

Meredith had felt that herself, just a few days ago when she'd run away from Heavendale to come to Boston for *more*.

And thus far, all her plans had backfired. She refused to dwell on that. There was time to still make those changes, to shed Meredith Shordon, Farm Girl, and turn her into someone who called her own shots, without interference from mothers, brothers ... or anyone else.

"Hey, there's nothing better to cure perpetual planner syndrome than eloping," Maria said, draping an arm over her friend's shoulder. "Not to mention the awesome sex you'll have from all the excitement of doing this on the spur of the moment."

"Michael does like a surprise ..."

"Then give him one he'll never forget." Maria winked. "But be sure to get a few pictures for those of us left here slaving away in the kitchen."

"I'll do better than that. I'll save you my bouquet."

"Not for me." Maria put up her hands. "I'm practically married already. I think that honor goes to Meredith."

"Whoa. No way. The *last* thing I'm looking for in Boston is a husband."

Maria and Candace exchanged glances. "Funny. That's exactly what we said."

"Where's our spokesmodel?" Larry asked on Friday morning, the minute Travis arrived at work.

Travis poured a cup of coffee from the pot in the break room, taking his time because he had an overwhelming urge to stuff Larry's apricot toupee from last November down his throat and watch him choke on it. "I don't know."

"You can't let her run out on us. We need her for the No-Moo Milk campaign. The president has already approved my ad ideas."

Travis wheeled around. "You ran an ad campaign by him without bringing in Kenny and me?"

Larry shrugged, reaching past Travis to grab two packets of sugar. He tore the tops off and dumped them into his red "Watch Out: Hot Stuff" mug, then stirred his sugar-coffee with a plastic spork. "Couldn't wait around for you two to get on the stick."

"You mean you wanted to get credit before we could get to work today."

Larry took a sip, then gave Travis a little smile. "Early bird gets the worm."

Travis would be willing to bet Larry hadn't been up half the night, unable to sleep because he'd been reliving the afternoon with Meredith and wishing he hadn't had an attack of conscience at the worst possible time. He'd finally fallen asleep sometime after four in the morning, then missed his alarm. Kenny had spent the night at Delia's house and woken Travis when he came by for a shower and a change of clothes before work.

Apparently Delia had forgiven him. Many times over, Kenny was happy to report, which explained the bags under his friend's eyes this morning.

"Doesn't matter anyway," Larry said. "I already got my money shot."

"What do you mean?"

"Hey I didn't get to be a vice president by being an idiot," Larry said, tapping at his peachy wig. "I set up a photographer inside the control room."

The control room sat above everything and oversaw the testing room. It had the one window into the room that wasn't a one-way mirror. "You did what?"

"I took a few photos." Larry leaned forward, his grin now a leer. 'That girl's a looker. Especially when you're looking down at her, if you know what I mean."

"Larry, you're an asshole."

He wagged the spork at him. "Careful, this asshole's your boss."

Travis laid his cup on the counter. "You know, I really don't give a shit. You have stooped to a new low here. I can't believe you'd do this."

"You're just jealous that you didn't think of it."

"I'm not that much of a jerk."

"Oh yeah? I've seen you and Kenny running out of here for the bar of the day and the woman of the night. You guys are the jerks, not me."

Travis looked at Larry, his paunch extending over his black leather belt and his tan permanent press pants. His bare left hand gripped the "Watch Out: Hot Stuff" mug and his right hand clenched in a fist, as if he had to hammer his point home.

Travis knew who was the jealous one in the eight-by-four break room.

He bit his temper back. Larry couldn't do anything with the pictures. "It's against the law to use her image without her permission," Travis said.

Larry draped his right arm over Travis's shoulders. It felt a lot like he imagined an octopus would if it grabbed him in the ocean and tried to drag him to the depths for an appetizer. "That's where you come in. You're going to convince her to sign off on the pictures of her dunking cookies and drinking No-Moo."

"No. I won't do it."

"Oh, you will. Because I have a trump card."

"You have nothing on me."

"Not on you." Larry let the words hang there until Travis connected the dots.

"My brother."

"Who I hear is getting married soon and needs his job." Larry removed his arm and went back to stirring his coffee. "He's applying for a mortgage, did you know that? I'd hate to see him get fired right when he's trying to buy a house for the little lady."

And then there was Kenny, who'd asked Travis not to mess things up at work because he needed the money, too. To pay for a marriage gone bad, instead of one to come.

Two people counting on him. When had this come about? Travis, the man who prided himself on never maintaining a commitment, suddenly had them springing up like weeds.

He looked at Larry, circling that "Watch Out: Hot Stuff" mug with the spork, a contented cat-who-had-the-mouse-in-a-corner grin on his face and decided this wasn't the end of the story. Larry might have the upper hand now, but he wouldn't maintain it.

Travis might suck at commitment but he was damned good at his job. And he had a plan.

Meredith's All-Hell's-Breaking-Loose Lobster Fra Diablo

2 tablespoons olive oil
1 lobster
1/4 teaspoon flour
6 cloves garlic, chopped
14-ounce can plum tomatoes
1/4 cup white wine
1 teaspoon crushed red pepper
1/2 cup fresh basil, chopped
1/4 teaspoon salt
1/4 teaspoon pepper
8 ounces linguine, cooked and drained

Just when you think you've got things under control, along comes a hearse and a tape measure to tell you that you don't. You have two options: run like hell or have some lobster. Me, I opt for the second one. It's easier to make decisions on a full stomach.

Start by heating the olive oil in a large saucepan. Split the lobster lengthwise, cut off the claws and remove the roe. Dust the lobster meat with flour, then put the claws and lobster, meat side down, into the hot oil. Mmm ... Can you smell the temptation already? Oh yeah, this is the way to solve your problems.

Cook on each side for three minutes or so, then add the garlic and sauté for a minute or two. Keep going, you've got more to put in the mix—the more the merrier, right? At least, that's what your mother thinks.

Next add the tomatoes, wine and red pepper. Let all these simmer, covered, until the flavors are blended and you've managed to bring land and sea together (it's a lot easier than getting your family to agree with you). Add the seasonings, give it a stir, then serve on a bed of linguine, being sure to arrange the lobster nicely.

Because if you can't get a dead lobster to cooperate, how do you expect to take control with those people who keep showing up to ruin your life?

CHAPTER EIGHTEEN

The hearse slowed to a stop in front of Gift Baskets to Die For. It was just after lunch on Friday and Candace had already left, bound for Vegas and wedded bliss, leaving the shop in Maria and Meredith's hands.

Dread sunk to the pit of Meredith's stomach. He was here, like the Grim Reaper himself, to kill any hope she had of a new life.

"Is that—" Maria began to ask.

"Yes," Meredith answered. They were standing in the front part of the shop, cleaning up after a tasting meeting with a potential new client.

Maria leaned forward, shielding her eyes against the bright sun streaming in through the shop's windows. "Who's that with him?"

When the passenger's side door opened, Meredith saw her new life head for the Port-O-Potty in the sky.

Her mother had arrived. Riding shotgun with Meredith's ex-fiancé all the way from Indiana to Massachusetts.

"Hey, it's Momma," Vernon said from the doorway. He and Ray Jr. had taken the T and shown up there shortly before noon, saying they were only there for the cookies and promising not to interfere if Travis came by. Meredith had threatened them with a cold-turkey sugar cutoff if they came near Travis with anything from a hardware store.

She needn't have bothered. Travis still hadn't come by or called. She refused to make the first move—again. She'd debased herself enough by whipping off her shirt and bra and practically prostrating herself at his feet to beg him to make love to her, only to be rebuffed in the end.

That wasn't the behavior of a city girl. Well, it was—but the kind of girl who maintained her office hours on a street corner.

Her entire plan had gone to hell. And now, looking out the window, she saw it was about to get a lot worse.

"Finally, we'll get a decent meal," Ray Jr. said. "I've missed Momma's cooking. 'Specially her pork-n-beans."

"Yeah. Aunt Gloria can't cook nothing." Vernon scowled. "Momma was right. The only thing her sister is the master of is the can opener."

The little bell over the door jingled a warning as the front door opened and Momma entered the shop, wearing a red floral print turtleneck and a long denim jumper—Momma's I-mean-business uniform.

From the neck down at least, the woman entering Gift Baskets looked like Martha Shordon. Above the neckline, she wore a surgical mask a la Michael Jackson.

"That smog out there would kill a cockroach." Once the door had shut behind her, Martha lowered the mask. "Here, I brought you one, too." She dug in her St. John's Bay tote bag and handed Meredith a second one. "Don't you walk around this cancer trap of a city without one. I swear, there's no fresh air here. Not like at home."

"Actually, Indiana has one of the highest smog rates in the country."

Her mother waved a hand of dismissal. "I don't believe that. Why this whole place is gray. Every building is gray. It's like they've got cancer."

"Uh, that's concrete, Momma."

"Just another word for permanent cancer. I know about dirty air. I saw that special on Three Mile Island on the Discovery Channel." She hoisted her mask back into place, muffling her words. "One breath of that and you might as well suck in a carton of Marlboros."

Meredith let out a sigh and laid the surgical mask on the counter without bothering to correct her mother's geography or her facts. Despite her mother's warnings of an impending long and painful death, she wasn't going to go outside looking like Dr. Kevorkian. Clearly, a change of subject was in order. "I can't believe you drove all this way. And with Caleb, too."

Changing subjects to Caleb probably wasn't the best of choices. If he was here, it was for one of two things: a dead body or her.

Since she didn't see any of the former lying around, she was willing to bet the next five winning Megabucks tickets that he was here to get her back.

At the mention of his name, Caleb, starched and stiff in a dark suit, came striding into the store. In one arm, he held a white Styrofoam vase with a spray of crimson roses.

Meredith recognized the type of container, the artful fanned arrangement of the red blooms.

Leftovers. *Eww.*

"We've come to take you back, Meredith," Caleb said.

"You can't play forever, honey," Momma chimed in. "It's time to face the music and be Miss Holstein, like you promised."

Maria stood against the counter, one eyebrow arched like a question mark. "Miss Holstein?" she mouthed.

Meredith gave her a look that said she'd explain later, then turned to face her ex-fiancé and her expectant mother. "I'm not going back. Rebecca needs me."

"I see a helper here," Momma said, gesturing to Maria. "I'm sure they can get by without you. Besides, your cousin didn't say you *had* to come. She told me you volunteered."

Oh, damn. Momma had gotten to Rebecca. She didn't blame Rebecca for caving. Her cousin was, after all, eight months pregnant and at an emotional disadvantage. "I did volunteer," Meredith said. "But I'm not ditching her now."

"You have an obligation, dear. J.C. needs you."

"And so do I," Caleb said. He raised the flowers in a hopeful gesture.

"And we need to get back to Momma's cooking." Vernon nodded. Ray Jr. elbowed him and told him to shush.

"I'm not leaving." Meredith crossed her arms over her chest. She knew if she gave in now, she'd never have another opportunity like this. It would be too easy to get sucked back into the world she'd left. Before she knew it, she'd end up married to Caleb with two kids and a casket for a coffee table. And no life outside of a three-bedroom ranch and baking pies for the spring church picnic.

Momma took a step forward, her eyes seeming as big as pie plates above the white oval of the mask. "But if you don't go home, who's going to ride Big Green?"

"I really don't care."

Silence descended over the shop, heavy and thick as beef stew. Vernon and Ray Jr. shrunk back against the front door, as if they were afraid Momma might lash out at them for substandard kidnapping. Caleb's roses drooped, lowering along with his jaw.

But Momma ...

Momma just stood there, not making a sound or a move for several long seconds. Meredith wished she could pluck the words out of the air and stuff them back down her throat, but knew if she did she'd end up right back in the same place she'd been before she'd left Heavendale.

"Well, you're not the daughter I thought you were," Momma said finally. Then she turned on her espadrilles and walked out of the shop. Like tin soldiers, the men followed behind, piling into the hearse.

After the long black car had pulled away from the curb, Maria draped an arm over Meredith's shoulders and drew her toward the kitchen. "Do you want to talk about it? Or see what we have in the fridge to ease the pain?"

Meredith laughed. "I think I just want to get back to work."

Maria tsk-tsked her. "Girlfriend, there are only three ways to deal with problems. You shop, eat or have sex until you forget what was bothering you."

Meredith pulled a tray of miniature cakes they'd made that morning out of the refrigerator, then grabbed a bag of chocolate buttercream icing. She busied herself with piping frosting onto each little chocolate circle. Her star tip stumbled and she created more of a mess than a delicate treat. "I can't do any of those things. My Visa is maxed out, my appetite is shot and sex is the one thing I can't seem to get no matter how hard I try."

"Whoa. Did you just say what I thought you said? What about Travis?"

"He won't do it."

"Is he *dead?*"

Meredith laughed and the frosting shivered on the end of the metal tip. "No. He's very much alive. But all of a sudden he has these morals and feels like we should wait."

"Wait? For what? The end of the world?"

"He wants my first time to be ... special. With someone I love." Meredith piped another cake, the dark chocolate icing creating a perfect celestial shape on the top.

Maria hesitated in putting the next sheet of cakes in front of Meredith. "Did you say 'first time'?"

"Yeah." She cringed. God, why did saying that sound like the equivalent of announcing she had a bad case of leprosy?

"What about Caleb? I thought he used to be your fiancé. Didn't you two ever ... ?"

"He wanted to, but in the hearse." Meredith shuddered. *That* had been the last straw.

"In the hearse?" Maria shuddered. "With or without an audience?"

"I never asked. I've known Caleb all my life and I thought I loved him, but when it came down to it, I just... couldn't. In a hearse or not, it didn't matter."

"He didn't ring your bells, huh?"

Meredith snorted. "He didn't even know where they were."

Maria laughed, a hearty, deep sound that came from far within her. "What about Travis?"

"Oh, he knows where the bells are," Meredith said with a sigh. She laid the piping bag down on the counter. "If I could only get him naked and onto a flat surface, I'd be all set."

Maria pushed the second tray over to Meredith. "What if. . .just for chuckles, you tried it his way?"

"What do you mean?"

"Fall in love." Maria wagged her left hand, showing Meredith the diamond engagement ring from Dante.

"I'm only here for a few weeks." A knot twisted itself around and around in her stomach.

"Sometimes it doesn't take long." A small, secret smile stole over Maria's face, as if she knew something special only to her.

As the shimmer of emotions washed over Maria's features, a stab of envy rushed through Meredith and for a fleeting second, she wondered if maybe she was wrong. Had Maria and Dante found that elusive feeling Meredith had read about in books but never believed *really* existed?

The same kind of love she had told herself she didn't need—or want. Because to Meredith, having it meant ending up in the exact prison she'd just escaped. The one that came with a ranch house and someone else's expectations, always waiting for her.

"Falling in love isn't as bad as it looks," Maria said, as if she'd read Meredith's mind.

Meredith turned away, reaching for the piping bag and busying herself with creating perfect stars instead of thinking about how happy Maria looked and how she'd never had that feeling herself, not in the three years she'd dated Caleb or any of the years before or the months since. Looking for it with Travis was ridiculous anyway. He'd made it abundantly clear he was a man who had zero interest in a long-term commitment.

Which was exactly why she wanted him.

"I'm not here to fall in love," she repeated.

"Then what *are* you here for?" Maria asked gently.

"Change. I want my life to be different than what it was all planned out to be from the minute I was born. I want... more."

"Nothing makes everything change more than love. And it's a good kind of change, Meredith. It only adds, it doesn't take away."

Meredith went on piping, ignoring Maria's words. Falling in love wasn't in her plans. If anything, it would ruin everything and send her right back to where she'd been before—engaged, tied down and headed for a life of ant-ridden town picnics and bean-dish-recipe exchanges on the church steps, and everyone telling her how to act, dress and behave.

If Travis wasn't going to keep his promise, then she'd find another man who would.

With that thought, the star beneath her tip crumbled into a sad mess of blotchy chocolate frosting.

Momma's Home-is-Only-a-Moo-Away Tuna Melt

2 6-ounce cans tuna, drained
2 tablespoons onion, chopped
2 tablespoons celery, chopped
1/2 cup mayonnaise
Salt and pepper
4 slices American cheese
8 slices good-old white bread, toasted
2 tablespoons butter

All you need is one of Momma's tuna melts and before you know it, you'll be back where you belong. Mix up the tuna, mayo, onion, celery and a little salt and pepper in a bowl. Spread on one slice of bread, top with the cheese and finish your sandwich with the other slice.

You can put these in a fancy toaster oven to brown them up if you want, but Momma does it the home-cooked way, with a little butter in a pan.

A tuna melt has everything you need in one place, same as home does. No need to go halfway around the country looking for anything more. Remember that, and you'll be just fine.

CHAPTER NINETEEN

On Monday morning, Momma was back, a determined set to her face—what Meredith could see of it—and no hint of their earlier argument in her eyes.

That meant trouble. When Momma ignored an argument instead of offering her hundred-dollar lecture, that meant she'd decided to utilize guerrilla tactics and would try to outflank her daughter with a surprise maneuver.

Momma gave Meredith's floral A-line skirt and red flutter-sleeve top a passing—but clearly disapproving—glance, then reached in her purse for a small metal object. There was a metal *vrrp* sound and suddenly Meredith found herself surrounded by numbers. "What—Hey! No! Stop measuring me!"

"I just want to make sure it's going to fit."

Oh no. Momma had gone to real extremes now. It explained Caleb's presence, and the hearse.

Meredith was being measured for a casket.

Momma wrapped the tape around Meredith's hips, then bit her lip. "Hmmm. I think we'll need to take in the udders a little."

Oh no. Momma wasn't measuring her for a casket. Her intentions were much worse.

"I am *not* going home to be Miss Holstein. Not right now."

"I knew you'd resist," her mother said. "You always were my defiant child. Must have been all those jalapeno poppers I ate when I was pregnant with you. Got my insides all in a twist and twisted up your brain cells, too."

Momma's idea of practicing medicine meant blending folklore with suspicions and astrological predictions. Her theories rarely made sense to anyone but herself. Nevertheless, Momma was convinced that too much rain made people bloated and walking backwards under a ladder brought instant death.

"Eating spicy food during your pregnancy didn't make me stubborn."

"Oh yeah? Then why are Vernon and Ray Jr. so sweet? Because I craved M&Ms with them." Momma nodded, as if that settled the issue. She ran the length of white and black tape around her daughter's head, managing to resist Meredith's attempts to bat it off. "At least the top will fit."

"I told you, I can't go home. Rebecca needs me."

"That's why I had J.C. overnight it to Aunt Gloria's." The bell over the door jingled again and Caleb entered, holding a long black-and-white spotted plastic bag. "You read my mind, dear. Thank you."

"I thought Meredith might come around."

"Come around to what?" But the dread in Meredith's stomach gave her the answer she needed.

Caleb unzipped the bag. It fell to the floor, leaving him holding a hanger—and the empty shell of a cow. "To being Miss Holstein." He gave her half a grin, since Caleb never had managed to work himself up to a full smile. "Here in Boston."

Meredith backed up several steps, hands up, warding off the udders, the hooves and the long white snout. "No. No. *No way.*"

"Honey, you competed and you won. You're my little cow girl," Momma said, her voice bursting with pride. "I talked to J.C. and he said if you couldn't be there to ride on Big Green, well, we were to get a picture of you and he'd blow it up to one of those life-size cutouts and affix it right on Big Green's radiator." Momma moved closer, making her case with a bright, Chapstick-adorned smile. "The Lincoln County Dairy Farmers Association got together and thought a little East Coast publicity wouldn't be such a bad thing." She waved out the door, indicating the city behind them. "These people don't drink enough milk. It's why they have such sour personalities."

Meredith shook her head. "What on earth does a lack of milk have to do with that?"

"Too little lactose," Momma said, laying a hand on her arm. "Doc Michaels thinks it can drive people mad. He says it isn't an apple a day you need, it's a quart a day. So the Lincoln County Dairy Farmers thought you could do them a favor and give the milk business a little boost while you're here."

"And just how am I supposed to do that?"

Her mother pressed the cow costume into her arms. "Why, dress up as Miss Holstein and get behind the counter here. People will stop on by, just to see the cow baking cookies and cakes."

Meredith knew if she put one foot into those hooves, she'd lose everything she had worked so hard for since arriving in Massachusetts. There was no way she could do this. Somehow, she had to get rid of Momma, Caleb, Vernon and Ray Jr.

Before they ruined her life forever.

"I can see the objection already in your mind," Momma said. "Damned jalapenos. I told your father I should have dipped 'em in ice cream first, but he said you would be a sweet baby no matter what."

Meredith knew the routine. Here came the guilt trip.

It wouldn't work, though. Not this time. They weren't going to suck her back in, no way.

"You simply have to do this, Meredith. The dairy farmers need you."

Meredith pushed the cow costume back at her mother, the udders flopping between them like little pink legs. "Let Annie Wilson be Miss Holstein. She did a great job last year."

"She can't, dear. She's in the family way," Momma said, lowering her voice to a whisper, just in case there were any of those little teapots around. "Her daddy marched her and Bobby Reynolds down to the courthouse and had them married, under the eyes of God and his best Remington."

Apparently that hernia screening hadn't hurt Bobby Reynolds's functionality.

Her mother looked away, but not before Meredith saw a flicker of worry in her green eyes. Stalwart Martha Shordon rarely betrayed any emotions, even when the family dog had been killed in a tragic La-Z-Boy accident.

But now, her eyes were misty and the cow costume shook in her hands, trembling like a new oak in a fall storm. "The milk business is suffering. Our farm is hurting, too, and whatever you could do..." Her mother's voice trailed off.

The Miss Holstein suit filled the strained space between them.

"But I thought Dad's farm was doing all right when I left," Meredith said.

Momma shrugged. "You know he doesn't like to worry us girls."

"How bad is it?"

"Do you think I'd come all the way out here and risk my life"—Momma pulled the surgical mask back over her mouth—"to bring you the Miss Holstein costume if it wasn't important?"

No, she wouldn't have, that Meredith knew. Martha had never left the town of Heavendale and she hadn't broken out in that much emotion since Ray Jr. graduated with honors in woodshop.

Not to mention, for her father to say anything at all about the farm's finances to her mother meant they had to be in trouble. Ray Shordon, Sr. worked hard, talked little and kept as much inside as he could. He took out his worries on a stubborn fence post or a stack of hay that needed baling. Not on his family.

That left Meredith in the exact same quandary where she'd been a week ago, only now the stakes were higher: live for herself...

Or help the people who loved her.

She stepped forward and took the bovine print out of Momma's hands. "What exactly does J.C. want me to do?"

The pile of crumpled paper beside the small desk in Travis and Kenny's living room nearly reached Travis's knee by the time he was pleased with the results. He sat back in the folding chair, rubbed at the crick in his neck, and studied the ad layout he'd created.

It could work. No. It *would* work.

And would work a hell of a lot better than Larry's crazy plan.

He'd worked all weekend—and avoided calling Meredith. He'd stayed home while Kenny hit the bars. Travis had thought it would be the best way to get Meredith out of his system.

He'd been wrong.

Every time he turned around, his brain resurrected a memory of her being in his apartment on Thursday. A hundred times, he'd reached for the phone, then put it back every time. Calling her would put actions behind his words, leaving him to either sleep with her without regard for the consequences or ...

Take everything to the next level and turn the words "making love" into a reality. That thought pretty much terrified Travis and left him with nightmares about wedding bells that rang "Ding, Dong, the Witch is Dead."

So he'd worked, staying up all of Sunday night, hammering out one ad concept after another.

Kenny wandered into the room, barefoot and sleep-rumpled, the morning's paper under his arm, the pages already out of order, Travis knew.

Before he even hit the toilet in the morning, Kenny grabbed the paper from the front stoop of the building. He said it was the one time of day when he could do some heavy thinking and after that, it was all downhill for his brain.

Kenny stifled a yawn with his fist. "Man, what the hell are you doing?"

"Working. Well, I was. But now I'm done." Travis held up a sheet with crude thumbnail sketches. The graphic designers would come up with something prettier, he was sure, but at least the concept was down on paper.

"You, working? *All night?*"

Travis glanced at the windows and saw, indeed, the first rays of sun beginning to stream through the second-floor apartment windows. "Yeah, I guess so."

"For a guy who says he doesn't want to get involved, I'd say you're involved up to your neck." Kenny drew a finger across his throat and made a cutting sound.

"This isn't about Meredith."

Kenny snorted. "Since when have you ever stayed up all night to work on any of the ad campaigns for Belly-Licious?"

"Never. But—"

"*Exactly.* Usually we bang them out after work on a cocktail napkin. Pretty much the same effort we gave to the Algebra Two problems we scribbled out in homeroom between the Pledge of Allegiance and waiting for Jeanine Cooper to raise her hand so we could see her belly button."

What Kenny said was true. Until now, neither one of them had poured much sweat into anything they'd done at Belly-Licious. Well, that wasn't exactly right They had worked hard on a few campaigns— until it became obvious that Larry would take all the credit, all the perks, and then run with his own stupid ideas at the last minute, tanking the company's latest beverage before it even had a chance to launch.

Still, the president kept Larry on, because Larry was, after all, family and at Belly-Licious, blood was apparently thicker than corporate profits.

Travis bent down and started tossing the crumpled ideas into the circular trash can beside his desk. "I'm tired of Larry's stupid ideas making all of us look bad."

"You mean you don't want Meredith plastered all over the *Globe* and the *Herald* drinking that fake milk crap as our company 'spokesmodel'?"

"That too." He didn't want *anyone* using Meredith. Not Larry, not the company. And especially not himself.

"Hate to tell you this, bud, but you're too late." Kenny withdrew the morning's *Globe* from beneath his arm and tossed it to Travis. "Check out page thirty."

Travis unfolded the paper and flipped through the pages. There, above the fold in a nice bold headline was the announcement of the launch of Belly-Licious's new synthetic milk product.

And right below that, a photo of Meredith, enjoying a glass. *Oh, shit.*

By the time Travis got to the caption, he was considering committing murder one.

"Meredith Shordon, this year's Miss Holstein for the Lincoln County Dairy Farmers Association,'' he read aloud, the anger boiling up in him with each word, "tasted a glass of No-Moo Milk at Belly-Licious Beverage Headquarters and pronounced it a 'delicious' substitute for the real thing."

Kenny took a seat on the edge of the desk. "Did you know she was a cow princess?"

"No. How the hell did Larry know?" Something low and dark began to rumble in Travis's gut. All those hours he'd worked on an idea—an idea he knew was good—and here was Larry, plummeting to new levels as a snake ... and all before breakfast.

"Google, I'm sure." Kenny shrugged. "The man is a sleaze. When he's not wasting his day losing at solitaire, he Googles like he's Blackmail Blackbeard."

Travis had stopped listening to Kenny. He stared at Meredith's unauthorized image but saw only red. He smacked the paper and jerked to his feet. "I can't believe he did this to her!"

"Whoa, cowboy. You sound pissed. And surprised. You know Larry. He does this shit all the time."

"That lousy son of a bitch. I swear, when I get into work today, I'm going to slam him into the wall and knock his goddammed hair off. Then I'll—"

"Hey!" Kenny jumped up, grabbed Travis's shoulder and gave it a shake. "Will you listen to yourself? This is our *boss* you're talking about. The guy who signs our paychecks, remember? Yours. Mine. *Brad's*."

The mention of his brother's name drew Travis back to reality. Travis couldn't afford to be killing Larry, not until Brad was secure with a new job. Hadn't Brad called him late last night to tell him he and Jenny had just been preapproved on that mortgage?

"There has to be a way around this," Travis said, pacing now, trying to burn off the anger before he did something he'd regret. "A retraction. Or something."

"You could buy up every copy of the *Globe* in the country."

"There's an idea."

"Or not, Rockefeller."

Travis circled the room, the paper in his hands, crumpling against his tightened fists. The urge to kill Larry hadn't dissipated.

"You really like her, don't you?" Kenny said.

"Who?" Travis kept walking, wondering if there was a way to plan the perfect murder.

"Miss Holstein."

He looked down at the picture in his hands. Meredith's pert pretty little mouth, poised to take a sip of the white beverage.

Hell, yes. He liked her. A lot. More than he'd liked anyone in a long, long time.

He stopped pacing and sunk into the black leather La-Z-Boy. "Yeah, I do."

Kenny shook his head and dropped onto the sofa. "All those years, wasted."

"What do you mean?"

"I worked so hard on making you into the perfect bachelor. Now you're going Commitment on me." Kenny shrugged. "I guess that's it. Our days of Coors, chicks and carousing are over."

"Hey, I'm not marrying anyone."

"Not yet, you aren't. It's just a matter of time, my friend. Just a matter of time." Kenny shook his head, then his moment of grief passed and he grinned. "Hey, but then the Apartment of Love is all mine."

Travis laughed. "*That's* what this is all about? Don't tell me you're in on this with Larry." He gestured toward the newspaper.

"Nah. I'd never cooperate with Hair Bear on anything. It's against my principles."

"I thought you didn't have any."

"Only ones that screw Larry." Kenny rose and padded across the floor to the kitchen and began making coffee. Travis followed, taking their only two mugs—still dirty from the morning before—and washing them out in the sink.

"Now, if I'm ever going to get my solo love pad," Kenny continued, "and you're ever going to get Larry back without ending up in Cedar Junction, then you need one thing."

"What's that?"

"A plan." Kenny poured the water into the brewer and turned the pot on, then leaned against the counter and crossed his arms over his chest. "Let's come up with one that brings about Larry's destruction and gets you that happy ending you're so damned determined to avoid."

Travis scowled at the mention of a happy ending. All he wanted was revenge right now, not a ring and a preacher. "Sounds to me like you end up winning in the end, not me. You, in your Apartment of Love."

Kenny stood and draped an arm over Travis's shoulders. "Hey, isn't that what friendship's all about?"

Meredith's How-to-Make-a-Fool-of-Yourself Cream of Shrimp Soup

3 tablespoons butter
1 onion, chopped
1 potato, diced
3 tablespoons flour
1 cup dry white wine
1 cup water
2 cups heavy cream
1 tablespoon Worcestershire sauce
Dash of ground nutmeg
Dash of Tabasco
Salt and pepper
2 pounds shrimp, peeled and deveined

Hiding out in the kitchen isn't cowardly. It's smart. You just made a total fool out of yourself, and the only way to fix it is to avoid everything and everyone.

Start by melting the butter and adding the onion and potato. Sauté for two or three minutes, then sprinkle with the flour. Add the wine, water, cream, Worcestershire, spices and all but a couple of the shrimp.

Cover the pot (wishing you could so easily be hidden) and simmer for twenty minutes. When it's done, puree in small batches in a food processor. Watch everything get sucked into a smooth, easy, pretty pink soup and dream of all your problems going into the same blender.

Return it to the pan, reheat and add more seasonings if necessary. Decorate with the reserved shrimp. Eat behind closed curtains and drawn blinds.

Don't answer the phone, the door or *any* of your mother's questions.

CHAPTER TWENTY

L ate Monday morning, Meredith stood in the middle of Government Center, adjusting her udders and trying not to feel like a complete fool. Hundreds of people watched her from the office buildings, while others had come out onto the plaza to gawk. A few were even taking pictures.

Apparently a woman in full cow regalia was not a usual sight in downtown Boston. Perhaps she should have brought Bongo Boy in to provide background music. Then there really would have been something worth seeing.

And heck, she might have even gotten a few tips out of it, too.

"A little to the left, Meredith, so I can get your right hoof in the picture," said the photographer from *Dairy Farmers Monthly.*

She obliged, shifting her body. The faux fur costume weighed at least thirty pounds and was starting to itch. Despite the cool fall weather, she was beginning to sweat, too. They'd already been at it for over an hour and had run through two and a half rolls of film. She prayed the photo shoot would end soon. How many shots did they need of her anyway?

"Okay, now keep those udders still. And smile. Remember, you're *the* Miss Holstein." The flash flared, the camera snapped, and then they repeated the whole thing over again, only this time with her leaning against a small brick pillar: Miss Holstein in Repose.

"Meredith, this time I want you to—" His words were cut off by a sudden flurry of activity coming from the right of them. A half dozen people, some with cameras, a few with notepads, rushed toward her, knocking the photographer from *Dairy Farmers Monthly* to the side.

Geez, these office people are getting out of hand. What do they want now? A hoof-print-graph?

A fuzzy black microphone was thrust into her face, bumping her chin. "Ms. Shordon, is it true you prefer fake milk over the real thing?" A long-legged blonde shouted. "Well, is it?"

"What? I—" Meredith shook her head. What were they talking about?

A slender man with glasses skidded to a stop beside her, along with a second man who was snapping a continuous stream of pictures. "Meredith! Aren't you afraid of what this will do to the dairy business in your home state?"

"Dairy business?" She spun around, looking for answers from the crushing crowd.

But no one explained; they just kept firing the questions at her like human M-60s.

"Why not do the same thing for real milk?"

"Doesn't this violate your agreement to be Miss Holstein for the year?"

"Aren't you worried about what the people back home will think of you?"

She put up her hands—hooves. "Please! Wait! I don't understand what you're talking about."

"The *Globe* this morning," one of the men in the back shouted. "The No-Moo Milk story."

"The *Globe?* What story?"

A second later, someone handed her a newspaper. The stupid hoof gloves made it impossible to grasp the thin pages, so she had to resort to reading it while the reporter held the paper open. The others jostled forward, waiting to write down her exact reaction.

The images hit her like one-two punches. The headline. The photo of herself. And then, the caption, saying essentially that Miss Holstein had given her stamp of approval to a synthetic milk product.

Oh God.

Everything around Meredith began to spin. The mob of reporters felt like a straightjacket, suffocating, scary. She tried to back up, but they were behind her. She stepped to the right, but found several blocking her way. She stepped to the left and they were there, too.

There was no room to move. To breathe. To think.

"What do you think about this, Meredith?"

"What are you going to do about it?"

"What are you going to tell the Lincoln County Dairy Farmers? They're counting on you to help the milk industry, you know."

And then, the one question that hit her like a right hook to the gut. "I understand your family owns a dairy farm. What are you going to tell them about all this?"

Meredith lunged forward, breaking through the crowd, using the hard plastic of her fake hooves to clear a path. The reporters parted slightly, but kept up their dogged pursuit, throwing questions at her retreating form like hunters with their quivers full of arrows.

Meredith did the only thing she could do—she ran. She heard the photographer from *Dairy Farmers Monthly* shouting at her but she didn't stop. Crowds of gawking strangers watched her hurried exodus, but she didn't care.

She ran for the first cab she saw and dove head-first inside the black-and-yellow Checker sedan like Michael Phelps going for gold at the Olympics.

"Let me guess," the driver said, his dark eyes meeting hers in the rearview mirror. "You want to go see the giant Hood Milk Bottle on Congress Street." He shook his head and put the cab in gear. "Some of you milk people are real fanatics."

Travis hadn't worked this hard in ...

Well, hell, his whole life. He suspected, no he knew, he'd gotten by at Belly-Licious on the occasional burst of brains and because he hadn't fought

Larry too much on his evil schemes to take over the beverage world. Larry had rewarded Travis and Kenny by tossing the two of them the occasional name-only promotion. It had been, as Kenny called it, a cake-walk of a job. Sweet and easy.

Until now.

Yet, even though he hadn't slept the night before, he felt renewed, energized. The ad campaign he'd come up with was damned good. Now all he had to do was find a way to sneak it past Larry—who would veto anything that didn't fit his plan to use Meredith— and up to the president's office. Then he'd get it into place fast and find a way to undo the damage done to Meredith by Larry's stupid version of a P.R. campaign.

He had finally given up on his other idea, which, in his defense, had come before he'd had any caffeine. At the time, though, it had seemed mighty smart to call in Ray Jr. and Vernon and their unlimited supply of duct tape.

Kenny had shot that one down, pointing out that an aggravated assault charge might not be the best way to keep his job.

Plus, Travis needed to get to Meredith and he couldn't do that if he was in jail for having Larry beaten up by the bruiser twins. Undoubtedly, she'd seen the debacle in the *Globe* and thought he'd arranged it. Somehow, he'd make her understand. After he found a way to fix this pile of crap—a pile that seemed to be growing faster than the one behind the Budweiser Clydesdales.

From outside his office, Travis heard the first stage of the plan he and Kenny had concocted being put into action. He rose and pressed himself to the wall near his door to listen.

"Hey, Larry," Kenny said, sidling up to their boss. "I'm going out to lunch with Delia and one of her friends. Travis can't make it, which leaves Delia's friend all alone. You want to come along?"

Kenny, as usual, had come up with the perfect bait to get Larry out of the office—a single, attractive woman. With Larry gone, Travis would head down to Jerome Herman's office and convince the president that Larry was not only a danger to himself, but also to the company. All Travis needed was five minutes with Jerome and he'd be able to sell him on the campaign he'd designed for No-Moo.

"I don't know, Kenny," Larry said. "I thought I'd sit by the phone. Wait for the orders for No-Moo to come pouring in. That *Globe* thing was sheer brilliance, I tell ya."

Travis's fist clenched at the sound of smugness in Larry's voice.

"That's what a secretary's for," Kenny said. "Come on, Lar. Delia's friend is a *flight attendant.* You know what that means."

A pause. "No, what?"

"She likes to have a man in every city. You never know. This might be your city."

It took another second before Larry made the connection. Clearly the glue in his hair products was starting to affect his neurons. "You really think she'd want to fly in and see me sometime?"

"If you don't come to lunch with us, you'll never find out." Travis heard the sound of Kenny playing with his keys. "Well, I'm running late, so if you don't want to go ..."

"Let me check my—" Larry cut himself off. "I, ah, have to make a quick stop in the little boy's room."

From his hiding place inside his office, Travis pumped a fist into the air. On the way home today, he'd buy Kenny a case of beer for this. No, make that two cases. His roommate was going to need the double alcohol after spending his lunch hour with the most annoying human being on the planet.

Ten minutes later, Travis was standing outside of Jerome Herman's office, the ad sketches he'd created in his hands. Herman's secretary had also gone to lunch, leaving no additional barriers. Travis knocked on the door, waited for the gruff, "Come in," then entered Larry's cousin's office.

Unlike Larry, Jerome had all his hair, neatly arranged in an artful gray wave across the top of his head. He wore tailored blue suits and pale blue shirts almost every day, usually with a tie in a contrasting dark color like maroon, or deep purple. Today he sported a violet shade.

Lining the shelf behind his head was a bottle of each of the products made by Belly-Licious through the years, some of which had actually done well— like the Kick-Butt Tomato Juice. There were also a few that had not, like the Hibiscus Spinach Juice.

"Travis," Jerome said. "What can I do for you?"

"I'd like to show you some ad campaign ideas for No-Moo Milk." Travis didn't waste any time getting to the point, just in case Larry came back for some hair glue or something.

Jerome shook his head. "Larry's got that under control. I love what he's doing. That coup of snagging Miss Holstein to be our spokesmodel is going to put our product on the map."

"We haven't exactly snagged her, sir."

"What do we mean we haven't? Isn't that her picture I saw in today's *Globe*?"

Travis took in a breath. It was now or never. He wasn't sure how Jerome, who was fiercely loyal to his family members, would react to Travis essentially being a tattletale. But there was no other way to get this idea of using Meredith off the table. "Larry took it without her permission."

Jerome templed his fingers and studied Travis. "This wouldn't be an attempt to undermine your boss, would it? Some weird way of assuring yourself a promotion or a raise or something? Larry assured me everything was on the up and up with this."

"Larry isn't telling you the truth."

A vein throbbed in Jerome's neck. "Are you saying my cousin is lying to me? My own flesh and blood?"

The silence in the room weighed more than the president's cherry desk. If Travis said yes, it would tick off Jerome because the Herman blood loyalty was as sticky as Super Glue. Jerome, for some reason, never saw a single fault in Larry, and if Travis was the one to point them out, he was quite sure the messenger would be the one shot in the end, not the cousin.

"I think Larry is just... misinformed," Travis said. "We can go about this another way."

"No." Jerome shook his head in such a way that left no room for disagreement. Not a hair on his head moved, evidence of a strong hairspray. What was it with these Herman men and their obsession with their hair? "I'm not entertaining any new ideas. I like the Miss Holstein one. We're running with it Larry thinks he might be even be able to get her into her cow outfit and get her in here, drinking some No-Moo."

What the hell was Larry planning on using for leverage? Meredith would never do that. She was probably already pissed that Larry had used her image illegally. The chances of her agreeing to anything more—

And then Travis realized what his plan should be.

Nothing.

Just step back, let Larry fall on his face, then step in with his own ad concept and save the day. Jerome would never see the bad side of his cousin, no matter what Travis said. And with Brad a few weeks away from getting married and buying a house, quitting or in any way shaking the No-Moo boat was not an option.

He'd just sit back and let the boat sink all by itself.

"It might just work," Travis said, plastering a smile on his face as he rose. He tucked the ad sketches under his aim. "I'll get with Larry and work on fleshing out the plan."

"That's what I like about you, Travis. You work so well with Larry. He says he barely has to bring you guys in to meetings with me because you and Kevin are such whizzes behind the scenes. Really run with his ideas and take 'em to the next level." Jerome punched a fist forward as if rah-rahing the team, even if he couldn't get the team members' names right.

Travis's smile started to hurt and he tried to keep his Larry-the-jerk feelings from showing on his face. "That's us, the behind-the-scenes guys."

And that's where he was going to stay, for now, Travis thought as he left Jerome's office. Larry could be front and center so he'd get all the attention when this blew up in his face.

In the meantime, Travis was going to look for a way out for himself, Brad and Kenny, and most important, he would find a way to fix this for Meredith.

She hadn't asked Larry to come along and ruin her life. Somehow, Travis was going to get revenge ... *and* get the girl.

Yeah. *That* should be a piece of cake. Right?

Candace's Time-to-Celebrate Lobster Thermidor

1 whole lobster, boiled
1/4 cup butter
2 shallots, minced
1/4 cup flour
1/4 cup white wine
2 cups milk
1 teaspoon Dijon mustard
Salt and pepper
1/2 cup Parmesan cheese, divided

When you've just made a major life change, it's time to celebrate. Preheat the oven to 375 degrees. Next, start by halving the lobster, removing the claws and all the meat. Save the half-shells and dice the lobster meat, setting it aside to add later.

In a separate pan, heat the butter, cook the shallots, then add the flour and stir until the flour is cooked through. Gradually add the wine and milk, then bring it up to a boil and reduce it to a simmer for about four minutes, until it's thickened. *Voila!* A sauce. You should be proud of your culinary skills. They're almost as good as your *other* skills.

Season with salt and pepper, then fold in the lobster meat and half of the Parmesan. Divide the mixture among the lobster shells and place them on a foil-lined baking sheet. Looks decadent and celebratory already, doesn't it? Believe me, you're going to have something to celebrate yourself soon, too. And if you don't, *create* something.

Sprinkle with the remaining Parmesan, then bake for 8 to 10 minutes, until it's golden brown and as ready to go to the next level as you are.

CHAPTER TWENTY-ONE

"**I** got married!"

The words brought work to a halt inside Gift Basket to Die For early Tuesday morning. Maria and Meredith turned to see Candace hurrying into the kitchen, wearing a white suit and flashing a diamond band above her engagement ring. "I'm officially Mrs. Michael Vogler!"

They rushed to hug her, exchanging cheers and whoops and a few tears. "Did Elvis do the honors?" Maria asked.

"You betcha. You can't get married in Vegas if you don't have Elvis marry you. It wouldn't be right." Candace grinned. "My grandmother cried when I told her I eloped."

"Because she missed your wedding?" Meredith asked.

"No, because I pulled the kind of stunt she's always doing. She told me she was proud of me for ditching the family, the plans and the whole big hullabaloo to do it my way."

"What about Michael?" Maria asked. "How'd he take the whole surprise thing?"

Candace blushed. "Quite well. You can say he thanked me many times over."

"See? I was right," Maria said. "As usual."

Candace grinned and drew her friend into a second hug. Then she turned and gave Meredith an extra one, too. "Two of us down, two to go."

"Hey, I set a date. Meredith hasn't even fallen in love yet," Maria said. "Or have you?"

Meredith got the distinct feeling they were ganging up on her.

"That's a little hard to do, considering I'm not even talking to Travis." She pivoted away and busied herself with wrapping a box of chocolates to add to the large wicker arrangement they were working on— a thank-you to a local plastic surgeon for a facelift gone right.

"Why? What happened?" Candace headed over to the counter, laying her purse on the opposite side and slipping onto one of the bar stools. "When I left, everything seemed to be going so well."

"*This* happened," Maria said, handing her the copy of the *Globe* with the picture of Meredith in it.

"I thought you promised to burn that," Meredith grumbled, stuffing a nose-shaped paperweight into the side of the basket.

"No, I promised to frame it." She grinned.

"Oh. Wow." Candace quirked a brow in Meredith's direction. "*Miss Holstein?*"

"That can be explained by this," Maria said, handing her that morning's *Boston Herald*. The photographers had gotten in several good snaps of the *Dairy Farmers Monthly* photo shoot, clearly using a telephoto lens to do so, and then another half dozen or so of her fleeing form, all beneath the glaring headline of DAIRY FARMERS' HOPES DASHED BY NO-MOO DEFECTION.

"Oh. That's much worse."

"It was even picked up by the Associated Press," Maria said, waving copies of *USA Today* and the *New York Times.* "Our Meredith's famous."

Certainly not the kind of fame she'd been seeking when she came to Boston, Meredith thought. She kept working on the basket, hoping that if she focused enough on the wireless mouse shaped like a breast (complete with a nipple for a wheel), she'd forget all about the debacle at Government Center.

"Is that why your brothers are out there again?" Candace asked.

Meredith nodded. "They've become my de facto bodyguards. The press won't leave me alone."

"Vernon and Ray Jr. work cheap, too," Maria added, handing Meredith a box of candies shaped like collagen-injected lips. "All it costs is a couple dozen cookies a day."

"Well, we better get baking," Candace said, taking off her jacket and rolling up the sleeves of her silky pink blouse. She grabbed an apron off the hook on the wall and a clean bowl for the KitchenAid mixer, then started pulling ingredients out of the cabinets. "We need to feed those men well if they're going to keep you safe."

Meredith let out a sigh, the gold ribbon bow in her hands drooping like a sad little portent of what was to come. "Maybe it would be best if I went back home."

"What, and miss all this fun?" Maria said. "You said you wanted a change. Well, you got one."

"I didn't want one that would destroy everyone's life getting it. My mother has been holding a vigil at Aunt Gloria's house for the ruin I have brought on our family, Aunt Gloria is trying to soothe everyone by making six different kinds of Hamburger Helper for dinner every night and Caleb won't stop re-reading *Romeo and Juliet.*" Meredith stopped working and buried her face in her hands, choking back the tears that had threatened at her for days. "I've ruined everything."

Candace patted her shoulder. "You haven't ruined anything for us."

Relief and a strong sense of kinship washed over Meredith. "Do you mean that? You want me to keep on working here?"

Maria grinned. "Of course we do. You're one of us, like it or not."

Tears stung at Meredith's eyes. "Oh, guys, I like being one of you. Really."

"Good," Candace said. "Now, let's work together on baking some cookies because there's one motto we have here at Gift Baskets."

"What's that?"

"Whatever trouble you get into, we're in it together. It's a lot more fun that way." After a quick group hug, Candace turned and got down some measuring cups, doing her part to help Meredith fix the massive mess her life had become.

For the first time in the past five days, Meredith began to think things might actually work out.

Maybe.

She changed her mind when her mother and Aunt Gloria showed up at the store that afternoon. Candace was out making a delivery; Maria was busy with a sales call, leaving Meredith to face the Shordon wrath alone.

Aunt Gloria strode in first, her white-blond hair poufed out around her face like a sunburst. Despite whatever *Glamour* had said was in for a fall facial palette, her eyes and cheeks were shaded with spring blues and pink. She had on a tight red two-piece sweat suit, with a hoodie and wide leg pants that were only wide from the knees down.

Aunt Gloria—the complete opposite to her younger sister, Martha. If Meredith hadn't seen the family pictures, she wouldn't have been able to pair them up, even in a lineup.

Her mother brought up the rear, clutching a stash of Kleenexes and pressing them to the space above her surgical mask. Momma's denim jumper and pumpkin-print turtleneck were a sign of one thing— she was through with the pity party and about to get serious.

"You have brought ruin upon our town, your father's business and the entire dairy industry," her mother said, giving her daughter the Evil Eye she'd perfected years ago. "How could you?"

"Momma, I told you. I had no idea there would be a photographer there when I went in for the No-Moo tasting. I was just doing a favor for a—" She cut herself off, unable to voice the word "friend." Travis wasn't a friend, especially after all that had happened.

"Your father said it's all over the papers back home. J.C. has about tied himself in fits. Caleb won't come out of the guest bedroom at Aunt Gloria's and the Lincoln County Dairy Farmers Association is talking about taking away your crown."

Aunt Gloria stepped forward, picking up the copy of the *Herald* that Maria had left out earlier. "Martha, I don't see a thing wrong with this."

Momma's face went from red to purple to white, her jaw muscles working up and down. "Have you *seen* the picture?" She slapped the newsprint image of Meredith's fleeing tail.

Aunt Gloria waved her pink manicure in dismissal. "If there's one thing Heavendale can use, it's a little hell to shake things up." She chuckled at her own pun.

Momma gasped. "How could you say that? You grew up there. You know what the town is like."

"Exactly. And that's exactly why I left it."

"You moved because of Mike's promotion," Momma said. "You had to leave."

"Mike *asked* for the transfer, Martha. Do you honestly think I wanted to be penned in by that town my whole life?" She planted her hands on her bright red hips. "Look at me. Do I look like Heavendale material to you?"

A shadow fell over Momma's face but she washed it away by thrusting her chin upward. "You used to."

"I used to be a lot of things. Then I realized I wanted more. And in my mind, there's nothing wrong with that," She turned toward her niece. "I bet all Meredith wants is a little more, too."

Momma looked from her sister to her daughter. Confusion knitted her brows, as if she no longer recognized either one of them. "That little bit more is costing some of us an awful lot," she said, then turned and left, a plain woman in a faded denim jumper who suddenly didn't know her family anymore. Meredith wanted to run after her, to somehow make this right, but didn't know what words could undo the damage she had done.

Vernon and Ray Jr. watched Momma go, then with a glance over their shoulder at Meredith, made their allegiance plain and followed their mother out of the shop. Clearly, Momma's chicken pot pie still held an appeal a baby sister couldn't match.

She'd gone too far. Her plan had backfired. She hadn't become a city girl at all. Instead, she'd become someone her own mother didn't recognize anymore. Tears stung at the back of Meredith's eyes. This wasn't what she'd wanted. Not even close.

A good portion of the blame rested on Larry and Travis's shoulders, but also on her own. She needed to do something—something drastic—to fix this. But the energy she needed to get angry with them, to do something, seemed to have left with her mother.

"Don't worry about it, sweetie," Aunt Gloria said, drawing her into a one-armed hug. "Your mother will come around."

Meredith shook her head. "I don't think so."

"What, you think she doesn't understand you?"

"I don't think we're on the same planet. Since I left Heavendale, I've screwed up every single part of my life."

Aunt Gloria shook her head, smiling. "That's what growth is all about. You screw up until you get it right. Sort of like learning to apply makeup."

Meredith glanced at Aunt Gloria's blue eye shadow and bright pink cheekbones. Perhaps it wasn't a good idea to take advice from someone who wore cerulean below her brows.

"I've got to find a way to fix this," Meredith said. "My dad, the town, everyone's counting on me to make it better. Somehow."

"That's a big load for such small shoulders," Aunt Gloria said, giving Meredith's skinny deltoids a squeeze. "You'd better keep the cow suit on, dear. You're going to need all the extra bulk you can get."

Brad's Settling-Down-Is-a-Piece-of-Crab-Pie

2 tablespoons butter
1/2 red bell pepper, diced
1/2 green bell pepper, diced
2 tablespoons onion, diced
2 cups crabmeat
8 ounces cocktail shrimp
1/2 teaspoon salt
1/2 teaspoon pepper
1 cup milk
1 cup heavy cream
4 eggs
1 cup Parmesan cheese
1/2 teaspoon Worcestershire sauce
1 ready-made pie crust

There's nothing better than coming home to a warm meal, a warm bed and a hot woman. Trust me on this. You might think marriage is as much fun as being a research rat in a maze with no treat at the end, but you're wrong. There are a lot of treats. Some sweeter than others.

This is one of them. If you want your wife to ... well, owe you one, you can make this yourself. It's easy, even for a guy who doesn't cook. Preheat the oven to 350 degrees. Melt the butter in a pan, then cook the peppers and onion until softened. Mix them and everything else in a bowl.

Yeah, major exertion there. This is the kind of cooking you can do during the half-time show. Put the pie crust in the deepest pie plate you can find (this makes a lot of pie. You're a man, you need a lot of pie). Then pour in the mix, put the pie plate on a cookie sheet in case you overdid it, and bake for 35 to 40 minutes.

If you cook dinner *and* do the dishes, she'll be showing her gratitude for days to come. Believe me, marriage has perks that bachelor life can't come close to matching.

Chapter Twenty-Two

"Hey, Travis, wait up." Brad's voice carried down the hall, catching Travis as he was about to exit the Belly-Licious building at the end of the day on Tuesday.

Travis turned and saw his younger brother coming at a slight jog down the carpeted hall. "What?"

"Let me follow you out to talk."

Talk? He and Brad didn't talk. They traded shoulder jabs in the break room, e-mailed each other bawdy jokes, slammed back a few beers after work. But talking? There wasn't much need for that. Never had been. They'd both figured they'd lived through enough hell that a conversation about it was pretty much redundant.

If Brad wanted to talk, though, it had to be important. Travis held the door for Brad to pass through first. The setting sun had cast the parking lot in lengthening shadows. Travis hated fall and the inevitable approach of the killer cold of Massachusetts's winter. For the four hundredth time, he thought of chucking it all and moving to Florida.

Meredith, however, didn't live in Florida.

Then again, she didn't live in Boston either. One of these days she'd go back to Indiana. He'd best remember that before he got in any deeper than he already was.

"I want to talk to you about the wedding," Brad said as they put some distance between themselves and the building. "And why you're so dead set against me getting married."

"I'm not dead set against *you* getting married. Just marriage in general." Travis grinned to take the sting out of his words.

"Just because Dad was a jerk who made marriage into a contact sport doesn't mean we're all going to do that."

"It's not about Dad," Travis said. "I'm simply not a marriage kind of guy."

Brad paused on the pavement by a Lexus. "Bullshit. Don't lie to me, Travis. I lived there, too. I watched him run through women like some people flip channels with a remote." He lowered his voice and took a half step closer. "Hell, you were bound to be affected. You were the older one; you saw more of it."

Travis scowled. "Don't go Dr. Phil on me. I'm an adult. I'm past all that."

"Oh yeah? Then why aren't you going after that pretty girl I saw you drooling over behind Big Ike the other day?"

"Meredith?" Travis started walking again. He reached in his pocket and pulled out his keys, a hint to Brad that he was going home, not continuing the conversation.

He'd forgotten how stubborn Brad was.

Brad fell into step beside Travis as they made their way to the back of the lot, a grin on his face. "If I've ever seen a guy who was falling for a woman, it's you. Every time you looked at her, you were like Steve Irwin with a new crocodile species."

Travis raised the remote on his key ring and clicked it in the direction of his convertible but he was too for away to unlock the car. "You're imagining things."

"And you're"—Brad scooted around the front of Travis and got right in his face—"chicken."

"I am not."

"*Bawk, bawk,*" Brad mocked. "Fall in love, big brother. It won't kill you. Some studies say it will make you live longer."

Travis shook his head and started walking again, skirting Brad's bad imitation of a mother hen. "There are a lot of days when I wish you weren't a scientist."

Brad chuckled. "Come on, you're twenty-nine. It's time to grow up."

"I am grown up."

"Sure you are. That's why you haven't been able to commit to a damned thing except your car. Hell, even your car's a lease." He gestured toward the silver convertible. "Not to mention a bachelor cliché."

"Hey, it was a good deal."

Brad arched a brow at that. "You're on a month-to-month with your apartment and you're a frequent flyer at Rent-A-Center. Then here I am, your baby brother, plunking down money for a Dutch Colonial in Newton."

"A mortgage is a thirty-year chain."

Brad waved a hand at him. "See? That's Dad talking. I'd like to believe you could be different."

"You're nuts."

"Nah, just eternally optimistic. Now stop being such a chicken and go after that woman." He tipped his chin at his older brother. "I dare you."

"What are you, ten?"

"You need someone who can keep you grounded." Brad clapped him on the shoulder, a touch that had the roughness of a brother but edged with the softness of caring.

Something thick filled Travis's throat. He shrugged it off. "You're just jealous I got the looks in the family—"

"And I got the brains."

Travis gave Brad a light jab in the upper shoulder. "Brains or not, I'm not going to fall in love."

"You want to bet?"

"Bet? Now I know you're crazy. You never bet, you Republican, you." They started walking the last few feet, reaching Travis's car a second later.

Regardless, Brad reached into his back pocket and pulled out his wallet. "I bet you a hundred bucks," he said, withdrawing two fifties, "that you fell in love with Meredith Shordon before my wedding."

"That's a bet you're going to lose. And I really hate to take money from a guy who's about to enter prison," Travis said, grinning.

"Hey, it's the kind of cage I want. And it doesn't have bars."

"You've been in that research lab too long, little brother. The fumes are starting to affect your brain. If there's one thing marriage is, it's a prison. For one person or the other." Travis thumbed his remote and unlocked his car doors.

Brad leaned one arm on the roof of convertible, preventing Travis from opening the door. "Do you know why tigers pace in their cages at the zoo?"

"What? What the hell are you talking about?"

"When they first get to the zoo, they think they've got it made. It's like the ultimate bachelor pad. No pressure to be the king of the pride. Or to take care of their women. They get three squares, a bed at night and a few visitors every day. Sounds like heaven. But pretty soon, they start to go crazy because they realize that the cage at the zoo is really fighting their natural instincts. Nature wants that tiger to pursue a female, settle down in a cave and have a few cubs. Not live the life of a sloth."

"Marriage is the cage, Brad, not bachelorhood."

"Uh-huh. And tell me how much you've been pacing lately, big brother." Brad didn't wait for an answer. He grinned and clapped Travis on the shoulder again. "Speaking of feeling constricted, be sure to leave next Wednesday open."

"Why?"

"That's when you're getting fitted for a tux."

Meredith left Gift Baskets after an especially long day at the shop on Tuesday and started walking in the opposite direction of where she'd parked the car she'd borrowed from Rebecca, hoping to avoid any news stalkers who'd been waiting for her.

It was after seven and night had already fallen. The street was quiet, bare. No reporters in sight. Good. Maybe some celebrity had done something stupid today so the media would be off on another trail.

She kept walking, not ready to go to Rebecca's yet. Going to Rebecca's meant facing her mother, her brothers and Caleb, all waiting for her in the house next door. They'd be expecting her to fix this mess. Meredith didn't have a solution. Not for this milk fiasco and not for the mess her life had become.

"I believe I still owe you a lobster."

She pivoted at the sound of Travis's voice. He stood on the sidewalk beside his parked car, dressed in jeans and a light blue T-shirtm topped by a weather-beaten denim jacket. He looked as comfortable as freshly washed linens and for a second, Meredith wanted to curve into the space between his arms and forget the events of the last few days.

Then she remembered who had gotten her into this predicament in the first place.

"I don't want to see you or talk to you," she said. "And I certainly don't want to eat a meal with you." Her stomach grumbled disagreement, though, and voted for lobster. And Travis. Together. Now her own body was turning traitor against her.

"I know you hate me right now, and probably rightly so, but if you'll give me a chance to explain—"

"Explain what? How you tricked me into representing No-Moo? How you helped me ruin my town, my father's livelihood and my relationship with my entire family, all in one day?"

"I had no idea Larry was going to do that." Travis came closer, his features defined by the moonlight. "You have to believe me."

"Why?"

Everything within Meredith told her to back away, to not listen. Yet she remained where she was, her gaze going to his as if an invisible tether controlled her. The connection she'd felt since that first night in the bar strengthened with every step he took.

"Because up until I met you, I wasn't exactly anyone's version of a model citizen." He rubbed the back of his head, a wry grin on his face. "You might not believe it, but you bring out the best in me."

She wanted to believe him, to allow his words to melt the wall in her heart, but she couldn't. Travis had brought her into Belly-Licious. Travis had asked her to do the No-Moo tasting. "Does the best of you involve using your friends to further your career?"

"No. I swear. I had no idea he was going to do that." Travis had moved closer again and now stood only inches from her.

Should she trust him? She had no idea if her instincts about people were good. Until two weeks ago, her entire world consisted of people she'd known all her life.

Clearly, she'd gotten that all wrong, considering most of the Shordon family had stopped talking to her.

"Give me a chance to explain. Five minutes, that's all." He took a step closer, reaching up to cup her chin. "I miss you."

She jerked back, out of his grasp. "You miss me? That's why you haven't called me in five days? You left me to the wolves? Was that part of the plan, too?"

"There was no plan, Meredith, at least not from me."

"I'd like to believe that, Travis. I thought I knew you, but from the start, you haven't done a single thing I expected you to do."

"What's that supposed to mean?"

"You won't sleep with me, but you're perfectly willing to use me in other ways." She took a step closer to him, tilting her chin until she looked him square in the eye. "What exactly do *you* want me for Travis?"

"For more, Meredith. Much more than a tumble in bed."

"Bull. You told me yourself that you're the king of non-commitment. There's no more, Travis. And you wouldn't want it if there were."

"What if I told you I'd changed my mind?"

"I'd say you were looking for a nice spread in the middle of *Boston* magazine."

A shadow washed over his eyes and he took a step back, as if she'd slapped him. Had she gone too far? Could he possibly have been telling the truth?

"I care about you, Meredith, whatever you might think about me. And somehow, I'm going to make all this up to you."

Then he leaned forward, placing a quick, chaste kiss on her lips before turning and walking away.

Leaving her as confused and distracted as a Golden retriever in a tennis ball factory.

Caleb's Ordinary-Isn't-so-Bad
Panfried Fish Fillets

2 pounds cod or other firm fish fillets
1 teaspoon salt
1/8 teaspoon pepper
1 egg
1 tablespoon water
1 cup cornmeal
Butter for frying

You don't always need fancy to be happy. Sometimes, a plain man in a dark suit who always has a Kleenex for you can be just as good. Best of all, he knows how to cook. Think that man in Boston knows how? I don't think so.

Start by sprinkling both sides of the fillets with salt and pepper. Beat the egg and water in a pie plate until blended, then dip the fish in the egg mixture. Coat with the cornmeal, then fry in the butter until brown on both sides and the fish flakes easily with a fork, sort of like your crazy relatives.

See, no need for spices and crazy concoctions. Just ordinary cooking from a regular guy who can handle a hearse with one hand. It's not something you find every day, so before you choose a man, think wisely about who will be there for you now... and in the hereafter.

CHAPTER TWENTY-THREE

When Meredith had been a little girl and gotten lost in the Great Corn Maze at Cecil's farm, she'd gotten hysterical, sure she'd never find her way home again. Her father had pulled her aside, dried her tears with the corner of his worn denim shirt and told her to go back to the place where she last remembered getting lost. "Start from there," he said, "and soon it will all make sense again."

She'd done that, with Ray Sr. following behind, and twenty minutes later, found the right turn to take her out of the green stalks.

When no other answers magically appeared by Wednesday, Meredith had called Caleb, hoping to figure out where she'd gone wrong, what turn she'd made that she could undo and start on the road toward fixing this mess ... and getting Larry Herman and the entire staff at Belly-Licious to stay out of her life.

It was nine in the morning and she and Caleb were sitting at the small glass table in the front portion of the gift shop. Maria and Candace were busy out back processing new orders, leaving them alone.

Caleb had on a cream-colored shirt and dark blue suit today, a definite sign he was beginning to come out of his Shakespearean depression.

"Is it really over?" he asked, lacing his fingers together.

"I told you back in Heavendale that it was."

"I thought you were kidding. I mean, Mr. Galloway was in the back and the roses can be pretty overwhelming. I thought maybe you weren't thinking straight."

"Caleb, we're not going to work out, you know that. I'm sorry." She reached for his hand, but he pulled it away, tucking both of them under the table. "Tell me something."

"What?"

Meredith traced a circle on the glass, then looked up at him. "Have you ever wanted to pin me up against the wall, jerk up my skirt and just... do it?"

His eyes widened with horror. "No!"

"See? That's why we shouldn't be together."

"Are you saying that because I don't want to have kinky *Kama Sutra* sex with you, you won't marry me?"

"Caleb, we never had any sex, never mind tried anything from the *Kama Sutra*. And why do you think that is?"

"Because we were waiting for our wedding night."

"We weren't waiting for anything. Except maybe a bolt of lighting to come along and make us ... different."

He shook his head. "Why do you want to be different? Everything was perfect the way it was."

"Everything was boring. Dull. Predictable as the size of Mary Lou Kendall's spring calves. I don't want that for my life."

"What if I do?" Caleb laid his hands flat on the table. His nails, as always were trim and perfect. He had always been a man who cared about tiny details. It was part of what made him a success with funerals... and what drove Meredith nuts.

"You need to find someone who loves the kind of life you do," she said. "Me, I want more. I want to feel that electric need for someone, I want to wake up in the morning and know that I did something today that I didn't do yesterday. And I want to look back in thirty years and feel like I lived my life when I was younger."

"I don't get it. You wake up every day in Heavendale. You live your life. I mean, if you hate your job at Petey's, go work at Louie's Grille."

She nearly slammed her hands on the table. "I don't want Petey's or Louie's! Or kissing in the back of the hearse while a dead body looks on."

"Uh, Meredith, dead people don't look on."

She bit back a scream of frustration at his correction. "I want more, Caleb. I want a life. And I found that here."

"With *him*?"

It wasn't even a question. She heard the sound of hurt in Caleb's voice and wondered if she was doing the right thing. He'd driven all this way to see her, to talk some sense into her. Because he loved her? Or because he *thought* he loved her?

"We've known each other all our lives," she said. Once, she'd thought that was reason enough to marry him.

He nodded. "I remember sitting next to you in Miss Henneman's class, listening to *Brown Bear, Brown Bear.* You wore that pink dress with those white shoes. You were ... an angel."

"And maybe that's the problem," she said.

"How is that a problem?"

"You see me as an angel. Not a sex object or a wife or a partner. An angel. Too perfect to spoil."

"So, you think I should date a woman that I only want to have mad, passionate sex with and forget about keeping her on a pedestal and treating her like gold?"

"Well, yeah." She smiled and reached again for his hand. This time, he let her take it, but she could feel the reservation in his touch. "Treating her right is always a good idea, but you should find that someone you want to put up against the wall. Trust me, you'll be a lot happier for it."

"I am happy."

Caleb's face was as dour as ever, a look he'd perfected in the years he'd been in the funeral business, all of it shadowed by the dark suit and perfectly brushed wave of his black hair. "Live a little, Caleb. Stop being as dead as the people in your back room."

He bristled and jerked back from the table and began to stand up. After a moment, the flush of anger faded from his face and he lowered himself back into the seat. "What... What does that kind of sex feel like?"

"The against the wall kind?"

"Yeah." A small, embarrassed grin crossed his lips. She knew it was a question he'd never asked anyone. If they hadn't known each other since the days they'd been wearing knee socks, she doubted he could have asked even her.

"I wouldn't know, I haven't done it yet." She shrugged, a mirror image to Caleb's smile on her own lips. "But I've thought about it a lot."

'You haven't had sex with him yet?" His brows arched in surprise.

"No. He thinks we should wait until we're in love."

Caleb's grin widened into the first genuine smile she'd seen on him in a long time. "Smart man to trap you with your own plan."

Then he said goodbye, wished her well and walked out of the shop, heading for his hearse. He still wore the dark pants and black dress shoes, but she'd swear there was a lighter step in his walk.

On his Wednesday drive to work, Travis nearly caused a five-car pileup when he spied a twelve-foot high image of Meredith in her Miss Holstein costume holding a glass of No-Moo, appearing to enjoy the synthetic beverage, for every car on 93 South to see.

Clearly, Larry had ramped up the stakes in the last twenty-four hours. The man was a menace. Travis was going to make sure he went down.

Him and his hair pieces.

Larry pounced on Travis as soon as he walked into the building. "Did you see our giant ad this morning? What'd you think of the moving arm? Wasn't that brilliant?" Larry chuckled. "Sometimes I scare myself with my ideas. Imagine if I were president of the You-nited States."

Travis didn't let his brain travel down that Armageddon path. "The whole damned thing is illegal, Larry. You can't use Meredith's image without her permission."

"I know. That makes it perfect. She'll sue us, we'll get tons of media coverage for the lawsuit, which will just get people talking more about No-Moo."

Larry's logic would confuse Einstein. "Does your cousin know you're risking a multimillion dollar lawsuit to promote a crappy drink no one is ever going to buy?"

"Oh, they're going to buy it. As long as Miss Holstein is telling them it's the drink to have. And I've got a whole lot more pictures where those came from that can be used to give this campaign some *bam!*"

Travis's hand crushed around the Styrofoam cup, ready to pulverize the little bit of coffee he held—instead of Larry's face. He opened his mouth to say he quit when he saw Brad passing by the door. Brad made the outline of a house with his hands, then a thumbs-up, indicating the mortgage had been approved.

Travis drew in a breath that stopped him from committing a felony, then chucked the rest of his coffee into the trash. "There are other ways to sell a product."

"Sounds like you don't support my little idea." Larry shrugged. "Fine with me. I don't need you. Or Kenny. Or Brad. All you three do is drag me down anyway."

He thought of Brad's thumbs-up, the sheer joy on his baby brother's face whenever he talked about getting married. Travis wouldn't be up for Best Man of the Year if he got Brad fired a few weeks before his wedding.

There had to be a way to dump this crazy ad campaign *and* save Brad's job. But what? Travis's mind raced through possibilities, and came up empty.

Aw, hell. Why did he have to go and grow principles at this late stage in his life? All they did was screw up what had been a very cushy existence.

Travis looked at Larry's grinning face as his boss opened up a folder and started blabbing about a layout for a print campaign featuring another doctored photo of Meredith.

The image of her raised a challenge inside him. She had taken a leap of faith, throwing away everything she knew to come to Boston and try for something different. She'd paid a hell of a price so far, one she hadn't asked for.

He'd be damned if he was going to let her pay it on her own.

It was time to call in Vernon and Ray Jr.

Rebecca's The-Right-Answers-Are-Right-There Seafood Newburg

3 tablespoons butter
8 ounces mushrooms, sliced
1/2 cup scallions
3 tablespoons flour
2 cups milk
1/4 cup sherry
1 tablespoon lemon juice
1/2 teaspoon salt
1/8 teaspoon paprika
8 ounces haddock, cut into one-inch pieces
6 ounces crabmeat
6 ounces scallops

Sometimes, when you're looking for the answer to what to do, it's best to just do something simple. Clear your mind and the solution will come to you. Start by melting the butter, then cooking the mushrooms and scallions. Add the flour and cook for one minute, then gradually stir in the milk.

Add the sherry, lemon juice and spices. If needed, season with salt and pepper. Simmer for five minutes ... long enough to start looking inside yourself for a few of the answers to the questions you keep asking everyone else. Add the seafood, then cook another few minutes, until all is done.

Serve on toast points and eat enough to fill your belly and help you find your way from the kitchen to the solution.

CHAPTER TWENTY-FOUR

The next morning, Meredith sat at Rebecca's kitchen table, watching Emily have fun with her oatmeal instead of eating it. The four-year-old clearly found a lot more enjoyment in tossing clumps at the beagle begging by her feet than in getting peaches-and-cream flavor into her mouth.

Rebecca sighed, watching the mess from her place in the opposite chair, a wet rag in her hand. "Em, are you sure you don't want any help?"

"Nope. Do it by myself," Emily said, beaming around the crust of Quaker on her face. "I'm a big girl."

Rebecca chuckled. "That you are. And determined, too."

Meredith laughed, getting to her feet and placing her empty coffee cup in the sink. "Wonder where she gets that from, huh?"

"Are you saying determination is a family trait?" Rebecca's eyes twinkled.

"No, making a mess is." Meredith started the dishes, rinsing the breakfast bowls and cups, then loading them into the dishwasher. "Did you hear about the billboard that Belly-Licious put up? They even showed it on Channel Seven last night. Me in my cow costume grinning over a glass of that chemical milk."

She was glad Caleb had gone back to Indiana last night. It had made for fewer people sobbing over Aunt Gloria's blueberry crumble dessert yesterday evening.

Rebecca turned in the chair, draping an arm over the back. "You know you can sue over this, don't you? No one can use your image without your permission."

"Suing would bring more attention to the whole thing. I want it to go away."

Rebecca put her feet up in the empty chair across from her. "I wonder..."

"Wonder what?" Meredith asked, shutting the dishwasher and turning around.

"If Belly-Licious did this on purpose."

"Of course they did. They set me up from the beginning. Had a photographer tucked away somewhere and everything."

"Yeah, but they had to know using your image is against the law. Maybe ... they *want* you to sue."

"Want me to sue? That's insane."

"No. That's called free publicity."

It took a minute for the meaning to sink in. Then Meredith realized that had likely been the company's plan from the start. Tick her off, get her into court and make the case drag on and on in the papers, giving No-Moo Milk a continual public relations boost. Though, that was a stupid plan in Meredith's opinion. One that could easily backfire—assuming it was even big enough news to hit the papers again— and make the company and the beverage look bad.

She grabbed a sponge and began wiping off the counters. "Well, that's one thing I've done right. I didn't sue and make them famous."

"So, if you aren't going to take them to court, what *are* you going to do?"

Meredith tossed the sponge into the dishwasher and took the last empty seat at the round table. "I don't know. I guess I've been too busy wallowing in my pity party."

"*You* don't have a plan for revenge? Is this the same girl who tied Andrew McConnell's shoelaces to his desk because he snapped your training bra strap?"

Meredith laughed. "That was a lot of years ago. And it was just a bra strap."

"Yeah, but now it's *just* your family and all of Heavendale, not to mention your life, too."

Rebecca was right. Meredith had been letting all these days go by, playing woe-is-me and not doing a damned thing about the situation. That wasn't the kind of person she wanted to be—or even used to be, for heaven's sake. Where had the old Meredith gone?

She didn't roll over and play dead. She got right up and chased the bad dogs out of her yard.

She'd tried to go back to the beginning, to become that old Meredith. It wasn't possible. And besides, it wasn't what she wanted. It wouldn't change the damage that had been done by Belly-Licious, it wouldn't make her happy and it wouldn't mend the tear in her relationship with her family.

She'd been stupid. She didn't need to go back. She needed to move forward. In a *big* way—with a Humvee and thirty-three-inch tires, not some tiny Honda that couldn't get out of the big boys' way.

Meredith rose, feeling invigorated for the first time in days. "You know, you're right. All I've done is worry about what can't be undone, rather than focusing on what I *can* do."

"To get revenge." Rebecca grinned.

"Exactly."

"And Travis, what about him?"

That thought brought Meredith back down into the chair. *Travis.*

He'd left messages, sometimes several a day, and sent flowers, but she'd ignored them all, resisting the urge to call him back. He, like everyone else in her life, wanted something from her that she couldn't give right now.

And yet, she missed him, more than she wanted to admit. Ever since he'd come by, offering a lobster and an apology, she'd been tempted to see him.

If she did, that would just throw another monkey wrench into her new life. She didn't want a relationship. She just wanted sex and a kiss good-bye at the end.

But that plan hadn't worked any better than the others. She *missed* him, damnit, as much as she didn't want to. And trying to go back to the beginning, to when she didn't care, was about as easy as giving a cat a bath in a fishbowl.

"I don't know," Meredith said. "I can't quite believe he didn't have anything to do with this."

That, Meredith knew, was more of an excuse than anything else. Deep down inside, she was sure Travis was the man she'd met in the bar, the man who'd help someone because he was a nice person, not for any personal gain. And yet...

Travis had been the one to invite her to Belly-Licious to try No-Moo Milk. He *must* have known about the photographer and the ad campaign. He had to be in on this with Larry.

Still, a part of Meredith—probably the part she'd so desperately wanted to leave back on the farm— wanted to believe differently, like Virginia with Santa Claus.

"Impossible," Meredith muttered. "I'm good at creating an impossible situation."

Rebecca reached forward to cover Meredith's hand with her own but before she could speak, Emily dumped the rest of her oatmeal on the floor for the family beagle. "Done!" the little girl said.

"Oh, Em," Rebecca sighed. "Keep your oatmeal to yourself, hon."

Meredith took the rag from Rebecca's hands, waving off her cousin's protest that bed rest didn't prevent her from cleaning off her four-year-old's face. "You should be in bed, too, you know, not sitting up. You keep breaking the rules and I'll have to call in Momma."

Rebecca gave a look of mock horror. "You wouldn't."

"I would. Now, I'll walk Em to preschool before I go to work. Aunt Gloria should be by later to check up on you, see if you need anything."

"What I need is for you to do something interesting and reckless." Rebecca wagged a finger at her. "I'm sick of living vicariously through Oprah reruns."

Meredith took a final swipe around Emily's face and paused. Rebecca was right. A surge of energy rushed through her veins. She felt like herself again— like the old Meredith, only with an added degree of strength.

She *could* do something about this besides moan over it. Something a lot bigger, and would get a lot more attention, than tying the class bully's shoelaces to a desk. "You're right. It's time I took the bull by the horns and wrestled him—and his hairpiece— right down to the ground."

Ray Jr.'s It's-Only-Fun-if-You're-Getting-Into-Trouble Crab Dip

8 ounces crab meat
8 ounces cream cheese, softened
1/2 cup pepper jack cheese
1/4 cup Parmesan cheese
1 tablespoon onion, minced
3 tablespoons Worcestershire sauce
2 tablespoons fresh lemon juice
1/2 teaspoon dry mustard
Dash of Tabasco
Salt and pepper

There's no sense living if you can't live by your own rules. Don't be shy now, get in the game and give 'em hell. Use good glue products when you do it, too. The results will be long-lasting. Know what I mean?

Before you head out to the hardware store with your list for fun in hand, try this little dip on for size. Preheat the oven to 325 degrees. Mix everything in a casserole dish (hey, I like my food simple and hot), then pop it in the oven for 40 minutes.

Dip whatever the hell you want in it. Most people get all fancy and do crackers. Me, I figure that's what God made fingers for.

CHAPTER TWENTY-FIVE

"I don't know, Ray Jr. Think we can trust him?" Vernon said, eyeing Travis, working thirty feet below them.

Ray Jr. grunted under the weight on his shoulders and glared at his younger brother, who had let go of his end. "It's a little late for that, don't you think? We're up here, he's down there. I'd say we trust him already."

"Yeah, but I think we're the ones having all the fun." Vernon grinned and tugged on the harness he had strapped around his hips and waist, then attached to a lifeline cable that ran along the length of the twelve by twenty-four feet sign.

In their hands were thirty poster sheets, to be assembled like a jigsaw puzzle over the image of Meredith. They were working in the middle of the night, gluing the new image into place before the morning commuters started their day's ride into the city.

A little subterfuge, just the kind of thing Ray Jr. liked. Best of all, he was helping to pay back what those bastards at Belly-Licious had done to his little sister. If he could have, he would have charged into the company's offices with Cecil's shotgun. That would have ended their plan to use Meredith for their kill-milk scheme.

He'd been all loaded up with buckshot and ready to go when Travis had stopped him, saying they took assault with a deadly weapon pretty damned serious in Massachusetts.

Liberals. Hell, how was he supposed to get any justice with those rules?

"Hey, this stuff works great," Vernon said, pasting another sheet into place, smoothing it out with a roller. "Might even beat out duct tape."

Ray Jr. raised the bucket of glue. "Think we can sneak a gallon into Cecil's truck and take some back home?"

"Oh, the trouble we could get into with this," Vernon said.

"You can say that again."

"Oh, the—"

"I didn't mean literally." Ray Jr. scowled. "Now hold this last piece up. There. That's it. We're done."

The two of them leaned back, but couldn't see much of their handiwork from the small catwalk surrounding the billboard. "That'll teach that Larry bastard to mess with our sister."

"Yep. And if he does it again, we'll glue *him* up here."

Ray Jr. chuckled. "Now there's an idea."

After a few special finishing touches, they collected their supplies, then climbed down the ladder to the ground. "All set," Ray Jr. told Travis. "You done on your end?"

"Yep. All wired and ready to go."

"Let's light her up then." Ray Jr. stepped back so he could get the full effect.

Travis flicked a switch at the base of the pole. Above them, the total destruction of Larry Herman came to life, complete with blazing lights and animatronics.

"Now *that's* revenge," Ray Jr. said. "You are one creative guy, Travis. Glad I'm not on your bad side."

Travis chuckled. "Thanks, guys. I appreciate the help."

"Just so you know, we're only doing this for Meredith," Vernon said, giving Travis a glare that said the younger Shordon had yet to be won over by Campbell.

Travis held out two fifty-dollar bills. Vernon snatched them up and stuffed them into the back pocket of his Levi's. "Well, for that, too," he admitted.

"Thanks again," Travis said. "I'll take care of things from here. Pick up the tools, return the supplies." He put out a hand for the leftover gallon of glue.

Ray Jr. didn't give up the wonder product quite yet. Instead, he shuffled a bit on his feet. Finally, he sucked in a breath and let out the words he hated the most to say. "I, ah, want to apologize."

"For what?"

"Calling you a city boy. You're not so bad. And if you want to marry Meredith, well, Vernon and I—"

he gave Vernon an elbow that caused his younger brother to grunt out an agreement, "—well, we'd stand up for you."

Travis raised a brow. "You mean be my ushers?"

"Hell no!" Ray Jr. scoffed. "We hate those damned penguin suits. I meant we'd stop drinking early enough at the bachelor party to stay standing. Keep you from making a fool of yourself with the strippers."

"Thanks ... I, ah, think."

Ray Jr. gave Travis a clap on the shoulder that caused the other man to stumble a bit. What this city man needed was a good piece of steak, at least a 22-ouncer, and a week on the farm to toughen him up. "Nothing to it."

"Let me know if you guys ever need a favor in return. You helped me, and Meredith, out tonight." Travis gestured toward the billboard, now flashing its message to the highway of passing drivers.

"Actually," Ray Jr. began. "There is one thing ..." Might as well take advantage of the situation. He gave Travis a devilish grin and clutched the gallon of glue to his chest. "If it's okay with you, I'd like to keep this. We got plans for this glue."

"Plans?"

"You could call it a competitive edge." Ray Jr. exchanged a glance with Vernon. His brother gave him a smirk that said he was sharing the same devious thought. "This year, Bobby Reynolds ain't going to be tractor pull champion. By the time we're done, he'll be lucky to pull out of the restroom."

Aunt Gloria's Mistakes-Can-Be-Baked-Away Fish Cakes

1 pound haddock fillet, cooked
1 pound potatoes, cooked and mashed
2 tablespoons butter
2 tablespoons onion, chopped
Juice of 1/2 lemon
1 tablespoon flour
1 egg, slightly beaten
1-1/4 cups breadcrumbs
4 tablespoons vegetable oil
Salt and pepper

Listen to your Aunt Gloria, who has made a mistake or two in her life. All you need to do is get the injured parties in the kitchen. Almost anything you've done wrong can be fixed over a hot stove.

Melt the butter in a pan and cook the onion. Flake the haddock into a bowl (making sure there are no bones about it, *ha ha*, a little humor there). Add the potato and butter mixture, then mix well. Stir in the lemon juice, then season with salt and pepper. Meanwhile, heat the oil in a frying pan.

Now's the time to get those hands working and take out any frustrations. Form eight little balls, then flatten them into a round shape. Dip each fish cake into the flour, then the egg, then the breadcrumbs. Fry them until they're golden brown all over and you can't see any of your mistakes in forming those patties anymore.

It's just like life. Cook something yummy and bad for your hips (and Lord knows, I have hips) and all your errors just seem to melt away.

Chapter Twenty-Six

"**M**omma, this is never going to work if you don't take that thing off," Meredith said, trying to keep Bessie still with one hand and pour milk with the other. It was early Wednesday morning and once again, Meredith was standing in a public place in her cow costume, only this time with the real version beside her.

Public humiliation, it seemed, had become her newest hobby.

"But what about the smog?" Momma asked. The words, muffled by the surgical mask, came out more like "What abudda smock?"

Meredith just eyed her mother, who got busy loading up a tray with three different kinds of cookies, donated by Gift Baskets and baked by Meredith and her mother in the wee hours of the morning. "You promised you'd help me. We aren't going to make any milk fans if we look like we're ready for the end of the world."

Momma sighed, then pulled off the surgical mask and tucked it into the pocket of her jumper.

"Oh, all right. But if I end up on my deathbed next week—"

"I promise to bring you chicken soup," Meredith said. "And even make it myself."

Momma relented and put an arm around her daughter's shoulders. "You are a good girl."

"No, I'm not. But I try my best."

"That's all I ask, you know."

Meredith laughed. "Momma, you ask more than that and you know it. You ask more than any one person can give. *And* a box of cookies."

Her mother pouted. "I do not."

Bessie swung her head around and let out a moo of contention. Meredith arched a brow that said, *See?*

"I can't help it if I have high standards." Momma took the gallon of milk out of Meredith's hands and took over the pouring duties. It had taken a lot of doing, and a lot of listening to Momma's lectures, but Meredith had finally smoothed the waters between her and her mother early this morning. It had helped that she'd brought home two pounds of fresh shrimp for dinner the evening before. Bribing her family with fresh seafood had worked—very well.

She knew that despite everything, she loved her mother and having a wall between them would make any outcome to this—good or bad—bittersweet. So they'd talked, and then they'd baked. Somewhere between adding the flour and stirring in the chocolate chips, Momma had paused and drawn her daughter into a hug, providing a temporary truce.

Even Vernon and Ray Jr. had relented, drawn in by the scent of fresh-baked cookies, and opted to help by picking up Bessie at a farm outside of Boston and transporting her and her trailer here. After that, her brothers had insisted on remaining along the fringes of the area, to provide crowd control—and grab an occasional bite to eat.

Momma still didn't understand Meredith's need to leave Heavandale, but she was here, helping Meredith repair the damage done by Larry Herman.

And that was a start.

"Are you sure this is going to work?" Momma asked, finishing with the paper cups.

"No. But it's the best plan I have."

Momma took a step back, swept an appraising glance over her daughter, then adjusted the cow-print hood. "You do look good in udders, sweetie."

"Gee, thanks."

Momma's hand lingered on the hood for a long second, then she let go. "Oh, your father would be so proud of you. Standing up to all these people like this."

Meredith caught a glimpse of phase two of her plan, heading toward them right on schedule. She adjusted her udders and tightened her grip on the leather leash that kept Bessie beside her in the middle of Government Center. "Brace yourself, Momma. Here comes the media."

Kenny came barreling into Travis's office, out of breath and waving his arms. "Have you seen the morning news report?"

"No. Why?" They'd both beaten Larry into the office this morning. Maybe he'd get lucky and see Larry hanging off the catwalk of the billboard, threatening to commit suicide by dairy product.

Kenny didn't answer. He just grabbed Travis's arm and dragged him down to the break room and over to the small TV mounted in the corner of the room.

There, on the nineteen-inch screen was Meredith, dressed in a cow costume, holding a leash connected to—

A cow?

Travis blinked. When he looked again he saw, indeed, it was a real live mooing cow standing beside Meredith. She and another woman, who had to be her mother judging by the similarity in their appearances, were pouring cups of milk and handing them out to the reporters, along with cookies.

"Well, I'll be damned," Travis said, chuckling.

"You'll be worse than damned if Larry sees this," Kenny muttered.

"I have a plan for that already." Travis crossed his arms over his chest and leaned against the counter, watching as Meredith talked to a reporter from Channel Seven.

"You can't beat the real thing," she was saying, "for nutrition. Real milk has been around for centuries and there's a reason for that. When you start drinking chemicals, who knows what it will do to your system down the road?"

"But Meredith, what about that picture of you drinking No-Moo Milk?" A lanky reporter in a too-big suit asked.

She smiled sweetly. "I was trying it out. You have to know your competition—in order to beat it." She handed him a paper cup of milk and a pair of chocolate chip cookies.

Damn. That woman was smart and sexy. Travis grinned, admiring her twenty times more than he had before. She could have bashed Belly-Licious, but that would have just stirred up the controversy more and given the company more press. Instead, she'd turned the conversation right back to her own cause.

"Travis..." Kenny said, interrupting.

"Hmm. What?" Travis didn't remove his gaze from Meredith's image.

"You mentioned a plan to take care of Larry. What did you do? Is it something that can get us fired?"

Travis shrugged. If all went well, no. But at this company, he didn't count on anything going well, so the answer was pretty likely yes. "Maybe."

Kenny shook his head, laughing. "My ex is going to hate me for saying this, but it's about time. I'm sick and tired of this job. Give me a good kick in the ass and I'm outta here."

Travis grinned and turned to Kenny. "No one's going to accuse you of being ambitious."

"Hell, no. That's what gets you into trouble. Working too late, drinking too little. And you know where that leads, don't you?"

Travis's gaze had returned to the image on the screen. Meredith had completely won the crowd of reporters over, he could see. Most of them held a cup of milk and several were starting on their second helping of cookies. The tone of the interview had shifted into something pleasant and soft, as if they were on a chatty talk show, not the morning Boston newscast.

"What?" Travis asked, when Kenny repeated his question.

"*No sex.*" He pronounced the words like a judge handing down a death penalty.

Travis glanced again at Meredith, her pretty pink mouth and wide blue eyes the only things he could see through the folds of the cow costume. Still, she looked cute as hell and, dressed like that, she could be his own personal Halloween fantasy. "That's not necessarily a bad thing, you know."

"Oh hell. Now you really have gone crazy." Kenny swiped a Styrofoam cup off the counter and poured himself some coffee. "What's it been, ten days? And here you are, saying no sex is a *good* thing? I think you need a shrink."

"Nope. What I need is her." Travis pointed at the screen.

Kenny raised his cup toward Meredith's image.

"She's not going to want a guy without a job. If there's one thing women want, it's a working man."

"Oh, she won't mind. Not once she sees what got me fired."

Kenny poured a second cup and pulled out a chair for himself, then gestured toward another one for Travis.

Travis didn't move until Meredith's image was replaced by one of the talking anchorheads, who went on to the weather forecast. High in the low fifties, partly cloudy.

But in Travis's heart, things had taken a decidedly sunny turn.

"All right, tell me what you did," Kenny said, sliding the second cup over to Travis. "I want to at least get in one good chuckle before I'm standing in the unemployment line."

"I—" Travis cut himself off, glancing again at the television. An ad for a soap opera filled the screen, nowhere near as exciting as the images he'd just been seeing.

A sense of urgency filled him. He'd done something to help Meredith, but had it been enough?

And besides, what the hell was he doing here, waiting for Larry to come in and blow a gasket, when he could be *there*—with her? *Duh*, as his teenage cousins would say. He was in the wrong place. He'd been in the wrong place for days.

"Sorry, Kenny. No can do." He got to his feet and pushed the chair back in against the table. "I have to go help a cow."

Travis's Apologies-Come-in-Little-Packages Seafood Puff Pastries

1 8-ounce package cocktail shrimp
8 ounces crabmeat
1 cup ricotta cheese
2 tablespoons each chopped parsley, dill and basil
2 tablespoons celery, minced
2 tablespoons onion, minced
1/2 teaspoon paprika
1 package puff pastry

You need something that's going to impress her, yet not take a lot of time or Emeril's skills to create. Preheat the oven to 400 degrees. Roll out the puff pastry to 1/8-inch thickness. Cut into 8 squares.

Mix all the other ingredients together. Fill each of the puff pastry squares with the seafood mixture, then twist the tops together to make a little package. (Hey, what'd you expect? Something that looked like a swan?) Put them on a cookie sheet and bake for 25-30 minutes.

Serve it fast, before she has time to think about all the reasons why dating you might not be such a good idea after all.

CHAPTER TWENTY-SEVEN

"Can a thirsty man have a drink?"

Meredith turned at the sound of the familiar voice. There was Travis, standing on the other side of the small table she and her mother had set up, wearing a white shirt and red tie and looking sexier than any man had a right to. She started to smile, then remembered her resolve to hate him for the rest of her natural life and kept her features stony. "Certainly."

She reached for a paper cup of milk, wishing Momma would tend to Travis instead. But her mother was busy chatting with a reporter from one of the local weekly papers, giving him her recipe for a vinegar and dishsoap all-purpose cleanser. The young man, who didn't look like he'd been out of college for more than a day, diligently took notes, as if he was girding up for major mildew battle.

"Here you are," Meredith said, handing Travis the milk. Then she turned to Bessie, giving the old Holstein a rub on her silky ears. The media crowd had petered out for the time being, leaving her and Travis alone. If she didn't count the cow.

"What? No cookies?" he said. "Everyone knows you can't have milk without cookies."

"Yeah, especially the fake kind." Her voice held a cutting edge to it that was unlike her and for a second, she wanted to take the words back.

"I deserved that." Travis took a step forward, the paper cup seeming so small in his large, strong hands. "But I also deserve a chance to make this up to you."

She let out a sigh. "Why can't you just leave me alone? You and that company you work for have ruined everything. All I can do now is try to repair the damage."

He arched a brow and grinned. "And you're going to do that with a... cow?"

Despite herself, she laughed. "Hey, it's a good idea."

Admiration shimmered in his eyes. "It is. I only wish I'd thought of it."

"Hey, if you want to trade places..." she said, plucking at the cow costume and gesturing toward him. For a second, the tension between them evaporated and Meredith could believe it was just like it used to be when they'd first gone out. Sweet Easy, with that ever-present hum of sexual electricity running between them.

"Uh, no. I think cowprint looks much better on you than it ever would on me." He gave Bessie a gentle rub behind the ears. "Nice cow."

Bessie let out a moo of agreement and clopped her hooves on the pavement as she moved from foot to foot.

"I don't see too many of these around here, and I bet neither do any of those people," Travis said, gesturing to the circle of gawkers who had spilled out of the office buildings and were pointing at the cow in wonder. Travis stroked Bessie's nose, which gave the Holstein an invitation to move closer to him.

"Welcome to my world," Meredith said. "If you lived in Heavendale, this would be about all you'd see. Cows, corn and crows."

Travis looked at Meredith, his gaze not on Bessie at all anymore. "I happen to think the view is very pretty."

Meredith turned away, refusing to be drawn back into the soft sound of his voice or the gentle way he gazed at her.

"Meredith," Momma scolded, turning to her daughter. "Why didn't you give this nice young man some cookies?"

"I've been trying to figure out the same thing, Mrs. Shordon," Travis said. He put out a hand to her. "Travis Campbell."

Momma smiled appreciation at his good manners, then shook with him. When she was done, she withdrew her hand and squirted a dab of Purell onto it from under the table, as she always did after any *mano-a-mano* contact.

Travis put out his hands for a dab of antibacterial gel to wipe off the cow germs. Momma obliged, flashing Travis a smile that said he and his good hygiene had been immediately accepted into her circle. "And which paper are you with?"

"None. I'm here to see Meredith. And to help you both with your milk campaign."

Momma looked from Meredith to Travis, and back again. "You're with my daughter?"

"He's not with me, Momma. He's—"

"Here to help," Travis interrupted, circling the table and grabbing a fresh gallon of milk from the cooler by their feet. He peeled off the seal, then started pouring. Momma beamed. There was nothing she liked better than a man who put some actions behind his words. "He's a nice looking one," she whispered into Meredith's ear.

"I thought you wanted me to marry Caleb."

Momma tugged Meredith over to help her arrange more cookies on the tray—and so she could put in her two cents without Travis overhearing. "As much as I'd like the family discount on a plot at Heavendale Gardens, what I really want is whatever will make you happy, dear."

"Even if it means not living in Heavendale anymore?"

Her mother paused, a raspberry thumbprint halfway between the Rubbermaid container and the silver tray. "Not living in Heavendale? But why?"

Oh, this wasn't the time. Or the place. Or how she wanted to tell her mother at all. She was wearing a cow costume, for God's sake, and clutching a leash attached to a 1,300-pound Holstein.

It wasn't exactly the right outfit for telling your mother you wanted to leave home for good.

And then there was Travis, two feet away and sending her a jumble of messages that had her heart running through a continuous spin cycle.

"We can talk about this later," Meredith said, waving a hoof at the group forming a perimeter around their public display.

Momma perched a hand on her hip. "I don't care if the entire free world is watching. My little girl just said she wants to leave me forever."

"It's not like I'd be moving to another planet."

Momma turned back to the cookies. "You might as well be." She sniffled. "Apparently Heavendale isn't good enough for you."

Travis, who had kept busy during the conversation by pouring milk, now crossed over to them. *Oh great.* He thought he could fix this, too?

"Boston's not such a bad place, Mrs. Shordon. We do have flights to Indiana, every day, too."

"It's not the same. I always thought my daughter would live right next door to me."

"You never know," Travis said, handing Momma a cup of milk and a smile. "Things can change down the road. Priorities change." At this, his eyes met Meredith's.

As if he had some kind of message to communicate.

She scowled at him, as best as one could scowl while wearing udders and holding a Holstein. What did he think he was doing? Every time this man got within five feet of her, he screwed up her life. Now he was practically telling her mother that if she left Heavendale, it would only be temporarily.

She'll be back on the farm in no time, Mrs. Shordon.

No, thank you. Meredith may have thought she was going back to Indiana when she'd first left, but now, she couldn't imagine leaving any of this for the predictable and confining life she'd had before.

"I like you," Momma said, patting Travis on the shoulder. "You must make your mother proud."

Travis let out a chuckle. "I don't know about that, Mrs. Shordon. I don't think she thinks about whether or not I'm making her proud."

"Doesn't she live near you?"

Travis finished with the milk, capped the jug and put it back into the cooler. "My mother is in Florida, doing a good job of retiring."

"Then who takes care of you?"

"Takes care of me?" Travis grinned. "Me."

Momma scoffed. "Well. That explains everything." She gave Travis an appraising glance that swept over his frame, taking in what Meredith saw as a trim waist but she knew Momma saw as a too-thin body. "You come to Aunt Gloria's house some night. I'll feed you right and take care of you."

This was not going well at all. Next her mother would be getting out her tape measure for Travis— for a very different reason.

And so, she imagined, would Caleb, should Travis ever come to Heavendale. But he'd be measuring to make sure he could fit Travis into the back part of the hearse.

Meredith grabbed the only thing she could think of to break the two of them apart. Bessie.

She tugged on the leash, but Bessie didn't want to move. The Holstein let out a whiny moo and stayed put. Meredith scooted around to the cow's flank and pushed, but Bessie didn't budge. Momma and Travis kept on chatting, going on and on about dinner possibilities, as if he'd been invited right into the family already.

Meredith spun to the right and grabbed some hay from the pile that had come with Bessie—the bribe that had gotten her off the trailer and into Government Center. Earlier that morning, she had trotted after the hay like a Greyhound after an electric rabbit, eager to go anywhere as long as she could have a bite.

But now, she couldn't care less.

"You'll just have to try my biscuits and gravy for breakfast," Momma was saying. "You haven't lived until you've had that. Meredith makes it even better than me, I think."

Travis smiled her way. "Is that so? Well, I'll just have to try some of both recipes. I bet they're both wonderful and Meredith learned some great cooking skills from you. I'm sure you run a tight ship in the kitchen."

Travis's comment sent him soaring to notches unknown on Momma's approval rating. Meredith's mother gestured to her to come over and play nice with him.

Instead, Meredith gave Bessie another shove. The cow looked back at the annoyance on her butt, flicked an ear and went back to chewing her cud.

Meredith muttered several curses under her breath. She'd moved cows at home before, hundreds of times. What was wrong with her?

"Travis has a cleaning lady to help him keep his place spic-n-span, did you know that?" Momma said, her voice bright with appreciation for this cleanliness luxury. "*A cleaning lady,* Meredith."

This time, Meredith slipped in front of Bessie, reached behind her own butt and wiggled her tail, then sashayed forward, tugging on Bessie's leash at the same time. The cow plodded after her, a lemming going wherever the other spots in front of it were headed.

Meredith and Bessie slipped right between Momma and Travis, effectively ending their conversation with the insertion of a half-ton beast. "I think Bessie's getting bored over there," Meredith said. "She wants a change of view. And company."

Momma frowned. "Travis, dear, could you put these cookies at the end of the table while I get another tray together?"

"Certainly." He took the silver tray and moved a few feet away.

"He's a good man," Momma whispered again. "You could do worse than marry him."

"Will you quit with that? God, I feel like a heifer at an auction. Highest bidder gets the bride."

Momma pursed her lips and kept stacking the round desserts in concentric circles.

From his place down the table, Travis sent her a grin. Meredith flapped a hoof at him and wished she could disappear into the ground, udders and all.

She was saved from a shotgun wedding by one of the reporters from the *Middlesex News*. He approached the table and Travis handed him a cup of milk and a couple of cookies.

"Hey, thanks," the guy said, introducing himself as Sherman Maxwell before taking a gulp. "This is good stuff."

"Real milk, it's the best way to go," Travis said. "And the healthiest."

Sherman finished one of his cookies, then put his cup down and readied his pen and skinny pad. "Yeah, but I thought I saw her," he said, indicating Meredith with the tip of the ballpoint, "on a billboard drinking some chemical crap."

Travis shook his head. "That billboard was a mistake. It's gone now."

Gone? When had it come down? No one had told Meredith anything about that. She glanced across the plaza at her brothers, realizing just now that they had never come over to eject, or duct tape, Travis. Which meant only one thing.

They were on his side.

When she caught Ray Jr.'s eye, he gave her a confident tip of his chin and a thumbs-up that said the Shordon boys had taken care of it.

"Miss Shordon, did Belly-Licious Beverages use your image without your permission?" Sherman asked.

She glanced at Travis. Saying yes would open up the firestorm she'd been hoping to avoid. And it would undoubtedly get him fired, especially because he was here, cavorting with the "enemy."

But saying no would essentially be lying, which went against who she was as a person. Meredith Shordon might have come here to Boston for a change, but she didn't want one that took with it her basic morality.

"Well, did they?" the reporter pressed, his pen poised to write down her next words. Apparently the cookie hadn't sweetened him up too much.

Lying might not save her soul, but it would save Travis. She watched him, the gallon of milk in his hand, and decided where her priorities lay. "Belly-Licious did nothing—"

"Did nothing but stop a bad ad campaign," Travis cut in. "They did use Miss Shordon but realized it would be a bad reflection on one of Nature's finest treasures. So they've come up with a better idea."

"They have?" the reporter asked.

"They have?" Meredith echoed.

"They sure have," Ray Jr. announced, stepping forward and grinning. That kind of smile on her brother meant only one thing.

Trouble.

"What do you know about this new ad campaign?" Sherman turned to Travis.

"I helped design it, with the amazing talents of Kenny Gerard, my assistant, and Larry Herman, the vice president. We launched it early this morning."

"And can you give me a sneak preview?" Sherman gave him a hopeful tip of his chin.

"Just get on 93 and head up to exit 26. All the answers you're looking for are right there."

Sherman shrugged, noted the information, and put his pad away before reaching for a couple more cookies. Apparently, he had what he'd come looking for.

But Meredith was more confused than ever. What had Travis meant by that? "All the answers you're looking for?"

When it came to figuring out Travis Campbell, Meredith doubted even a psychic in a fortune cookie factory could help her.

Momma's Matchmaking-Two-Peas-in-a-Pod Shrimp and Snow Pea Stir-Fry

2 tablespoons canola oil
1 tablespoon garlic, minced
1 tablespoon fresh ginger, minced
1/4 cup chicken broth, separated
2 cups broccoli florets
1 cup cauliflower florets
2 carrots, sliced
1 red bell pepper, julienned
1 pound shrimp, peeled and deveined
1 pound fresh snow peas
3 tablespoons soy sauce
1 teaspoon sesame oil

See, even Momma can learn a new recipe or two. If I can learn to love food that doesn't come from a farm, then you can learn to love that man who has the best hygiene habits I've seen in a long time.

Start by heating the oil in a wok (yes, I said "a wok." Told you Momma could change ... some). Add the garlic and ginger and sauté for about 30 seconds, then add a tablespoon of the chicken broth and toss in all the vegetables except the snow peas. Stir-fry until they're crisp-tender.

Mix in the shrimp and the snow peas and blend them all, nice and harmonious, in the wok. Sort of like bringing Indiana and Massachusetts together in one place. Add the remaining ingredients, heat for another minute or so, then serve over hot rice.

And stop being so stubborn. You know that Momma always knows best. The sooner you start listening to her wisdom, the sooner you'll be happier.

CHAPTER TWENTY-EIGHT

An hour later, Vernon, Ray Jr., Travis and Meredith had loaded up Bessie—using the hay and Meredith's tail as bait—into the borrowed trailer attached to the back of Cecil's pickup truck and were heading out of the city and back to the Happy Acres farm.

Travis and Meredith followed behind in Travis's car. The seating arrangement had been completely arranged by Momma, who had shooed off the boys, then jumped into Meredith's car and put it into gear, shouting that she needed to rest her feet and Meredith should just go along with Travis to bring up the rear and see Bessie home.

He could tell Meredith wasn't happy. She refused to talk to him, sitting in the passenger's seat of his car in stony silence, letting the air conditioner cool her body—and hopefully her temper, too.

She'd stripped off the top half of the cow costume, revealing a white fitted T-shirt. He wanted to run the back of his hand down the soft cotton fabric, tracing the outline of her curves, but he knew if he came anywhere near her right now, she'd likely pound him into the ground with one of those plastic hooves.

They followed the pickup for a few minutes, until they approached the exit for Storrow Drive and Fenway Park. Travis veered off, while Vernon and Ray Jr. kept going, barreling on up I-93 in the bouncy pickup, their heads bopping up and down with the bad springs like human popcorn. Travis slowed and parked his car on the shoulder of Exit 26, then killed the engine.

"What are we doing? We have to go with them to return Bessie."

"I want to show you something."

He got out of his side, came around and opened her door, leading her out of the car before she could protest. The traffic hummed along by them, the tires making their own kind of music against the pavement. The city bustled around them, buildings looming like sentries. "Look up."

She did. "I see sun. Clouds. Sky." She pivoted back, hand on the door's latch. "Okay? Let's go."

"Turn a little to the right."

She let out a gust of breath, but did as he asked, a question on her lips that never got voiced. When her gaze connected with the massive sign that overlooked the highway, Meredith's jaw dropped open.

"*That's* what replaced you," he said.

"How... What... When?"

He chuckled. "Vernon and Ray Jr. helped me last night."

"But..." She gaped at the moving parts, the gleaming smile above her head. "This is not what the company was planning for No-Moo. You're going to get fired for this."

He shrugged. "Probably."

"Doesn't that worry you?"

"Not anymore." Travis circled around to the front of Meredith and reached for her hands. When she didn't resist, he felt a tiny surge of hope that maybe all this tension between them was as fixable as the billboard had been. "I did it for you."

"Me? Why?"

He took a deep breath. "You were right; I did use you for the No-Milk focus group."

"You were behind the whole thing, weren't you? The newspaper articles, the billboard. All of it." She tried to tug away from him but he held fast.

"No, I wasn't. I met you and I thought you'd be great for helping us figure out how to sell No-Moo to people in the Midwest, the hardest market to crack." He shook his head, knowing that if he had met Meredith today, two weeks after all the changes he had made in his life, he would not have even thought of doing the same thing. "At the time, I thought it was a fair trade. You wanted me, I wanted you."

"But you never came through on your end of the bargain."

A smile crossed his lips. Oh how he'd wanted to. Then, and even more so now. "We'll get to that later," he said. "I promise."

For the first time in days, he saw a spark in her eyes. Maybe all wasn't lost with Meredith, maybe they could indeed fix the mess they'd made of everything.

She arched a brow. "You promise?"

"Here in front of God and Larry." He gestured toward the billboard.

She laughed. "I'm not sure that's much of a promise."

He nodded, agreeing. "Probably not. But it's the best I can do standing on the highway."

She grinned. "It'll do."

A bus sped past them, so close to the shoulder it nearly sideswiped his car. The whoosh of air going by sent Meredith's hair whipping around her face. Travis reached up and brushed the tendrils off her soft, peaches-and-cream cheeks, allowing his hand to linger for a long moment. "I was a different man when I met you," he said. "Back then, I didn't notice if people got hurt by the stupid things I did. I made idiotic choices, lived a life without many consequences and basically skated along, doing what I had to, to keep my job and pay my bills."

"And now?"

"And now I want more. More out of me, and more out of my life."

"And this"—she motioned toward the twelve-by-twenty-four image—"is part of that?"

He chuckled. "That's mainly revenge. The point is, I'm not so worried about losing my job anymore. I've got a plan to take care of my brother and Kenny, if that happens. But I am worried about one thing."

"What's that?"

"Losing you."

She swallowed and broke away from him. 'There is no *losing* me, Travis. I wasn't yours to begin with."

"Why not?" The lunchtime traffic began to multiply and speed down the road, looking a lot like animals going two-by-two into an all-you-can-eat buffet on Noah's ark. "Why not, Meredith?"

"Because I don't want any of that."

"Why? Because you're too busy running away?"

"I'm not running away. I'm just looking for something different for a while."

"Oh yeah? Then why are you so scared of me?"

"I'm not scared of you." She took a step closer to him and brought her chest within a few inches of his. "If anything, I'd say *you're* the one scared of *me*."

"Bull."

"You've put me on this pedestal like I'm some kind of china doll that you can't break. I know you're not a virgin; I know you've slept with other women... but you won't sleep with me. And don't tell me it's because you're afraid of taking my virtue or any of that nineteenth-century crap."

"That isn't crap, it's being a gentleman."

"No. It's being *afraid*.'" Her hair blew around her face again, but this time she was the one to brush it impatiently out of the way. "I'm the one woman that you can't have unless it's true love and doves in the air and rings on our fingers." She let out a gust and shook her head, as if the entire idea were absurd. "Do you know what you're afraid of, Travis?"

"What?"

"Breaking my heart."

He stepped back, stunned, and she knew she'd hit the nail on the head. For a long time, he didn't say anything. He stared at the traffic going by them, as if the procession of semis and SUVs was the Macy's Thanksgiving Day parade.

"My father did that, you know," he said after a long time. His voice was so low, she could barely hear it above the engines of the cars.

She came up beside him. "Did what?"

"Broke women's hearts. All the time. It was like a hobby for him, Get them to love him, then leave them and move on to another prize. He was a hunter, looking for bigger game every time. And me and Brad, we'd be left with some woman weeping in our living room, asking us why. Hell, we didn't know. We were six and seven or ten and eleven, twelve and thirteen. Didn't matter. It happened about every year, like he got an itch in January."

The pieces clicked into place in Meredith's mind. "And you don't want to be him."

Travis shook his head. "No. Not one bit."

"You don't have to worry. You're not going to break my heart, Travis," she said softly, taking his hand in hers. "Because I have no intentions of falling in love with you. Or anyone."

Yet even as she said the words, the first little crack shimmied through her heart and she wondered who was lying now.

Kenny's All-Hell-Is-Breaking-Loose Beer-Poached Salmon

1 pound salmon fillet
2 teaspoons garlic salt
3 tablespoons brown sugar
3 tablespoons butter
1 12-ounce beer

When you see the boss's hair standing on end, and he swivels his head a full 360 degrees, you know it's not gonna be a good day at work. Time for a beer. And a beer-based meal.

Preheat your grill to medium-high. Then get crafty (in your kitchen, not with the boss. You do need that job, you know). Make a foil boat for your salmon, leaving the top open. Put the fish inside it, season it with the garlic salt, then sprinkle on the brown sugar and dot with butter.

Place your boat on a grill. Make sure you don't have any leaks, because the last thing you want to do is waste the brewski. Pour the beer into the boat, cover it with more aluminum foil, then bring down the grill lid and cook on medium-high for about ten minutes.

There. The salmon's happy, you're happy. The boss isn't, but after a beer or two, it doesn't bother you as much.

CHAPTER TWENTY-NINE

When Travis's cell phone started ringing like the hunchback at Notre Dame had ingested a little too much wine before hitting the bells, he knew the shit had hit the billboard at work. He heard the faint sound of the ringer through the windows of his car and reached inside for his Motorola.

Three missed calls from Larry. Four from Kenny. As he was flipping it open to call Kenny back, the phone rang again.

"You have to get back here, Travis," Kenny said. "All hell is breaking loose and the demon is coming out of his cave to chop off heads."

"Jerome?"

"Yeah. Oh, gotta go. I see the axe coming at me." Kenny clicked off, leaving Travis with dead air and the certain knowledge that he had, indeed, gotten everyone fired.

"I hate to do this," he said to Meredith, "but I have to take you home, or back to the shop. I have to get back to work."

She nodded, as if she were glad for the interruption. Truth was, he was too. She'd hit pretty close to home with what she'd said and he wanted a little time to breathe. Maybe think about it.

After he'd gotten to work and dealt with the wrath of the Herman family.

"The shop is fine," Meredith told him. "It's closer to Belly-Licious and I can get a ride back to Rebecca's on the T or with Maria."

"Or I can come by after work and pick you up." It was a question, one that hinted at a future between them.

She didn't answer. Travis opened her car door, then came around to his own side. In a second, they were back on the expressway, heading in the opposite direction, through the new tunnel and then over to Atlantic Avenue. Again, she said almost nothing on the ride over there, as if she'd said everything already.

Well, he'd be damned if he was done.

Though it didn't take long to get from the Storrow Drive exit to the little shop off of Atlantic Avenue, it was long enough for Travis to realize Meredith had been right. He *was* afraid of breaking her heart.

He'd never felt that way about a woman before. Always, he'd met the kind of woman who knew he wasn't there for much more than a good time and a kiss good-bye at the end.

Meredith, though, as much as she protested otherwise, was different. And Travis, as much as he protested otherwise, realized he liked that about her. A lot.

As soon as he parked the car in front of Gift Baskets to Die For, Meredith hopped out, offered him a quick good-bye and headed into the shop. Travis ignored the insistent ringing of his phone and headed in after her.

"I want to see you again, Meredith."

She pivoted towards him and shook her head. "No. I'm sorry, Travis. I made the wrong choice."

He grabbed the frame of the door and ducked into the shop, not allowing her to escape so easily. Not yet. "What do you mean, the wrong choice?"

"You're not the right man for the job. And I'm not the right woman for what you think you want." Her smile had turned bittersweet and something within Travis's chest constricted like a rubber band had been wrapped around his lungs. "I'm sorry."

She crossed the room, past a curious Maria and Candace, and headed straight for the kitchen.

He followed behind her, so she kept going until she'd reached the little office in the back. There was nowhere farther to go. They were alone in the quiet, small room that held little more than a desk, a few filing cabinets and a couple of shelves.

Travis shut the door. "Don't run away, Meredith."

"I'm not running away."

"Bullshit. You are, too. You're scared out of your mind that you might just fall in love with me."

She lifted her chin, defiant. "I am not."

"Oh yeah? Prove it."

"How do you prove something like that? What do you want me to do? Take a love lie-detector test?"

"Yeah. And I have just the equipment for it right here." He leaned forward and pressed his lips to hers, putting all his doubts and fears on the same distant shelf where he kept his out-of-season clothes and the yellow boots that his mother had sent him for his birthday but he'd never worn.

At first, Meredith didn't respond and a flicker of fear rushed through Travis. Maybe he'd read her wrong. Then her eyes drifted shut and she shifted forward, letting her head fall back and tip to the side, curling into the perfect position to open her mouth against his and dart her pert little tongue in to dance.

His arms went around her waist, hands pressing against her back, urging her closer. She dropped her purse, then her jacket to the floor, each landing with a soft clunk on the vinyl flooring. Her hands skated up his back, lifting and tugging at his shirt, clutching at the cotton as if it was all a bothersome hindrance to the thing she wanted most.

Him.

Travis went hard against Meredith, the fire he'd felt since the first minute he'd met her roaring to life within him. She dropped one hand into the space between them, stroking him through the fabric of his pants, her mouth still on his, her tongue previewing what could happen if they were recumbent instead of upright.

He grasped her thighs and wrapped her legs, still clad in the silly bottom half of the costume, around his waist. Then he strode to the nearest available flat surface—the desk—pressing her against it, fitting his pelvis against the space of hers, never losing the connection with those sweet, delicate lips that tasted like cherry soda.

Meredith's arms went around his neck, her fingers toying with the hair at his nape. Her legs straddled his waist, pelvis tilted up and pressing against his erection. Her hands traveled down, to fling his tie to one side and start in on the buttons of his shirt.

Travis pulled back and looked up at Meredith's flushed face, so serious with concentration and yet so vulnerable with want... and realized he was past being scared.

He'd already fallen in love with her.

Somewhere between the steamers and the shrimp, Travis Campbell, avowed bachelor, had found a woman who made him want to be more of a man.

He reached up and cupped her face with his hands. "Meredith," he said, his voice half caress, half growl.

"Hmm?" She had two of the buttons undone and had already started on the third.

"Meredith," he repeated, louder, more insistent. The urge to tell her, to share the feelings that seemed to be bursting inside his chest, was as strong as the urge coming from the rest of his male anatomy.

She paused in her unfastening work, confusion in her eyes. "What?"

Travis felt a smile steal across his face. "I'm falling in love with you."

He'd expected her to smile, to maybe say the same thing back. At the very least, he'd expected her to look happy.

But instead Meredith jerked off him and scrambled away. "Why did you have to say that?"

"Because it's true."

"But... I don't want you to fall in love with me."

He grinned. "Too late."

The words were out. A lightness filled his chest. He, of all people, *he* had fallen in love, with the one woman who had connected with him outside of a bedroom. He was glad he hadn't slept with her, as crazy as that sounded, because it meant he loved her. Not her body, not the thought of her in his bed, but *her*.

Yet, as he looked into Meredith's eyes, he saw doubt and fear reflected in the deep blue depths.

"You took a huge risk coming out here," Travis said, clasping her hands, trying to bridge the gulf between them. "Take another one now. Fall in love with me."

She pulled away from him, crossed the room and toyed nervously with a stack of books on the end of the third shelf. "I... I don't know. To me, that's going backward, not forward."

He chuckled. "For me, this is a giant leap forward for mankind."

Her shoulders shook a little and a light echo of his laughter escaped her. "Why do I do this to myself?" she said softly.

"Do what?"

"Pick the wrong man at the wrong time."

"Who says I'm the wrong one?"

She turned around, her blue eyes connecting with his. "Who says you're the right one?"

He reached up and drifted the back of his hand down her cheek. "You gonna find another man who thinks you're sexy as hell when you're dressed as a cow?"

She grinned. "If I visit enough mental hospitals, yeah, I probably will."

With one finger, he tipped her chin up and brushed a light kiss across her lips. "Jump off the bridge with me, Meredith."

"Oh, Travis," she sighed against his mouth, "why can't you be the cliché? Just love me and leave me?"

He grinned. "Now where's the fun in that?"

Travis *had* left Meredith a few minutes later. Though he'd switched it to vibrate, his cell phone had rung so many times, it was hot to the touch and he was pretty sure the thing would explode from overuse.

As Travis headed north again on 93, he let out a gust of breath and ran a hand through his hair. Why had he gone and told her he was falling in love with her? All it had seemed to do was scare Meredith off more than before.

But it was the truth, and Lord help him, he knew there was no going back.

It was as if he'd turned a new corner in his own evolution. Homo sapien man walks upright and learns to have deeper feelings.

Boy, Brad was really going to enjoy winning this bet. Probably would never let him live it down, either. For the first time in his life, Travis figured he was the real winner—or he would be if he could convince Meredith that taking a chance on love wasn't the equivalent of walking blindfolded down the center line of the Callahan Tunnel.

He pulled into the Belly-Licious parking lot just as his cell phone went off again. He ignored it and broke into a slight jog, heading into the building and down the hall to the offices.

He could hear the shouting from around the corner.

"Whose idea was this?" Larry screamed. "That's my face up there! I'm going to sue somebody and then I'm going to kill them." He turned his gold-spun-red head just as Travis rounded the corner and entered the room. "*You,*" he said, the word coming out like spit. "You did this."

Travis nodded. "I did. And Kenny and Brad had nothing to do with it. So don't fire them." He'd had a little help from the graphic design guys, too, who had taken great pleasure in creating the image of Larry for the billboard, but Travis left them out of it.

"I'll fire whoever the hell I want." Larry took two steps forward. His face was red and puffy from the exertion of anger. "Starting with you."

Jerome Herman crossed his arms over his chest and leaned against a metal desk. His face was as cold and stony as a block of ice. "Do you care to explain yourself, Travis, before we have security drag you out of here?"

"You know, Jerome, I'd love to do that, but I think I'll let the sales report speak for me." Travis loosened his tie and gestured to Heather, the office assistant. "Can you get me the manila folder on my desk, please?"

Heather, her eyes wide with fear that she was about to get caught in the pink slip crossfire, scurried away to do as he asked. Kenny, who was sitting in one of the empty chairs on the other side of the room, gaped at Travis and mouthed, "Are you insane?" at him. Brad had wandered into the room, along with the rest of the R&D team, and leaned against the doorjamb, a bemused smile on his face.

"Just get the hell out of here," Larry said, pointing the way in case Travis had forgotten it. Travis took a seat in an empty chair, just to tick Larry off. "We don't want to hear your—"

"Sales report?" Jerome cut in. "What sales report?"

Heather hustled through the center of the room as fast as her three-inch pumps could carry her and dumped the folder into Travis's lap before backing away again just as fast. Travis leaned back in the chair, flipped open the cover of the manila folder and scanned a finger down the first page. "Let's see ..."

He already knew what was inside the folder. He'd written the report himself late yesterday. Out of the corner of his eye, he saw Larry's face turn a light shade of purple. Kenny looked ready to have a heart attack; Jerome's features had only gone colder. Brad, however, was grinning.

Brad was the only one who had been in on it from the beginning. Travis never would have done something so risky without his brother's blessing. The two of them had concocted the plan two days ago and while Travis put the sales calls into motion, Brad oversaw the surreptitious graphic design. It had been fun, Travis realized, working with his brother, and he made a vow to get his act—and his bank account— together to someday soon make that dream of owning their own company a reality.

"Uh, yeah. Right here," Travis said, after he'd delayed enough to send Larry into an apoplectic fit. "A three-hundred-thousand-dollar order from Soy-Ya Wanna Drink beverage stands. Another two-hundred-thousand-dollar order from the Living Without Lactose clinic. Oh, and a few other little ones, adding up to a couple hundred grand more." Travis shrugged, like it was nothing. "Just a few sales."

The glacier melted on Jerome's face and his jaw dropped to his chest. "That's... more than half a million dollars in sales."

"Yep." Travis rose and tossed the folder onto the desk in front of Kenny, who just stared at in amazement

"How did you do that?"

"By developing a whole new ad campaign around our new spokesman for lactose intolerance." Travis draped an arm around Larry's shoulders and gave him a grin.

"Me? Are you insane? Who gave you permission—"

"Shut up, Larry," Jerome said. He chewed on his lip, assessing Travis. "Was this the idea you came to me about the other day?"

"You went behind my back?" Larry sputtered. "You bastard. I'll have you fired."

"I said shut up, Larry." Jerome swiveled toward his cousin. "Or *I'll* fire *you*."

Larry opened his mouth, closed it. Opened it again, and left it like that for a long, shocked second.

"Yes, sir, it is," Travis answered.

Jerome nodded. "And you went ahead with it on your own, without permission?"

"I did."

Jerome's eyes narrowed. "Why?"

"Because I knew it would work. And it wasn't going to get us sued."

"Like another certain ad campaign might?"

"Maybe."

Jerome circled the room, thinking. Larry, Travis could see, wanted so badly to say something that he had his hands clenched at his sides, but he did as his cousin said and kept his mouth shut. Kenny was flipping through the folder, nodding his head in admiration.

"It was a clever idea," Jerome said. "Using Larry. I especially liked the moving parts."

"You mean the way he made a fool out of me?" Larry squeaked.

"The moving arm, the opening and closing mouth. Incredible idea," Jerome said. "Looks like he's really drinking No-Moo Milk."

"That's the effect I wanted. And the buyers really liked the image push we were giving it. That's where the big orders came from."

Jerome paused, his hands on the back of Kenny's chair. "So you solicited orders from customers using an unapproved ad campaign?"

Travis shrugged. "I knew I'd never be able to sell you on it, if I couldn't prove it would work."

"Well, I can't say I like your methods," Jerome said. "But the results, I can't argue with those. I like the idea, I like the billboard and I like the sales." He gave a short, quick nod. "We're going with it."

"Are you *nuts?!*" Larry shouted. "Did you see what he did to me?" He grabbed a Polaroid photo of the billboard off one of the desks and waved it around. "Did you see this? I'm bald!"

That had been the graphic designers and Brad's idea. They'd had a lot of fun doctoring the photo of Larry from the annual report. *Quid pro quo,* Travis thought.

Jerome rolled his eyes. "Yeah. And you look a hell of a lot better that way, too, instead of with the hair dye of the month."

"It's not a hair dye. I'll have you know these are quality follicle enhancers," Larry said, patting his head.

Jerome snorted. "Larry, get used to being bald. Because you're going to be that way in all our ads from here on out." He picked up the sales report from Kenny's hands and scanned the paper. "If these early sales figures are any indication of No-Moo's potential with the lactose-intolerant market, then you're going to be busy for a long time."

"But—"

"Don't *but* me. You were the one behind this product, remember?" Jerome gave his cousin a knowing grin. "And now you've got a hell of a team to take it to the next level. With Travis as the new Director of Marketing, I'd say we're set. He's in charge of all ad campaigns from now on and *you*," he pointed at Larry, "answer to *him*." With that, Jerome left the room.

"But I'm bald!" Larry screamed, clearly not hearing the news about his demotion.

Kenny rose and crossed to Larry. "Don't worry, Lar. Delia's friend told me she actually prefers men with a little acreage up top. She thinks Patrick Stewart is the sexiest man alive."

Larry paused as he took that in. "Really?"

"Yep. And now you're famous. She's going to want you bad, man."

Larry's chest puffed out like a bantam rooster's. "I *am* famous, aren't I?"

Oh God. There 'd be no living with him now. Travis may have saved three jobs, but in the end, he'd created a monster.

Cordelia's Change-ls-in-the-Air Fish and Chips

1 cup flour
1 cup beer
2 egg whites, whipped to stiff peaks
9 ounces haddock or cod, cut into serving sizes
2 pounds potatoes, peeled and julienned
Vegetable oil, for frying
Salt

When you want a taste of a new place, start with a bite of what they eat there. As you know dear, the food can be the very thing that teases your senses and begs you to stay, even when you're resisting what your heart wants.

Put the vegetable oil into a deep pan and heat it until it reaches 300 degrees. Cook the potatoes in the oil for 5 or 6 minutes, until they're soft but not brown, then remove them and drain. Yes, we will finish them. Have patience.

In a bowl, mix the flour and beer, then fold in the egg whites to create the batter. Dip the fish in the batter and fry about 6 to 8 minutes until golden brown.

Finish the chips (I know, you call them "French fries") by frying for about two or three minutes.

Drain on paper towels (do worry about your arteries; you only get one heart, you know), then sprinkle the fish and chips with salt and serve with tartar sauce.

Taste the new world awaiting you ... and take a giant leap forward into it!

Chapter Thirty

As soon as Travis left, Meredith changed out of her cow costume and into the clothes she'd left at the shop that morning. She poured herself into work, not knowing what else to do. She'd solved the dairy dilemma, but the one with Travis was going to take more than a Holstein and a couple cookies to fix.

Now Meredith, Maria and Candace were in the front part of the shop, going through a box of fall decorations and making a list of what needed to be replaced before the Thanksgiving season came. Cordelia Gershwin had stopped by for her morning cup of tea ... and never left.

"Cordelia, I think you have customers waiting for you to open your shop," Candace said, looking out the window.

Cordelia took off her little pillbox hat, toying with the bobby pins that had held it in place. Then she pursed her lips and shook her head. "No. I'm not going over there today."

"Are you sick?" Maria asked. "One of us can cover for you if—"

"No. I'm not sick. Not in the traditional sense." Cordelia's face softened and she turned to Meredith, clasping her hand. "You inspired me, young lady."

"Me? What did I do?"

"You started a whole new life for yourself and you did it with strength and conviction."

Meredith snorted and tossed the bent paper turkey in her hand back into the box. "I ran away, screwed up everything and now I'm just barely putting the pieces back together."

"No, that's not it at all." Cordelia shook her head. "You left, but you brought all the best parts of you with you from Indiana to Massachusetts. You didn't abandon your roots, you just... expanded them." She smiled. "And look at the tree you're turning into."

Meredith blinked. "Tree?"

Maria and Candace had stopped working and come around to form a human circle around them.

"Okay, so my metaphors aren't the best," Cordelia went on, "but my point is you did what I've been wanting to do since my Richard died. I've been stuck here, doing the same thing I always did because ..." at this, she paused and glanced out the window, her eyes misting and filling with memories. "It was easier."

"It's okay," Candace said, draping an arm over Cordelia's shoulders. "We like having you as a neighbor. And you can stay our neighbor for as long as you want."

"I love you girls, you know that, right?" Cordelia said, taking in their faces one at a time. "And that's why I'm doing this." She put her hat on the counter, then reached into her little bag and withdrew a key on a small round silver ring and placed it into Candace's palm. "I'm closing up shop and giving you the key back."

"But, but—" Maria sputtered.

"No buts. It's time for a change for me. If Meredith can put on a cow suit and take on Boston, then I think I can put on my walking shoes and see England."

Candace stared at the key. "Who'll run your shop?"

"No one. I'll sell off the inventory to a friend of mine who's been begging me for years to let him add it to his store. Then I'm on the next plane across the world. And for you girls, well, let's hope a new adventure moves in next door."

Maria and Candace stared at their neighbor, as shocked as if she had just told them she was the president of the local nudist camp.

"Now what about you?" Cordelia asked, turning to Meredith.

"Me?"

"When are you going to go for it with that sexy hunk of a man I've been seeing you with?"

"Ms. Gershwin!" Maria said, laughing. "I don't think I've ever heard you talk like that."

"What? I'm not dead, dear. I can still appreciate a good man. And a woman who's in love even if she refuses to believe it."

In love? Her? That would be impossible. Meredith had done everything in her power *not* to fall in love with Travis Campbell.

And yet, she thought of the way she felt when he kissed her. Not the hard, hectic kisses on Castle Island, the ones he'd given her to prove a point but the ones where he'd cupped her jaw with his hand and captured her lips with a tender, almost reverent touch.

She'd complained about him putting her on a pedestal. And yet he hadn't really done that at all. He'd simply been showing her how he felt. He was in love with her, as he'd said earlier today.

In love with her. The words hummed inside her, scary and joyous all at once.

"I'm not in love," Meredith said.

Maria and Candace each arched a brow of disbelief.

"I can't be. I came here for a change from my old life, not—"

"Were you in love with anyone in your old life?" Cordelia asked.

"No. Not at all."

She smiled brightly. "Then I'd say this is a change."

"Well... yeah, but..."

Cordelia put one hand on her hip and pursed her lips. "What do you want, Meredith? A billboard to drop on your head?"

A billboard. The mention of the word brought to mind the one Travis had shown her. The one he'd risked his job for... and his life, considering he'd gone to her brothers for help. He'd done it for her.

"Uh-oh," Maria said, looping an arm through Candace's. "I know that look."

"What look?" Meredith asked.

Candace nodded. "Yep, it's happening. I think it's the chocolate in this place."

"No," Maria said, shaking her head, "it's the pasta in these neighborhoods. It'll get you every time."

"What are you guys talking about? All I've eaten since I got here is seafood. Travis took me for steamers. And shrimp and lobster. No, wait, he still owes me a lobster."

He still owed her a lobster. It was a debt he hadn't paid and one she could collect on, any time she wanted. She looked around at the three women who were far wiser than she and realized that she was in the right city, but in the wrong place.

"I need to go," Meredith said. "I... Well, I don't even know what I want to say to him, but at least I'll tell him I want the lobster. We'll start there." She smiled and felt the joy of it run through her heart.

As Meredith left the shop, Maria turned to Candace and Cordelia. "Looks like we'll be paying a visit to the JCPenney bridal registry soon."

Candace laughed. "Hey, I'm a frequent shopper there."

Cordelia swung her little purse in her hands. "I'll have to send my gift airmail, because I'm off to England." She gave them each a tender hug and a light kiss on the cheek. "Take care of yourselves and the little place next door."

As Cordelia left, Maria and Candace looked at each other. "Well, who knew?" Candace said.

"Oh, come on, you did. Didn't you?"

"I had my doubts there for a while, but I figured it was just a matter of time. Meredith is bound to find a happy ending, considering she's surrounded by them."

Maria picked up the key to Cordelia's shop and turned it over and over in her palm. "I wonder who's going to move in next door?"

"As long as our new neighbor likes chocolate—" Candace began.

"We'll all get along just fine," Maria finished.

Rebecca's What's-All-the-Fuss Crunchy Baked Cod

1 pound cod fillet, cut into four pieces
2 tomatoes, sliced
1 lemon, sliced
1 cup fresh bread crumbs
Salt and pepper
2 tablespoons chopped fresh parsley
2 teaspoons vegetable oil

I swear, when a crisis hits, my mother is like a tornado warning system. The entire neighborhood is put on alert that "Rebecca is going through an event." Meanwhile, Ma is running up and down the street like a panicked chicken.

The best thing to do is to bake something easy and quick. Ma's going to need the sustenance anyway, because she'll keep going until her Nikes wear out. So, preheat the oven to 400 degrees.

Place the cod fillets in a baking dish, then arrange the tomato slices and lemon slices on top. Sprinkle with salt and pepper. In a separate bowl, mix the bread crumbs, parsley and oil, then crumble all that on top of the fish. Pop it in the oven for 15 to 20 minutes.

Now, if only dealing with my mother could be that simple.

CHAPTER THIRTY-ONE

If an alligator had crawled into the pond at Boston Garden, the public reaction wouldn't even have come in a close second to the pandemonium at Rebecca's house when the cab pulled up in front. Since Momma had taken Rebecca's car back, Meredith had hailed a taxi for the ride to Cambridge.

She paid the man, and he took off fast, probably because it looked like an asylum on the loose on Rebecca's street. Aunt Gloria was running back and forth between the two houses, waving her hands, her hair a mess, her bright turquoise pants set making her look like a bird of paradise run amok. "My baby is having another baby!" she shouted. "Quick, call the ambulance!"

Momma came out onto Rebecca's porch, a cordless phone in one hand. "Gloria, you're not doing anyone any good out here. You need to get in there and help Rebecca." She started dialing again. "Where are those boys?"

"Vernon and Ray Jr. aren't back yet?" Meredith asked, heading up the stairs. She tried not to let the worry that Rebecca's baby was coming so early show on her face.

Momma let out a sigh. "They're having a little trouble saying good-bye to the cow. And Jeremy already left on a business trip this morning, so that leaves just us women."

Meredith smiled. "I think we're capable."

Momma nodded. "You're right. You come in here and help me with Rebecca. Gloria's no good in a crisis."

Meredith was already a step ahead of her mother and halfway into the house. Rebecca was on the sofa, laying back, a hand on her belly. "Is all that commotion out there for me?" She managed a weak smile.

"I'm afraid so. Your mother wants to call an ambulance."

Rebecca shook her head. "I'm okay. Really. The contractions are still pretty far apart, just ten minutes. The doctor said I can get a ride to the hospital because it's not far from here. Why don't you drive me in, before my mother calls out the National Guard?"

"Sounds like a plan." Meredith slipped an arm around Rebecca's waist and helped her cousin to her feet. She wobbled a bit, breathing hard, then managed to put one foot ahead of the other.

"I'll ride in the back," Momma said, hurrying into the house. "I can't drive in this city. These people are insane. I barely made it home alive this morning."

Before they could take a single step, Aunt Gloria came rushing into the house. "Oh, baby! Are you okay? Do you have the overnight bag? Did you call Jeremy? Do you want me to take Emily? *Oh!* Emily! Where is she?"

"At school, Ma. Don't worry."

"Someone has to go get her." Aunt Gloria ran a hand through her hair, displacing the blond strands into an Einstein-like frazzle. "Uh ... what was our plan again?"

"You get her at school, and—" Rebecca paused to breathe through a contraction, then couldn't go on.

"I'll get her, Gloria," Martha said. "You go with your daughter."

"But..."

"No buts. This is what you need to do." Momma gave her younger sister a little push toward the door and then grabbed Aunt Gloria's coat, swinging it over her shoulders.

"But you don't know where to go and someone has to call the school and—"

Momma grabbed Aunt Gloria's shoulders and gave them a little shake. "Your daughter needs you now. So listen to me. Pull yourself together and go be her mother."

Aunt Gloria's vision fixed on her sister's, then she drew herself up and stopped panicking. "You always were the bossy one, weren't you?"

"We all have your strengths." Momma grinned.

"Okay." Aunt Gloria drew in a breath. "Directions to Emily's school are behind my phone. Rebecca and I will call the office from the car and let them know you're coming."

Momma smiled. "There. That's the family spirit." She gave her sister a quick hug, then pulled back.

Rebecca let out a low moan. "I don't mean to interrupt, but I do need to go to the hospital."

"Oh! Oh yes! Now, shoo," Aunt Gloria said, waving at Meredith and Rebbeca. "I'll get the door. And the suitcase. And the—"

Seven hours later, Maria, Candace and Meredith had been dubbed godmothers to Jackson Hamilton, whose six-pound, four-ounce perfection had completely won over all three women as well as his grandmother and great aunt. Rebecca and Jeremy, who had flown back just in time to see his son born, were firmly ensconced in the hospital room with their new baby. Aunt Gloria and Uncle Mike were busily plunking change into the pay phones and spreading the news.

Before she left, Meredith peeked in on Rebecca one last time. Jeremy lay on the bed curled against his wife, marveling over every toe and finger on the newborn in their arms. The look on the faces of Rebecca and Jeremy was one of such complete joy that Meredith felt a stab of envy so sharp that it could have been a knife in her heart.

She leaned her head against the wall and took in a deep breath. She'd thought she could come here and leave behind the things that had seemed to be keeping her from living the life she wanted. Things like family. Commitment. Relationships. She'd purposely sought out the complete opposite.

And where had it left her?

As empty as a deflated balloon.

She knew exactly where she needed to go to fill that empty place in her heart. Meredith didn't walk out of Mount Auburn Hospital.

She ran.

She paused outside the house. There was one more bridge to repair before she went forward with her own life. Meredith climbed the stairs to Aunt Gloria's house and saw her mother inside the living room, sitting on the couch.

Meredith let herself in. "Hi, Momma."

"Meredith! How's Rebecca?" Her mother was folding a basket of laundry that looked like it had already been haphazardly done by Aunt Gloria.

"Rebecca's great and the baby's going to be just fine, even though he came a little early." Meredith sunk into the chair opposite her mother and reached for a T-shirt, spreading it on the ottoman before her and neatly pressing each sleeve back, then either third of the shirt before flipping up the bottom half, turning it over and giving the front a final smoothing. Just the way her mother liked it

"Everything's still all right?"

"Yep. Aunt Gloria and Uncle Mike are still there, calling all the relatives and cooing over the baby every chance they get."

Momma laughed. "I don't blame them. Grand-children are an amazing thing." Her face turned wistful, even envious, and Meredith knew there was one thing that chaotic, exuberant Aunt Gloria had that Martha didn't.

Yet.

"Momma, I wanted to talk to you." Meredith paired two socks, tossed the roll into the basket, then sat back.

"Uh-huh." Momma went on folding a pair of pants, straightening the hems again and again, try-ing to get the crease perfect.

"Can you stop folding for a minute and look at me?"

Momma shook her head and tugged at the cuffs of the pants harder.

"Momma," Meredith said softly, laying a hand on her mother's.

She stilled, the pants shaking a bit in her grip. Finally, Momma looked up, her eyes misty. "I don't want to hear what you're going to tell me. I know you're going to say that you're never coming home and I'm never going to be next door when you're hav-ing your first baby. I'm going to miss it all." The pants fell into a crumpled heap in her lap and a sob escaped her. "I'm sorry I've been so... difficult. I guess I want the best for you and sometimes that best comes with a lot of—"

"Clorox?" Meredith finished, adding a lighter note. She slid forward onto the ottoman, reaching to take one of her mother's hands in both her own. "I know that. And I haven't been very understanding or nice to you. I kept thinking if I could get far enough away from Heavendale, I could change who I was."

"But why would you want to do that?"

"Because I wasn't happy."

Momma looked stricken, as if she took personal fault for Meredith's unhappiness. "Unhappy?" she echoed.

"With who I was, not with where I was. Well, I thought it was where I was. But I realized since I got here, and well, *all of you* got here too, that it doesn't really matter where I am, but *who I am*."

Momma cocked her head. "What do you mean?"

Meredith let out a breath and tucked her legs underneath her in the chair. "I needed to get to know myself. What I was capable of, outside of that perfect little box of Heavendale. Growing up there, I never really had to try hard to make friends or succeed or heck, even get a job. Because it's so small a world. Then I got here and I had to try harder, stretch those wings a little more. And you know what I found out?"

Momma put the pants aside and sat back against the couch. For the first time Meredith could remember in her life, her mother wasn't doing anything while they were talking. She was giving her undivided attention. Not washing dishes. Not folding laundry.

Not cooking dinner. It was just the two of them, talking in the silent house. "What?" Momma asked.

'That I'm capable of so much more than I thought. And I can weather a lot more of a storm than I thought."

Momma nodded, as if she'd known that all along. "I was really proud of you for the way you handled that. I know I didn't sound it at the time, but I am."

"Thanks." Meredith smiled. "And thank you for helping me."

"You know," Momma said, taking a sip from a glass of water beside her, "you're not the only one who learned a thing or two here. I found out I can go halfway across die country in a hearse and survive—"

Meredith laughed.

"And that I can breathe the air here and live—"

Meredith chuckled again.

"And that I can help my daughter out of a jam and be really proud of what a strong, capable woman she's turned out to be."

"With your help, Momma," Meredith said, rising. She wrapped her arms around her mother and drew her familiar scent to her. "You had a little to do with that, you know."

Momma returned the embrace, then after a long while during which Meredith was sure she heard a sniffle or two, she pulled back. "A little? If I hadn't put those bumper pads on the coffee table and stored all the hazardous chemicals out of reach, why you wouldn't have even made it to your second birthday."

"Momma..."

Her mother's face sobered and she cupped Meredith's face. "You're all grown up now. I guess it's hard for me to let go."

"I won't be so far away."

"Anyplace that isn't next to me is too far." She brushed a lock of hair off her daughter's temple in a gesture reminiscent of when Meredith had been five and fallen off her bike. She'd had the wind knocked out of her, and been too afraid to get back on the two-wheeler. Her mother had sat with her and done that same thing, pushing the hair off her face and telling her that she could, indeed, get back up and ride again, and be just fine, because Momma would always be there with some Betadine.

"I'll be as close as I can be," Meredith said. "And when I'm having my first baby, how about I fly you out to stay with me until your new grandchild arrives?"

Momma beamed. "I'd like that. I could help you get the baby's room ready and do the disinfecting of all the surfaces and—"

"One thing at a time, Momma." Meredith laughed. "Let me get married first."

"Oh! Speaking of that," Momma said. "I forgot. Travis has been waiting for you to come home. He's over at Rebecca's. I fed him some dinner—that boy is too skinny, you know—then I let him in." Her mother smiled. "I figured you wouldn't mind."

"Travis is here? Waiting for me?" Meredith scrambled to her feet, the laundry forgotten. She pressed a kiss to her mother's cheek, not waiting for an answer.

Then she bounded out of Aunt Gloria's house, down the steps, across the sidewalk and up into Rebecca's house.

Finally, she was in the right place. At exactly the right time.

Meredith's When-the-Mood-Is-Right Lobster Stew

3 tablespoons butter
1 pound lobster meat
1 cup heavy cream
3 cups milk
1/2 teaspoon salt
1/4 teaspoon white pepper
Paprika

Pull out all the stops now with the most decadent dish you can create. This one is rich ... in everything you've been denying yourself. Melt the butter and fry the lobster meat until it's warm and heated through. Add the cream and milk, gradually, stirring it carefully over low to medium-low heat.

Don't rush it! The end result will be worth every second you put into it. Season with salt and pepper, then let this simmer gently for about 15 to 20 minutes. Sprinkle a little paprika on top.

Since this dish is so indulgent, be careful who you serve it to. He might just come back for seconds. And thirds. And ... *more.*

CHAPTER THIRTY-TWO

Meredith skidded to a stop in the living room. Travis was sitting on the sofa, his head propped on one arm, asleep. The beagle snored at his feet.

Travis looked ... peaceful. At home. And for just a second, she allowed herself to imagine seeing this sight every night for the rest of her life. It wasn't such a bad image after all.

She slid into the space beside him, careful not to wake him, and slipped her head into the alcove created by his shoulder and neck. It felt comfortable here. Right.

Travis stirred, dropping his arm to wrap around her. "I thought you'd never come home."

"I was talking to my mother. I didn't know you were here." She snuggled closer, seeking his warmth, his touch. Everything about him.

Instead, he moved away and slid off the sofa, kneeling beside it and taking her hands in his. His green eyes met hers. "I have to tell you something."

"No, wait, Travis. I want to tell you something first."

He pressed a finger to her lips. "Please. If I don't tell you, I know I'll regret it." He took in a breath, then let it out. "I know you don't want to fall in love with anyone. But I love you, Meredith. And if I can't be with you, I think I'll go insane. So if you don't want a relationship right now, I'll live with that. Just don't walk away. Because then," he gave her a grin, "you'll be breaking my heart and—"

This time, she pressed a finger to his lips. "Stop. Don't say another word."

"Let me finish."

"No." She smiled. "All you have to do right now is kiss me."

He did as she asked, leaning forward and taking her mouth with his own. His lips caressed hers softly at first, then with more insistence, fueled by all the teasing and the desire that had been brewing between them for two weeks.

The feel of his mouth on hers was different somehow—sweeter, more tender, as if by telling her he loved her, he had added a new dimension to his touch. She'd been attracted to him before, but now she felt a comfortable warmth layering over the heat and passion between them.

"I want you, Meredith," he said, pulling back to tangle his hands in her hair and trail kisses along her neck.

Oh, those were the *other* words she'd waited to hear. "Then what are you waiting for?"

He grinned. "Directions to your bedroom."

She pressed her lips to his throat, to the throbbing pulse in his neck. "Second door at the top of the stairs."

Travis scooped her up and took the stairs two at a time, while Meredith started early on to get him naked. This time, there weren't any damned buttons to slow down her progress. She tugged at his T-shirt, wrestling it out of the space between them and when they got to the top of the stairs, she slid out of his arms, then pulled the shirt up and over his head and tossed it to the floor.

He had a glorious chest. Hard and defined. Perfect for her head, her chest. In fact, she could imagine almost any of her body parts against that wonderful space. She placed her hands against his torso, then her lips, kissing down the length of him, lingering at the V of hair that met his waistband.

"Oh God, Meredith." He groaned. "Which door was it?"

She chuckled, then took his hands and hauled him into the guest bedroom. "Here. Though I would have settled for the stairs."

"I wouldn't have let you," he said, tipping her chin to place a soft kiss on her lips.

She smiled. "Trying to make sure I have a good time?"

"And that I don't end up with a broken back."

She laughed again, then reached to take off her shirt.

"Oh no you don't," Travis said, grasping her hands and stopping her. "I've been wanting to do that myself ever since I met you. You always have all the fun."

He tugged the pale blue shirt up and over her head, then allowed his hands to drift down her throat, along her neckline. He teased the valley there for a long, hot second, then slipped his fingers under the slim satin of her bra straps. They slid off her shoulders, revealing her breasts to his gaze. The warm air of the room drifted over her naked skin, tickling against her.

Travis bent down, teasing a circle around each breast with his tongue, then taking one pert nipple in his mouth, sucking it gently for a long, sweet second before moving on to do the same to the other one.

Fireworks exploded in her brain. She wanted him to stop. Do it again. Do something even better.

Meredith moaned and tilted her pelvis up against his, asking for more, for anything. "Oh, Travis. Oh, God. Oh ... more."

"In a hurry?"

"Oh yeah."

"Patience, sweetheart." He grinned, then released the hooks from the back of her bra and let it fall to the floor. His hands drifted down her torso, his mouth following suit, until he reached the snap of her jeans. She raced her palms over every part of him that she could reach, dying to have more of him in her grasp.

One agonizing second after another passed as he undid the snap, then the zipper, then peeled the denim back and slid it down, inch by inch. He kissed a trail of seduction down her hips, her thighs, her legs, as he made his way down with the jeans to the floor.

She wanted to tear off her underwear, grab him and throw him on the bed. But when she reached for him, he caught her hands in his and came up to kiss her mouth again, bringing his naked chest to hers. The infusion of warmth and Travis's long, slow kisses sent her heart down a tender path. Desire still throbbed within her, but the easy, gentle way he was touching her made her feel like a queen.

He released her hands and she slid them between their bodies, undoing the buttons of his Levi's and sliding them off his hips. He wore silky red boxers, something that surprised and delighted her. For a moment, she simply rubbed her hands against them, enjoying the fabric slipping against her grip while their mouths continued to dance.

Then she slid her hands into the back of his waistband, feeling the taut, warm skin of his buttocks and nearly died with want for him.

He pulled back, his hands holding her face and his dark, smoldering gaze connecting with hers. "Are you sure, Meredith?"

"I've never been more certain of anything in my life. I want my first time to be with you." She wanted every time to be with him, but dared not voice that. Not yet. She didn't want to spoil anything with thinking about tomorrow.

"It's my first time too," he said.

"Oh, don't lie to me." She shook her head and looked away.

He tipped her head, bringing her gaze back to meet his. "I'm serious. It's the first time I've ever been in love. And for me, this is a sweet, sweet first."

Tears welled up in her eyes at his admission. She blinked them back and brought a smile to her lips. She would not cry. Absolutely would not cry during her first time. Even tears of happiness. "Well then, I'm glad your first time is here, with me."

He grinned. "Me, too."

And with that, Travis Campbell swept Meredith off her feet and into the bed.

When Meredith awoke a few hours later, Travis was gone. The house was empty with Rebecca still in the hospital, Jeremy likely spending the night there with his wife and new baby, and Emily asleep next door. Meredith pulled on a robe and padded downstairs.

And realized with a sinking feeling that Travis had done exactly what she'd asked him to do: loved her and left her.

She had what she wanted. And it sucked.

Meredith opened the refrigerator, hungry for something that would fill this empty feeling. When she'd been with him in bed, it had been wonderful.

Perfect. She'd never imagined that making love with someone could be so fulfilling.

And yet, all of those feelings had disappeared the moment she realized he was gone. She shut the door. There was nothing in the Frigidaire that would take care of this. What she wanted was to wake up with Travis. Today, tomorrow, and every day.

She'd been lying to herself, and to him.

Meredith Shordon, who had convinced herself she didn't need or want love, had gone and fallen in love anyway.

She'd been so afraid that love would be constricting and controlling. That she couldn't be herself, or try her wings at new things, and still be with a man who loved her. That it would be like her family, always surrounding her with advice and good intentions that seemed to go in the complete opposite direction Meredith wanted to travel.

She'd been wrong. As she thought back over the days since she'd met Travis, she realized he had given her the one thing she wanted—freedom. And the second thing she hadn't even known she wanted—

A love that didn't ask for anything in return.

Oh, how stupid she had been. She'd been too busy worrying about the trees to see the forest. Why couldn't she have seen all this before ... before Travis had left?

"You're up. I was hoping to surprise you."

She pivoted at the sound of Travis's voice, happiness bubbling up inside her so fast and so hard, she thought she'd explode.

He'd come back.

He stood in the entryway to the kitchen, holding a paper bag from a local seafood restaurant. A whisper of steam escaped from the top, bringing with it the scent of the luscious meat inside. "I made you a promise."

She crossed to him. "What promise?"

"A lobster dinner. It may be late, but in Boston there's always someplace that's open in the middle of the night."

She smiled at the thoughtfulness and sweetness of what he'd done, going out in the middle of the night to track down a lobster, just for her. "Thank you. I'm famished."

"Me too." He grinned. "For more than just seafood." He pressed a kiss to her neck and she nearly lost her resolve and the pretty little speech she'd been composing in her head before he got here.

"Before we eat," Meredith said, taking the bag from Travis's hands and laying it on the counter, "I want to take back what I said earlier."

"Take it back?"

"Yeah. I don't want to do this with you anymore."

His face dropped. "You don't?"

"No. No more of this sex-only thing. The rules have changed. I want more now."

He blinked, clearly confused. "More?"

Oh, she was going to enjoy teasing him. Every time he thought he knew what she wanted, Meredith went and turned the tables on Travis Campbell. "Yep. I want the whole enchilada now. The ring, the preacher, the house in the suburbs. Even the damned dog."

"A dog?" He opened his mouth, closed it, opened it again. "What are you saying?"

"Oh, did I forget to tell you?" She smiled. "I love you too, Travis. And I don't want a one-night stand anymore."

A wide grin broke across his face. "You love me, too?"

She nodded. The joy exploding in her heart surely showed on her face. "I tried to fight it, but you're one tough guy to resist."

"It's all that natural charm."

"Yeah, right." She gave him a jab in the arm. "You know what this means, though, don't you?"

"What?"

She crossed her arms over her chest and gave him the Evil Eye that Momma had taught her so well. "We're going to have to get married. Because as much as I tried, I couldn't quit being a traditional girl."

He took a step forward, hauling her into his arms and breaking her into a fit of laughter. "No, I disagree. You're not traditional at all."

"Really?"

"I think *you* just asked me to marry you." He leaned forward and brushed his lips against hers.

She drew back and put a hand on her hip. "I did not!"

"Are you sure?" He arched a brow.

"Positive. I'd never do that." Though she knew she *technically* had done exactly that, she wouldn't admit it.

"Good." Travis dropped to one knee and took her left hand in his. "I didn't just go out for a lobster.

I was hoping maybe you might have changed your mind." He reached into his back pocket withdrew a small velvet ring box and turned it around to face her. A round diamond, surrounded by a dozen smaller stones, blinked back at her from a platinum setting. "I bought this earlier today, hoping you might ah, want to break a family curse with me."

She laughed. "What kind of proposal is that?"

"After all this, you want me to be formal?" She nodded. "Okay, here goes." He cleared his throat, grinning up at her. "Meredith Shordon, will you marry me?"

"Only if you promise me one thing."

"Anything."

She took the ring, slid it onto her finger and hauled him up to kiss her. "I always get the last bite."

Then she brought her mouth to his and gave him a sweet taste of the future to come.

Ray Jr.'s Happy-Ending-for-Everyone Garlic Scallops and Shrimp

6 large scallops, halved
8 large shrimp, peeled and deveined
2 tablespoons flour
3 tablespoons olive oil
1 clove garlic, minced
1 tablespoon basil, chopped
3 tablespoons lemon juice
Salt and pepper

Before you make your great escape, you have time for one more meal. Everyone in your family is finally happy now, and it's up to you to bring that happy ending to a Holstein with a heart.

Rinse the scallops under cold water and pat them dry. Season all the seafood with a little salt and pepper, then dust with flour, shaking off the excess.

Heat the oil in a pan large enough to give each scallop his own space. Then add them and their shrimp neighbors to the pan. Reduce the heat to medium-high and cook for two minutes, then flip. Add the garlic and basil, then finish cooking for another two minutes. Shower it all with lemon juice and you've created a non-beef masterpiece.

Serve to all your friends and show them there's an option out there besides just cows for dinner.

Then get the hell out of town before anyone looks to see what you're hiding in the back of your truck.

CHAPTER THIRTY-THREE

"I don't think this is a good idea, Ray Jr.," Vernon said as they hurried west on the toll road in Cecil's truck. They'd left in the middle of the night, barreling out of Massachusetts as fast as the old pickup could go.

Ray Jr. flicked the wipers on to brush away the light rain that had started. "Hush up, Vernon. We couldn't let her stay there. God only knows what that guy would have done to her."

"Yeah, but kidnapping her in the middle of the night? There are laws against that."

"Let 'em try and catch me. I'll just rebrand her and put her on our farm. Nobody will know the difference."

Vernon shook his head and let out a sigh. "You're an old softie, you know that, don't you?"

"I am not." Ray Jr. hesitated, then shrugged. Maybe Vernon was right. How many times had he gone out hunting and come back empty-handed because he couldn't bear to hurt an animal? 'Course, he had to pretend to miss, so his friends wouldn't think he was a complete weenie. "I just... Well, I couldn't see her get slaughtered like that."

Vernon raised his hands in frustration. "She's a *cow*, Ray! That's what happens to them."

"Not to my Bessie. She's coming home with us to Indiana."

"Momma's gonna be mad. She told you, no more pets."

"Bessie's a... souvenir."

Vernon waved his Patriots hat around. "*This* is a souvenir. *That* is a side of beef." He sent a thumb in the direction of the trailer they were hauling.

"Not anymore, she isn't. I have plans for that cow."

"Plans?"

"Yep. Since Meredith is a little busy in Boston—"

"With that city boy." Vernon scowled.

"He's not so bad, you know. Any man who can take care of Meredith and love her like that is worth a place at our dinner table."

Vernon gave a grudging shrug. "As long as he doesn't eat the last biscuit."

Ray Jr. rolled his eyes. "Anyway, I think I solved Meredith's last problem."

"What do you mean?" Vernon gave a little wave as they passed the "Thank You for Visiting Massachusetts" sign and headed across the state line.

Ray Jr. gestured toward the unsuspecting cow chewing her cud in the trailer behind them. "Meet Bessie, the *new* Miss Holstein. She's gonna look mighty good on the front of that tractor."

"How are you going to do that?"

Ray Jr. grinned. "We have the glue. We can do just about anything now."

Vernon's grin was just as devilish. "Oh the trouble we can get into ..."

"You can say that again," Ray Jr. said. Then before Vernon could open his mouth, Ray Jr. picked up the foam Patriots finger and flashed it at his brother. "But don't. It's a hell of a long ride home."

EXCERPT FROM
THE PLAYBOY SAVORED SEDUCTION

Book Four in the Sweet and Savory Novel Series

"Sold!"

The auctioneer's gavel came down with a final slam, and Boston's 28th most eligible bachelor walked off the stage of the Worth Hotel ballroom— and straight into the open arms of his new female owner.

Her prize was one Jerold Klein, a forty-year-old rare bird dealer with a hooked nose and graying head to match his prize cockatiels. Geraldine Hawkins let out a squeal of joy at her successful purchase, as if she'd just nabbed a four-thousand dollar ermine bargain on the fur rack at Macy's.

Daniel Worth IV scowled. Why the hell he'd signed up for this, he didn't know. Actually, he did know. He'd agreed after the third or fourth round of a damned good Scotch, too mellowed by the liquor to refuse when Kyle Montague had asked him to participate in the early February "charity" event.

Yeah, it was a charity all right. One where men who knew better gave away their dignity and called it a tax deduction.

All night, the women had been straining forward in their seats, waving their checkbooks like dollar bills while the auctioneer listed the assets of the each bachelor with the drama of Bob Barker giving away a Caddie.

This was as much charity as a Chippendales performance was a garden party.

"For our next eligible bachelor, we have Percival Howard the Third," the auctioneer began. Percival, who'd always been on the pink side of shy, lingered beside Daniel in the shadows, his white-knuckled hands glued to the wrought iron railing.

Daniel shook his head. What the man in front of him needed was a good shot of testosterone, or at least a fourteen-ounce rib eye. Babied by his mother, because of his "weak constitution" and his inability to digest anything containing protein, Percival's diet was filled mostly with carrots, his vegetable of choice. The result—a perpetual orange tint in his skin.

It gave "you are what you eat" a whole new meaning.

Percival's dietary choices had had the dual effect of greatly improving his eyesight but leaving him with the unfortunate nickname of "Persimmon." Being known as a fruit hadn't exactly helped Persimmon develop his social graces. The poor orange man shook and sweated his way up the two steps to the stage.

Regardless of his menu restrictions, the audience wanted its next bachelor. Particularly one who had a second house in Tuscany and a reputation for treating women like crystal. Still, Persimmon lingered outside the glare of the spotlights, the color in his cheeks deepening from under-ripe carrot to crimson.

"Where is he? Give him to us!" shouted someone in the back.

"Yeah, get him on stage!"

"Are these the same women who organize the annual Support an Orphan party?" asked Jake Lincoln, sidling up beside Daniel. "That fancy shindig where we pay a grand a head to eat Marcy Higgins's cousin's crappy version of standing rib roast and listen to her father drone on about the tragedy of growing up alone?"

"Wasn't he raised in a family of twelve?" Daniel said.

Jake chuckled. "The rich empathize with everyone, don't you know that?"

Daniel knew that spiel. Particularly around tax time, when Grandfather Worth was looking for an extra deduction.

"Give us your poor, tired and hungry," Daniel said. "Just don't make us walk in their knock-off high heels or eat their store-brand canned food."

The auctioneer went over to coax Percival onto the stage. A cheer went up from the crowd, checkbooks raised in tribute. Moments later, a price was put on Percival's persimmon-colored head.

"Ain't that the truth." Jake shook his head. "You want to mosey on over to the bar or continue watching our peer group being sold off like prize livestock?"

"Sold!" The auctioneer declared again, giving Boston's 29th best a nod and a slam of his gavel. "And now, our final bachelor of the night, our *piece de resistance,*" the auctioneer said, waving his hand to add a touch of drama to his words, "and the man you ladies have been waiting to see. The one *Boston* magazine called 'the most eligible bachelor in the city.'"

"Can't," Daniel said to Jake. "I'm up."

"*You're* the *piece de resistance?*" Jake laughed. "The icing on the cake? The cherry on the sundae? The—"

Daniel raised a finger in warning. "Don't forget, I know about that slightly illegal thing you did trading small caps last year. So if I were you, I'd stop right there."

Jake clapped him on the back. "Go get 'em, tiger. Remember, this is for..." He paused. "What the hell charity is this for, anyway?"

"I don't know." Daniel let out a long breath that said he'd been to too many of these things in recent weeks. It seemed *this* had become his job. It wasn't a job Daniel liked, but it was one Grandfather Worth insisted Daniel do, exerting his iron grip on everything in Daniel's life, as he had for twenty-eight years.

Daniel could think of several things he'd much rather be doing, but Grandfather would have his head—and his inheritance—if he stepped off the carefully planned family path.

The prep school Daniel had attended, the college he'd graduated from, even the courses he'd taken, had all been decided by Grandfather. All Daniel had to do in exchange was abide by the elder Worth's rules and the money would continue to flow into Daniel's bank account, as regular as Old Faithful.

But one misstep—such as the time Daniel had dated a woman whose pedigree Grandfather had deemed "inadequate", like she was a substandard poodle at Westminster—and the money vanished. A simple break-up, and the floodgates were opened once again.

When Daniel had been young and more concerned with his social life than his future, Grandfather's rules had been a tolerable annoyance. Slug back a whiskey with friends and he'd forget the future waiting for him at the helm of Worth. Forget how much he'd hated business school. Forget that every element of his adult life was set in a pattern as unchangeable as a DNA strand.

But today, as he waited for the auctioneer to finish listing his assets like he was a 2006 Escalade, the whole thing grated. And made Daniel wish for…

Something. *Anything* but this.

"Why are you selling yourself anyway?" Jake asked, as they waited for the auctioneer to finish his spirited recap of Daniel's personal résumé.

"My grandfather makes me do this crap. Says it makes the family look good."

Jake's raised eyebrow as Daniel walked away told him what he thought of that.

The women whooped and catcalled Daniel as he made his way across the ballroom stage. He'd known many of these women all his life and they'd never acted like this. What the hell had the waiters been passing around in the drinks anyway?

Was it just the thought of turning the tables, of being in control? Of having a man at their beck and call?

Twin canister lights were directed at the spot where he was to stand—conveniently marked with a duct-taped X. White beams shone like a police interrogation in his face, making it hard for him to see the audience. Just as well. He didn't want to know if it had been Mary Jo Williamson or Lauren Templeton who'd let out that wolf whistle.

After all, he had to face them in mixed doubles tennis on Tuesday.

"As you ladies know, Daniel Worth the Fourth is single," the auctioneer paused long enough to allow a few appreciative hollers from the crowd. "He's twenty-eight years old, and, as a member of the Worth family, valued at ninety-three million dollars."

Technically, that wasn't correct. He only had that net worth *if* his grandfather kept him on the family dime. As long as Daniel towed the family line, there wasn't any reason to think that would change, considering Daniel had been born into wealth, as had his father, and his grandfather, and all the Worths before them, ever since the first Worth had started a chain of hotels in Boston and made a mint, practically from the day the colonists were looking for housing.

The Worth family excelled at one thing: finding what people wanted in a bed. And charging them a damned good rate for a pillowtop, room service and a maid who would pop in and turn down the covers just before you were ready to retire. A dreamy experience, Grandfather Worth called it, chuckling all the way to the bank.

Now there were Worth hotels in seventeen countries, each pouring a steady stream of money into the family coffers.

Which meant that yes, Daniel Worth was, pun intended, worth a hell of a lot of dough, and he didn't have to do a whole lot to get the money—besides show up at things like this and eventually take the reins of the family business, carrying on the Worth mantle of ownership.

Daniel had already done all the hard work by being born into the right family. His father had died of a heart attack at forty-eight, leaving a gap between Daniel Worth the Second and Daniel the Fourth—and placing an extra generation of expectations on Daniel's shoulders.

Expectations he hadn't been very good at fulfilling. Hell, he wasn't much good at anything beyond playing the bachelor, as his grandfather reminded him on a weekly basis. That was probably why *Boston* magazine had done that stupid article on him last month. His reputation, it seemed, had seeped into the collective media.

"Now, who'd like to start the bidding?" The auctioneer looked out over the crowd. "Remember, ladies, this is all going to a good cause: the Juvenile Diabetes Foundation."

Oh yeah, that's what they were raising money for. Explained the lack of cake, too.

"Two thousand dollars!" said a woman in the back who sounded a lot like Lauren Templeton.

"Two thousand, five hundred!"

"Three thousand!"

"Four!"

"Four thousand, five hundred!"

Daniel's stomach twisted. When he'd arrived at the hotel tonight, he'd thought this might be fun. Some woman, maybe one he'd dated before, would buy him, they'd go out, have a few laughs and a few drinks, and he'd have done his charitable work for the year. Might even be able to write off the bar tab.

But with the women yelling out price tags on him—

"Six thousand!"

"Six thousand, three hundred!"

—like he was a twelve-carat yellow diamond they all wanted, he felt—

Cheap.

Hell, this wasn't fun. It was freaky.

"Eight thousand!"

"Nine."

"Nine thousand, five hundred!" Whoever raised that price gave out a little whoop-whoop at the end.

When this was over, he was going to strangle Kyle. Surely Grandfather had enough money and influence to get Daniel off on self-defense. Or at least temporary insanity.

"Twelve thousand, three hundred and twenty-two dollars!" called a woman's voice Daniel didn't recognize. He scanned the crowd but couldn't see past the blazing lights. A heavy hush descended over the elaborate ballroom.

Everyone was probably wondering the same thing he was—who had put that large, precise dollar tag on Daniel Worth…and why?

More importantly, what did she intend to do with him once she had her bachelor? Each woman was paying for the right to twenty-four hours with the man of her choice.

Twelve grand… What was she expecting to get for her five hundred dollars an hour?

"Do I hear twelve thousand, five hundred?" The auctioneer looked around the room. Apparently, most of the bank accounts in the room had been drained by the first twenty-nine offerings. None of the women leapt to the next level in bidding. Granted, not a man tonight had gone for more than eight grand. Why should he think *he'd* go for the equivalent of two dozen pairs of Jimmy Choos?

Hell, he'd already dated half the women in the room. Sort of took the air of mystery out of the equation. He stepped forward, out of the glare in his eyes, and scanned the group again, all seated in a room as familiar as the back of his hand. Okay, half might be an exaggeration.

Of sorts.

"Twelve thousand, three hundred and twenty-two going once, going twice," the announcer paused, his gavel hovering over the wooden stand, "and sold! To the woman in the back row."

Just like that, it was over.

ABOUT THE AUTHOR

New York Times and *USA Today* bestselling author Shirley Jump spends her days writing romance and women's fiction to feed her shoe addiction and avoid cleaning the toilets. She cleverly finds writing time by feeding her kids junk food, allowing them to dress in the clothes they find on the floor and encouraging the dogs to double as vacuum cleaners. Visit her website at *www.ShirleyJump.com*, follow her on Facebook at www.facebook.com/shirleyjump. author or follow her Twitter at www.twitter.com/ shirleyjump.

www.ingramcontent.com/pod-product-compliance
Lightning Source LLC
Chambersburg PA
CBHW070353260626
47161CB00001B/129